THE AIRS OF EARTH

Also by Brian Aldiss and available in the NEL series:

EARTHWORKS
THE INTERPRETER
SPACE, TIME & NATHANIEL
THE DARK LIGHT YEARS
THE CANOPY OF TIME
THE COMIC INFERNO
EQUATOR

The Airs of Earth

Brian W. Aldiss

NEW ENGLISH LIBRARY
TIMES MIRROR

First published in Great Britain by Faber and Faber Limited in 1963

*

First Four Square edition September 1965
An NEL Edition May 1971
This NEL Edition May 1975

*

NEL Books are published by
New English Library Limited from Barnard's Inn, Holborn, London, E.C.1.
Made and printed in Great Britain by Hunt Barnard Printing Ltd., Aylesbury, Bucks.

45002097 5

ACKNOWLEDGEMENTS

My thanks for permission to reprint these stories—and for granting me the hospitality of their columns in the first place—go to the editors of two magazines:

'A Kind of Artistry' and 'Shards': *The Magazine of Fantasy and Science Fiction*; 'How to be a Soldier' (previously 'Soldiers Running'), 'Basis for Negotiation', 'O Moon of My Delight' (previously 'Moon of Delight'), 'The Game of God' (previously 'Segregation') and 'Old Hundredth': *New Worlds Science Fiction*. Many of the stories have been revised and altered since their first appearance.

CONTENTS

INTRODUCTION

To be a science-fiction writer is to be a curiosity not only to one's neighbours—all men are curiosities to their neighbours—but also to the national press.

Many reviewers do not know how to take science-fiction writers. The man who wrote in *Reynolds News* of one of my previous books that it 'contained not one important new forecast' was obviously hoping for a cross between Old Moore and the Air Ministry roof. Then there was that delightful concluding sentence of Mr. John Coleman's friendly review in *The Spectator*: 'Mr. Aldiss knows all about chromosomes, but he seems, agreeably enough, to be almost totally uninterested in sex.'

What a wild goose starts up here, inviting chase! Is it possible to strike the right tone of voice so that sex and chromosomes combine happily in one story? For more years than one cares to remember, this matter has been debated in sf circles.

And the other strange delusions that reviewers suffer. What tales one might tell if one would! There was, for instance, the amiable gentleman on *The Dudley Herald* who was perceptive enough to compare my writing with Olaf Stapledon's, only to spoil the good work by complaining of the rest of the field that 'every author with a couple of mediocre detective tales to his discredit seems to be climbing on to the sf bandwagon'. (The actual situation is that a few mediocre sf writers have become mediocre in other fields, producing thrillers among other work. Nobody minds.)

Other critics imagine that science fiction sells phenomenally well in this country. Others think it is all a dreadful conspiracy.

I hate to say anything against my publishers, for one does not bite the hand that starves one, but they have been very slow to issue disclaimers and explain that sf writers are human, never write best-sellers, and get published under the mundane arrangements that apply to other authors (arrangements roughly classifiable as Survival of the Fittest). They have, however, allowed me a space in which to say something about sf.

Perhaps the one thing worth saying is that it is almost impossible to say anything very fruitful about sf in general.

There is only X's science fiction and Y's science fiction (not to mention Z's space opera), and because X and Y may be of very different temperaments, their stories will contain different qualities.

Sf is not all of a piece. One can make not only the valid distinction that some of it is very good and much of it very poor; one has also to say that every worth-while writer makes an individual contribution. Thus, Arthur C. Clarke's sf is often concerned with forthcoming technological innovations. He is, indeed, likely to go down in history as the man who first thought of telstar. One has also to say that John Wyndham's and John Christopher's sf is in some respects the very opposite of this; that such novels as their *Day of the Triffids* and *Death of Grass* are symptoms of a revolt against an increasingly technological and inhuman society (I suspect that this is one reason why they have achieved their great popularity). One has to say that William Tenn is most interested in a techno-logical society when it emphasizes human weaknesses already apparent. One has to say that Frederik Pohl exposes present-day economic evils by projecting them on to the future. And so on. To each his own *métier*.

Only when these authors can be dealt with as individuals and not as some sort of outcrop of a vast mass mind that occasionally defecates a burst of 'space fiction' will criticism come out of its paleolithic era.

All the same, there are some interesting figures stirring in the early dawn. The number of critics who can say something worth while about sf grows. It includes, for instance, Kenneth Allsop, John Bowen, Alan Brien, G. D. Doherty, Robert Conquest, Miss Stevie Smith, Colin Wilson, Angus Wilson, and Kenneth Young. (We all know about Messrs. Amis, Boardman, and Crispin, who were up before first light.)

These critics—and happily the list is incomplete—know that if an sf story fails by ordinary literate standards, it has failed; they also know that it needs something extra to succeed. And this extra demand has to be allowed for.

To define this 'extra something' is not easy without falling into generalization. But look at it this way.

A writer of traditional fiction writes a book, a novel. It centres round the problem three men have in seducing a girl, their various approaches and her various retreats.

A writer of sf writes a novel. He begins by creating a new solar system and a future time to set it in. In that system he sets one planet in particular, gives it an appropriate biosphere and an ecology within that biosphere. He gives his creatures life and purpose, gives them a social system, domestic life, architecture, and a local substitute for Coca-Cola. He brings in some visiting Earthmen. Then he sets to work on Chapter One.

An sf writer works hard for his living. He may be excused if he becomes impatient when a reviewer reads his work and says, 'No characterization'. He may be excused if he replies, with the well-known humility of any author facing any strictures, 'You mean you want characterization *as well*?'

The odd thing is that much sf does contain at least adequate characterization. What one is less entitled to expect is that interplay of character which marks the novels held in highest esteem by the Leavis school of criticism, novels by Jane Austen, Henry James, and D. H. Lawrence. The interplay of relationships that goes on in a lot of sf is between man and X the unknown; and in such cases there is no room for any depth between personal relationships.

And so I come to these airs of Earth. Some of them do seem to be about personal relationships—the first one, for instance, centres round them. Yet they are always about something else as well. It's a confusing situation about which a few words might well be said—by someone else.

I don't think these airs on a G-strain are much like any other writer's, though they show some variety among themselves. The majority of them have not been given benefit of escape velocity, and take place on Earth, though the Earths differ considerably, some being tomorrow's possible Earth, some the Earths of the remote future. Space is a bit *passé* these days, now that the Russian and American tourist season is getting into full swing. One of the two that are set away in the galaxy, 'The Game of God' is an attempt—and attempt I make too seldom—to write 'proper sf', with a problem that introduces parasitology, or in this case para-parasitology. And 'O Moon of my Delight!' is a shot at imagining a personal case history not covered by Havelock Ellis because it could only occur under special extra-terrestrial circumstances.

Of the other stories, I must push 'Old Hundredth' forward by saying that it was written for the centenary issue of Britain's oldest sf magazine, *New Worlds*.

'Basis for Negotiation' also appeared in the same magazine, and caused much discontent there. It concerns the outbreak of a Third World War in which Britain remains neutral. I was accused of holding certain attitudes to certain political parties, and to certain sexual propensities, even of taking the name of C.N.D. in vain; one reader, bolder than the rest, suggested I had written in my cups. Not all these charges do I deny, though I hope a perceptive reader will find the story fights its

11

real battle on other battlefields. Anyhow, the story remains; I have even included here an ironic echo to it. 'The International Smile'. I should say that 'Basis' is somewhat revised. For that I must thank John Baxter, an Australian reader whose criticisms have been very useful. Often the most perceptive critics come from within the ranks of the so-called fans. Which is understandable; they share the major kink of sf writers—a deep and irrational devotion to science fiction.

But between the critics and the fans lies the mysterious land where the ordinary reader lives. This is the land wherein the writer can never tread; it is almost impossible for him to have commerce with it (populous though the place is, its people go masked). So he sends into it an occasional tender, hoping it may prove of value, hoping the natives will prove friendly.

Oxford,
October 1962

A KIND OF ARTISTRY

It is better to repose in the earth betimes than to sit up late.
W. S. LANDOR

I

A GIANT rising from the fjord, from the grey arm of sea in the fjord, could have peered over the crown of its sheer cliffs and discovered Endehaaven there on the edge, sprawling at the very start of the island.

Derek Flamifew Ende saw much of this sprawl from his high window; indeed, a growing unease, apprehensions of a quarrel, forced him to see everything with particular clarity, just as a landscape takes on an intense actinic visibility before a thunderstorm. Although he was warmseeing with his face, yet his eye vision wandered over the estate.

All was bleakly neat at Endehaaven—as I should know, for its neatness is my care. The gardens are made to support ever-greens and shrubs that never flower; this is My Lady's whim, that likes a sobriety to match the furrowed brow of the coast-line. The building, gaunt Endehaaven itself, is tall and lank and severe; earlier ages would have found its structure impos-sible: for its thousand built-in paragravity units ensure that column, buttress, arch, and wall support masonry, the mass of which is largely an illusion.

Between the building and fjord, where the garden contrived itself into a parade, stood My Lady's laboratory, and My Lady's pets—and, indeed, My Lady herself at this time, her long hands busy with the minicoypus and agoutinis. I stood with her, attending the animals' cages or passing her instru-ments or stirring the tanks, doing always what she asked. And the eyes of Derek Ende looked down on us; no, they looked down on her only.

Derek Flamifew Ende stood with his face over the receptor bowl, reading the message from Star One. It played lightly over his countenance and over the boscises of his forehead. Though he stared down across that achingly familiar stage of his life outside, he still warmsaw the communication clearly.

13

When it was finished, he negated the receptor, pressed his face to it, and flexed his message back.

'I will do as you message, Star One. I will go at once to Festi XV in the Veil Nebula and enter liaison with the being you call the Cliff. If possible I will also obey your order to take some of its substance to Pyrylyn. Thank you for your greetings; I return them in good faith. Good-bye.'

He straightened and massaged his face: warmlooking over great light distances was always tiring, as if the sensitive muscles of the countenance knew that they delivered up their tiny electrostatic charges to parsecs of vacuum and were appalled. Slowly his boscises also relaxed, as slowly he gathered together his gear. It would be a long flight to the Veil; and the task that had been set him would daunt the stoutest heart on Earth; yet it was for another reason he lingered: before he could be away, he had to say a farewell to his Mistress.

Dilating the door, he stepped out into the corridor, walked along it with a steady tread—feet covering mosaics of a pattern learnt long ago in his childhood—and walked into the paragravity shaft. Moments later, he was leaving the main hall, approaching My Lady as she stood gaunt, with her rodents scuttling at breast level before her and Vatna Jokull's heights rising behind her, grey with the impurities of distance.

'Go indoors and fetch me the box of name rings, Hols,' she said to me; so I passed him, my Lord, as he went to her. He noticed me no more than he noticed any of the other parthenos, fixing his sights on her.

When I returned, she had not turned towards him, though he was speaking urgently to her.

'You know I have my duty to perform, Mistress,' I heard him saying. 'Nobody else but a normal-born Earthborn can be entrusted with this sort of task.'

'This sort of task! The galaxy is loaded inexhaustibly with such tasks! You can excuse yourself for ever with such excursions.'

He said to her remote back, pleadingly: 'You can't talk of them like that. You know the nature of the Cliff—I told you all about it. You know this isn't an excursion: it requires all the courage I have. And you know that only Earthborns, for some reason, have such courage. . . . Don't you, Mistress?'

Although I had come up to them, threading my subservient way between cage and tank, they noticed me not enough even to lower their voices. My Lady stood gazing at the grey heights inland, her countenance as formidable as they; one

14

boscis twitched as she said, 'You think you are so big and brave, don't you?'

Knowing the power of sympathetic magic, she never spoke his name when she was angry; it was as if she wished him to disappear.

'It isn't that,' he said humbly. 'Please be reasonable, Mistress; you know I must go; a man cannot be for ever at home. Don't be angry.'

She turned to him at last.

Her face was high and stern; it did not receive. Yet she had a beauty of some dreadful kind I cannot describe, if weariness and knowledge can together knead beauty. Her eyes were as grey and distant as the frieze of snow-covered volcano behind her, O My Lady! She was a century older than Derek: though the difference showed not in her skin—which would stay fresh yet a thousand years—but in her authority.

'I'm not angry. I'm only hurt. You know how you have the power to hurt me.'

'Mistress——' he said, taking a step towards her.

'Don't touch me,' she said. 'Go if you must, but don't make a mockery of it by touching me.'

He took her elbow. She held one of the minicoypus quiet in the crook of her arm—animals were always docile at her touch—and strained it closer.

'I don't mean to hurt you, Mistress. You know we owe allegiance to Star One; I must work for them, or how else do we hold this estate? Let me go for once with an affectionate parting.'

'Affection! You go off and leave me alone with a handful of parthenos and you talk of affection! Don't pretend you don't rejoice to get away from me. You're tired of me, aren't you?'

Wearily he said, as if nothing else would come, 'It's not that. . . .'

'You see! You don't even attempt to sound sincere. Why don't you go? It doesn't matter what happens to me.'

'Oh, if you could only hear your own self-pity.'

Now she had a tear on the icy slope of one cheek. Turning, she flashed it for his inspection.

'Who else should pity me? You don't, or you wouldn't go away from me as you do. Suppose you get killed by this Cliff, what will happen to me?'

'I shall be back, Mistress,' he said. 'Never fear.'

'It's easy to say. Why don't you have the courage to admit that you're only too glad to leave me?'

'Because I'm not going to be provoked into a quarrel.'

'Pah, you sound like a child again. You won't answer, will you? Instead you're going to run away, evading your responsibilities.'

'I'm not running away!'

'Of course you are, whatever you pretend. You're just immature.'

'I'm not, I'm not! And I'm not running away! It takes real courage to do what I'm going to do.'

'You think so well of yourself!'

He turned away then, petulantly, without dignity. He began to head towards the landing platform. He began to run.

'Derek!' she called.

He did not answer.

She took the squatting minicoypu by the scruff of its neck. Angrily she flung it into the nearby tank of water. It turned into a fish and swam down into the depths.

II

Derek journeyed towards the Veil Nebula in his fast lightpusher. Lonely it sailed, a great fin shaped like an archer's bow, barnacled all over with the photon cells that sucked its motive power from the dense and dusty emptiness of space. Midway along the trailing edge was the blister in which Derek lay, senseless over most of his voyage.

He woke in the therapeutic bed, called to another resurrection day that was no day, with gentle machine hands easing the stiffness from his muscles. Soup gurgled in a retort, bubbling up towards a nipple only two inches from his mouth. He drank. He slept again, tired from his long inactivity.

When he woke again, he climbed slowly from the bed and exercised for fifteen minutes. Then he moved forward to the controls. My friend Jon was there.

'How is everything?' Derek asked.

'Everything is in order, My Lord,' Jon replied. 'We are swinging into the orbit of Festi XV now.' He gave the co-ordinates and retired to eat. Jon's job was the loneliest any partheno could have. We are hatched according to strictly controlled formulae, without the inbred organizations of D.N.A. that assure true Earthborns of their amazing longevity; five more long hauls and Jon will be old and worn out, fit only for the transmuter.

Derek sat at the controls. Did he see, superimposed on the face of Festi, the face he loved and feared? I think he did. I think there were no swirling clouds for him that could erase the clouding of her brow.

Whatever he saw, he settled the lightpusher into a fast low

orbit about the desolate planet. The sun Festi was little more than a blazing point some eight hundred million miles away. Like a riding light of a ship it bobbed about a turbulent sea of cloud as they went in.

For a long while, Derek sat with his face in a receptor bowl, checking ground heats far below. Since he was dealing with temperatures approaching absolute zero, this was not simple; yet when the Cliff moved into a position directly below, there was no mistaking its bulk; it stood out as clearly on his senses as if outlined on a radar screen.

'There she goes!' Derek exclaimed.

Jon had come forward again. He fed the time co-ordinates into the lightpusher's brain, waited, and read off the time when the Cliff would be below them again.

Nodding, Derek began to prepare to jump. Without haste, he assumed his special suit, checking each item as he took it up, opening the paragravs until he floated and then closing them again, clicking down every snap-fastener until he was entirely encased.

'395 seconds to next zenith, My Lord,' Jon said.

'You know all about collecting me?'

'Yes, sir.'

'I shall not activate the radio beacon till I'm back in orbit.'

'I fully understand, sir.'

'Right. I'll be moving.'

A little animated person, he walked ponderously into the air lock.

Three minutes before they were next above the Cliff, Derek opened the outer door and dived into the sea of cloud. A brief blast of his suit jets set him free from the lightpusher's orbit. Clouds engulfed him like death as he fell.

The twenty surly planets that swung round Festi held only an infinitesimal fraction of the mysteries of the galaxy. Every globe in the universe huddled its own secret purpose to itself. On some of those globes, as on Earth, the purpose manifested itself in a type of being that could shape itself, burst into the space lanes, and rough-hew its aims in a civilized extra-planetary environment. On others, the purpose remained aloof and dark; only Earthborns, weaving their obscure patterns of will and compulsion, challenged those alien beings, to wrest from them new knowledge that might be added to the pool of the old.

All knowledge has its influence. Over the millennia since interstellar flight had become practicable, mankind was insensibly moulded by its own findings; together with its lost innocence, its genetic stability went out of the galactic window.

2   17

As man fell like rain over other planets, so his strain lost its original hereditary design: each centre of civilization bred new ways of thought, of feeling, of shape—of life. Only on old Earth itself did man still somewhat resemble the men of pre-stellar days.

That was why it was an Earthborn who dived head-first to meet an entity called the Cliff.

The Cliff had destroyed each of the few spaceships or light-pushers that had landed on its desolate globe. After long study of the being from safe orbits, the wise men of Star One evolved the theory that it destroyed any considerable source of power, as a man will swat a buzzing fly. Derek Ende, going alone with no powering but his suit motors, would be safe—or so the theory went.

Riding down on the paragravs, he sank more and more slowly into planetary night. The last of the cloud was whipped from about his shoulders and a high wind thrummed and whistled round the supporters of his suit. Beneath him, the ground loomed. So as not to be blown across it, he speeded his rate of fall; next moment he sprawled full length on Festi XV. For a while he lay there, resting and letting his suit cool.

The darkness was not complete. Though almost no solar light touched this continent, green flares grew from the earth, illumining its barren contours. Wishing to accustom his eyes to the gloom, he did not switch on his head, shoulder, stomach, or hand lights.

Something like a stream of fire flowed to his left. Because its radiance was poor and guttering, it confused itself with its own shadows, so that the smoke it gave off, distorted into bars by the bulk of the 4G planet, appeared to roll along its course like burning tumbleweed. Farther off were large sources of fire, impure ethane and methane most probably burning with a sound that came like frying steak to Derek's ears, and spouting upwards with an energy that licked the lowering cloud race with blue light. At another point, blazing on an eminence, a geyser of flame wrapped itself in a thickly swirling mantle of brown smoke, a pall that spread upwards as slowly as porridge. Elsewhere, a pillar of white fire burnt without motion or smoke; it stood to the right of where Derek lay, like a floodlit sword in its perfection.

He nodded approval to himself. His drop had been success-fully placed. This was the Region of Fire, where the Cliff lived.

To lie there was content enough, to gaze on a scene never closely viewed by man fulfilment enough—until he realized that a wide segment of landscape offered not the slightest

18

glimmer of illumination: He looked into it with a keen warm-sight, and found it was the Cliff.

The immense bulk of the thing blotted out all light from the ground and rose to eclipse the cloud over its crest.

At the mere sight of it, Derek's primary and secondary hearts began to beat out a hastening pulse of awe. Stretched flat on the ground, his paragravs keeping him level to IG, he peered ahead at it; he swallowed to clear his choked throat; his eyes strained through the mosaic of dull light in an effort to define the Cliff.

One thing was sure: it was large! He cursed that although photosistors allowed him to use his warmsight on objects beyond the suit he wore, this sense was distorted by the eternal firework display. Then in a moment of good seeing he had an accurate fix: the Cliff was three-quarters of a mile away! From first observations, he had thought it to be no more than a hundred yards distant.

Now he knew how large it was. It was enormous!

Momentarily he gloated. The only sort of tasks worth being set were impossible ones. Star One's astrophysicists held the notion that the Cliff was in some sense aware; they required Derek to take them a pound of its flesh. How do you carve a being the size of a small moon?

All the time he lay there, the wind jarred along the veins and supporters of his suit. Gradually it occurred to Derek that the vibration he felt from this constant motion was changed. It carried a new note and a new strength. He looked about, placed his gloved hand outstretched on the ground.

The wind was no longer vibrating. It was the earth that shook, Festi itself that trembled. The Cliff was moving!

When he looked back up at it with both his senses, he saw which way it headed. Jarring steadily, it bore down on him.

'If it has intelligence, then it will reason—if it has detected me—that I am too small to offer it harm. So it will offer me none and I have nothing to fear,' Derek told himself. The logic did not reassure him.

An absorbent pseudopod, activated by a simple humidity gland in the brow of his helmet, slid across his forehead and removed the sweat that formed there.

Visibility fluttered like a rag in a cellar. The slow forward surge of the Cliff was still something Derek sensed rather than saw. Now the rolling mattresses of cloud blotted the thing's crest, as it in its turn eclipsed the fountains of fire. To the jar of its approach even the marrow of Derek's bones raised a response.

Something else also responded.

The legs of Derek's suit began to move. The arms moved. The body wriggled.

Puzzled, Derek stiffened his legs. Irresistibly, the knees of the suit hinged, forcing his own to do likewise. And not only his knees: his arms too, stiffly though he braced them on the ground before him, were made to bend to the whim of the suit. He could not keep still without breaking bones.

Thoroughly alarmed he lay there, flexing contortedly to keep rhythm with his suit, performing the gestures of an idiot.

As if it had suddenly learnt to crawl, the suit began to move forward. It shuffled forward over the ground; Derek inside went willy-nilly with it.

One ironic thought struck him. Not only was the mountain coming to Mohammed; Mohammed was perforce going to the mountain. . . .

III

Nothing he could do checked his progress; he was no longer master of his movements; his will was useless. With the realization rode a sense of relief. His Mistress could hardly blame him for anything that happened now.

Through the darkness he went on hands and knees, blundering in the direction of the oncoming Cliff, prisoner in an animated prison.

The only constructive thought that came to him was that his suit had somehow become subject to the Cliff. How, he did not know or try to guess. He crawled. He was almost relaxed now, letting his limbs move limply with the suit movements.

Smoke furled him about. The vibrations ceased, telling him that the Cliff was stationary again. Raising his head, he could see nothing but smoke—produced perhaps by the Cliff's mass as it scraped over the ground. When the blur parted, he glimpsed only darkness. The thing was directly ahead!

He blundered on. Abruptly he began to climb, still involuntarily aping the movements of his suit.

Beneath him was a doughy substance, tough yet yielding. The suit worked its way heavily upwards at an angle of something like sixty-five degrees; the stiffeners creaked, the paragravs throbbed. He was ascending the Cliff.

By this time there was no doubt in Derek's mind that the thing possessed what might be termed volition, if not consciousness. It possessed too a power no man could claim: it could impart that volition to an inanimate object like his suit. Helpless inside it, he carried his considerations a stage further. This power to impart volition seemed to have a limited range: otherwise the Cliff would surely not have bothered to move its gigantic mass at all, but would have forced the suit to traverse all the distance between them. If this reasoning were sound, then the lightpusher was safe from capture in orbit.

The movement of his arms distracted him. His suit was tunnelling. Giving it no aid, he lay and let his hands make swimming motions. If it was going to bore into the Cliff, then he could only conclude he was about to be digested: yet he stilled his impulse to struggle, knowing that struggle was fruitless.

Thrusting against the doughy stuff, the suit burrowed into it and made a sibilant little world of movement and friction which stopped directly it stopped, leaving Derek embedded in the most solid kind of isolation.

To ward off growing claustrophobia, he attempted to switch on his headlight; his suit arms remained so stiff he could not bend them enough to reach the toggle. All he could do was lie there helplessly in his shell and stare into the featureless darkness of the Cliff.

But the darkness was not entirely featureless. His ears detected a constant *slither* along the outside surfaces of his suit. His warmsight discerned a meaningless pattern beyond his helmet. Though he focused his boscises, he could make no sense of the pattern; it had neither symmetry nor meaning for him. . . .

Yet for his body it seemed to have some meaning. Derek felt his limbs tremble, was aware of pulses and phantom impressions within himself that he had not known before. The realization percolated through to him that he was in touch with powers of which he had no cognizance—and, conversely, that something was in touch with him that had no cognizance of his powers.

An immense heaviness overcame him. The forces of life laboured within him. He sensed more vividly than before the vast bulk of the Cliff. Though it was dwarfed by the mass of Festi XV, it was as large as a good-sized asteroid. . . . He could picture an asteroid, formed from a jetting explosion of gas on the face of Festi the sun. Half-solid, half-molten, it swung about its parent on an eccentric orbit. Cooling under an interplay of pressures, its interior crystallized into a unique form. So, with its surface semi-plastic, it existed for many millions of years, gradually accumulating an electrostatic charge that poised . . . and waited . . . and brewed the life acids about its crystalline heart.

Festi was a stable system, but once in every so many thousands of millions of years, the giant first, second, and third planets achieved perihelion with the sun and with each other

21

simultaneously. This happened coincidentally with the asteroid's nearest approach; it was wrenched from its orbit and all but grazed the three lined-up planets. Vast electrical and gravitational forces were unleashed. The asteroid glowed: and woke to consciousness. Life was not born on it: it was born to life, born in one cataclysmic clash!

Before it had more than mutely savoured the sad-sharp-sweet sensation of consciousness, it was in trouble. Plunging away from the sun on its new course, it found itself snared in the gravitational pull of the 4G planet, Festi XV. It knew no shaping force but gravity; gravity was to it all that oxygen was to cellular life on Earth; yet it had no wish to exchange its flight for captivity; yet it was too puny to resist. For the first time, the asteroid recognized that its consciousness had a use, in that it could to some extent control its environment outside itself. Rather than risk being broken up in Festi's orbit, it sped inwards, and by retarding its own fall performed its first act of volition, an act that brought it down shaken but entire on the surface of the planet.

For an immeasurable period, the asteroid—but now it was the Cliff—lay in the shallow crater formed by its impact, speculating without thought. It knew nothing except the inorganic scene about it, and could visualize nothing else, but that scene it knew well. Gradually it came to some kind of terms with the scene. Formed by gravity, it used gravity as thoughtlessly as a man uses breath; it began to move other things, and it began to move itself.

That it should be other than alone in the universe had never occurred to the Cliff. Now it knew there was other life, it accepted the fact. The other life was not as it was; that it accepted. The other life had its own requirements; that it accepted. Of questions, of doubt, it did not know. It had a need; so did the other life; they should both be accommodated, for accommodation was the adjustment to pressure, and that response it comprehended.

Derek Ende's suit began to move again under external volition. Carefully it worked its way backwards. It was ejected from the Cliff. It lay still.

Derek himself lay still. He was barely conscious.

In a half-daze, he was piecing together what had happened. The Cliff had communicated with him; if he ever doubted that, the evidence of it lay clutched in the crook of his left arm.

'Yet it did not—yet it could not communicate with me!' he murmured. But it had communicated: he was still faint with the burden of it.

The Cliff had nothing like a brain. It had not 'recognized' Derek's brain. Instead, it had communicated with the only part of him it could recognize; it had communicated direct to his cell organization, and in particular probably to those cyto-plasmic structures, the mitochondria, the power sources of the cell. His brain had been by-passed, his own cells had taken in the information offered.

He recognized his feeling of weakness. The Cliff had drained him of power. Even that could not drain his feeling of triumph. For the Cliff had taken information even as it gave it. The Cliff had learnt that other life existed in other parts of the universe.

Without hesitation, without debate, it had given a fragment of itself to be taken to those other parts of the universe. Derek's mission was completed.

In the Cliff's gesture, Derek read one of the deepest urges of living things: the urge to make an impression on another living thing. Smiling wryly, he pulled himself to his feet.

He was alone in the Region of Fire. The occasional mourn-ful flame still confronted its surrounding dark, but the Cliff had disappeared; he had lain on the threshold of conscious-ness longer than he thought. He looked at his chronometer, to find it was high time he moved towards his rendezvous with the lightpusher. Stepping up his suit heating to combat the cold that began to seep through his bones, he revved up the paragrav unit and rose. The noisome clouds came down and engulfed him; Festi was lost to view. Soon he had risen beyond cloud or atmosphere.

Under Jon's direction, the space craft homed on to Derek's radio beacon. After a few tricky minutes, they matched veloci-ties and Derek climbed aboard.

'Are you all right?' the partheno asked, as his master staggered into a flight seat.

'Fine—just weak. I'll tell you all about it as I do a report on spool for Pyrylyn. They're going to be pleased with us.'

He produced a yellowy grey blob of matter that had ex-panded to the size of a large turkey and held it out to Jon.

'Don't touch this with your bare hands. Put it in one of the low-temperature lockers under 4Gs. It's a little souvenir from Festi XV.'

IV

The Eyebright in Pynnati, one of Pyrylyn's capital cities, was where you went to enjoy yourself on the most lavish scale possible. This was where Derek Ende's hosts took him, with Jon in self-effacing attendance.

23

They lay in a nest of couches which slowly revolved, giving them a full view of other dance and couch parties. The room itself moved. Its walls were transparent; through them could be seen an ever-changing view as the room slid up and down and about the great metal framework of the Eyebright. First they were on the outside of the structure, with the bright night lights of Pynnati winking up at them as if intimately involved in their delight. Then they slipped inwards in the slow evagination of the building, to be surrounded by other pleasure rooms, their revellers clearly visible as they moved grandly up or down or along.

Uneasily, Derek lay on his couch. A vision of his mistress's face was before him; he could imagine how she would treat all this harmless festivity: with cool contempt. His own pleasure was consequently reduced to ashes.

'I suppose you'll be moving back to Earth as soon as possible?'

'Eh?' Derek grunted.

'I said, I supposed you would soon be going home again.' The speaker was Belix Ix Sappose, Chief Administrator of High Gee Research at Star One; as Derek's host of the evening, he lay next to him.

'I'm sorry, Belix, yes—I shall have to head back for home soon.'

'No "have to" about it. You have discovered an entirely new life form; we can now attempt communication with the Festi XV entity, with goodness knows what extension of knowledge. The government can easily show its gratitude by awarding you any sort of post here you care to name; I am not without influence in that respect as you are aware. I don't imagine that Earth in its senescent stage has much to offer a man of your calibre.'

Derek thought of what it had to offer. He was bound to it. These decadent people did not understand how anything could be binding.

'Well, what do you say, Ende? I'm not speaking idly.' Belix Ix Sappose tapped his antler system impatiently.

'Er . . . Oh, they will discover a great deal from the Cliff. That doesn't concern me. My part of the work is over. I'm just a field worker, not an intellectual.'

'You don't reply to my suggestion.'

He looked at Belix with only slight vexation. Belix was an unglaat, one of a species that had done as much as any to bring about the peaceful concourse of the galaxy. His backbone branched into an elaborate antler system, from which six sloe-dark eyes surveyed Derek with unblinking irritation.

24

Other members of the party, including Jupkey, Belix's female, were also looking at him.

'I must get back to Earth soon,' Derek said. What had Belix said? Offered some sort of post? Restlessly he shifted on his couch, under pressure as always when surrounded by people he knew none too well.

'You are bored, Mr. Ende.'

'No, not at all. My apologies, Belix. I'm overcome as always by the luxury of Eyebright. I was watching the nude dancers.'

'I fear you are bored.'

'Not at all, I assure you.'

'May I get you a woman?'

'No, thank you.'

'A boy, perhaps?'

'No, thank you.'

'Have you ever tried the flowering asexuals from the Cephids?'

'Not at present, thank you.'

'Then perhaps you will excuse us if Jupkey and I remove our clothes and join the dance,' Belix said stiffly.

As they moved out on to the dance floor to greet the strepent trumpets, Derek heard Jupkey say something of which he caught only the words 'arrogant Earthborn'. His eyes met Jon's; he saw that the partheno had overheard the phrase too.

In an instinctive gesture of his left hand, Derek revealed his mortification. He rose and began to pace round the room. Often he shouldered his way through a knot of naked dancers, ignoring their complaints.

At one of the doors, a staircase was floating by. He stepped on to it to escape from the crowds.

Four young women were passing down the stairs. They were gaily dressed, with sonant-stones pulsing on their costumes. In their faces youth kept its lantern, lighting them as they laughed and chattered. Derek stopped and beheld the girls. One of them he recognized. Instinctively he called her name: 'Eva!'

She had already seen him. Waving her companions on, she came back to him, dancing up the intervening steps.

'So the brave Earthborn climbs once more the golden stairs of Pynnati; Well, Derek Ende, your eyes are as dark as ever, and your brow as high!'

As he looked at her, the wakeful trumpets were in tune for him for the first time that evening, and his delight rose up in his throat.

'Eva! . . . And your eyes as bright as ever. . . . And you have no man with you.'

25

'The powers of coincidence work on your behalf.' She laughed—yes, he remembered that sound!—and then said more seriously, 'I heard you were here with Belix Sappose and his female; so I was making the grandly foolish gesture of coming to see you. You remember how devoted I am to grandly foolish gestures.'

'So foolish?'

'Probably. You have less ability to change in you, Derek Ende, than has the core of Pyrylyn. To suppose otherwise is foolish, to know how unalterable you are and still to see you doubly foolish.'

He took her hand, beginning to lead her up the staircase; the rooms moving by them on either side were blurs to his eyes.

'Must you still bring up that old charge, Eva?'

'It lies between us; I do not have to touch it. I fear your unchangeability because I am a butterfly against your grey castle.'

'You are beautiful, Eva, so beautiful! And may a butterfly not rest unharmed on a castle wall?' He fitted into her allusive way of speech with difficulty.

'Walls! I cannot bear your walls, Derek! Am I a bulldozer that I should want to come up against walls? To be either inside or outside them is to be a prisoner.'

'Let us not quarrel until we have found some point of agreement,' he said. 'Here are the stars. Can't we agree about them?'

'If we are both indifferent to them,' she said, looking out and impudently winding his arm about her. The staircase had reached the zenith of its travels and moved slowly sideways along the upper edge of Eyebright. They stood on the top step with night flashing their images back at them from the glass.

Eva Coll-Kennerley was a human, but not of Earthborn stock. She was a velure, born on the y-cluster worlds of the dense Third Arm of the galaxy, and her skin was richly covered with the brown fur of her kind. Her mercurial talents were employed in the same research department that enjoyed Belix Sappose's more sober ones; Derek had met her there on an earlier visit to Pyrylyn. Their love had been an affair of swords.

He looked at her now and touched her and could say not one word for himself. When she flashed a liquid eye at him, he assayed an awkward smile.

'Because I am oriented like a compass towards strong men, my lavish offer to you still holds good. Is it not bait enough?' she asked him.

'I don't think of you as a trap, Eva.'

'Then for how many more centuries are you going to re-frigerate your nature on Earth? You still remain faithful, if I recall your euphemism for slavery, to your mistress, to her cold lips and locked heart?'

'I have no choice!'

'Ah yes, my debate on that motion was defeated: and more than once. Is she still pursuing her researches into the trans-mutability of species?'

'Oh yes, indeed. The mediaeval idea that one species can turn into another was foolish in the Midlde Ages; now, with the gradual accumulation of cosmic radiation in planetary bodies and its effect on genetic stability, it is correct to a cer-tain definable extent. She is endeavouring to show that cellular bondage can be——'

'Yes, yes, and this serious talk is an eyesore in Eyebright! Must I hear of her when I want to talk of you? You are locked away, Derek, doing your sterile deeds of heroism and never entering the real world. If you imagine you can live with her much longer and then come to me, you are mistaken. Your walls grow higher about your ears every century, till I cannot cannot—oh, it's the wrong metaphor!—cannot scale you!'

Even in his pain, the texture of her fur was joy to his warm-sight. Helplessly he shook his head in an effort to shake her clattering words away.

'Look at you being big and brave and silent even now! You're so arrogant,' she said—and then, without perceptible change of tone, 'Because I still love the bit of you inside the castle, I'll make once more my monstrous and petty offer to you.'

'No, please, Eva! . . .'

'But yes! Forget this tedious bondage of Earth, forget this ghastly matriarchy, live here with me. I don't want you for ever. You know I am a eudemonist and judge by standards of pleasure—our liaison need be only for a century or two. In that time, I will deny you nothing your senses may require.'

'Eva!'

'After that, our demands will be satisfied. You may then go back to the Lady Mother of Endehaaven for all I care.'

'Eva, you know how I spurn this belief, this eudemonism.'

'Forget your creed! I'm asking you nothing difficult. Who are you to haggle? Am I fish, to be bought by the kilo, this bit selected, this rejected?'

He was silent.

'*You* don't need me,' he said at last. 'You have everything

27

already: beauty, wit, sense, warmth, feeling, balance, comfort. *She* has nothing. She is shallow, haunted, cold—oh, she needs me, Eva. . . .'

'You are apologizing for yourself, not her.'

She had already turned with the supple movement of a velure and was running down the staircase. Lighted chambers drifted up about them like bubbles.

His laboured attempt to explain his heart turned to exasperation. He ran down after her, grasping her arm.

'Listen to me, will you, damn you!'

'Nobody in Pyrylyn would listen to such masochistic nonsense as yours! You are an arrogant fool, Derek, and I am a weak-willed one. Now release me!'

As the next room came up, she jumped through its entrance and disappeared into the crowd.

V

Not all the drifting chambers of Eyebright were lighted. Some pleasures come more delightfully with the dark, and these pleasures were coaxed and cosseted into fruition in shrouded halls where illumination cast only the gentlest ripple on the ceiling and the gloom was sensuous with ylang-ylang and other perfumes. Here Derek found a place to weep.

Sections of his life slid before him as if impelled by the same mechanisms that moved Eyebright. Always, one presence was there.

Angrily he related to himself how he always laboured to satisfy her—yes, in every sphere laboured to satisfy her! And how when that gratification was accorded him it came as though riven from her, as a spring sometimes trickles down the split face of a rock. Undeniably there was satisfaction for him in drinking from that cool source—but no, where was the satisfaction when pleasure depended on such extreme disciplining and subduing of himself?

Mistress, I love and hate your needs!

And the discipline had been such . . . so long, also . . . that now when he might enjoy himself far from her, he could scarcely strike a trickle from his own rock. He had walked here before, in this city where the hedonists and endemonists reigned, walked among the scents of pleasure, walked among the ioblepharous women, the beautiful guests and celebrated beauties, with My Lady always in him, feeling that she showed even on his countenance. People spoke to him: somehow he replied. They manifested gaiety: he tried to do so. They opened to him: he attempted a response. All the time, he hoped they would understand that his arrogance masked only shyness—or did he hope that it was his shyness which masked arrogance? He did not know.

Who could presume to know? The one quality holds much of the other. Both refuse to come forward and share.

He roused from his meditation knowing that Eva Coll-Kennerley was again somewhere near. She had not left the building, then! She was seeking him out!

Derek half-rose from his position in a shrouded alcove. He was baffled to think how she could have traced him here. On entering Eyebright, visitors were given sonant-stones, by which they could be traced from room to room; but judging that nobody would wish to trace him, Derek had switched his stone off even before leaving Belix Sappose's party.

He heard Eva's voice, its unmistakable overtones not near, not far. . . .

'You find the most impenetrable bushels to hide your light under. . . .'

He caught no more. She had sunk down among tapestries with someone else. She was not after him at all! Waves of relief and regret rolled over him . . . and when he paid attention again, she was speaking his name.

With shame on him, like a wolf creeping towards a camp fire, he crouched forward to listen. At once his warmsight told him to whom Eva spoke. He recognized the pattern of the antlers; Belix was there, with Jupkey sprawled beside him on some elaborate kind of bed.

'. . . useless to try again. Derek is far too entombed within himself,' Eva said.

'Entombed rather within his conditioning,' Belix said. 'We found the same. It's conditioning, my dear.'

'However he became entombed, I still admire him enough to want to understand him.' Eva's voice was a note or two astray from its usual controlled timbre.

'Look at it scientifically,' Belix said, with the weighty inflections of a man about to produce truth out of a hat. 'Earth is the last bastion of a bankrupt culture. The Earthborns number less than a couple of millions now. They disdain social graces and occasions. They are served by parthenogenically bred slaves, all of which are built on the same controlled genetic formula. They are inbred. In consequence, they have become practically a species apart. You can see it all in friend Ende. As I say, he's entombed in his conditioning. A tragedy, Eva, but you must face up to it.'

'You're probably right, you pontifical old pop,' Jupkey said lazily. 'Who but an Earthborn would do what Derek did on Festi?'

29

'No, no!' Eva said. 'Derek's ruled by a woman, not by conditioning. He's——'

'In Ende's case they are one and the same thing, my dear, believe me. Consider Earth's social organization. The partheno slaves have replaced all but a comparative handful of true Earthborns. That handful has parcelled out Earth into great estates which it holds by a sinister matriarchalism.'

'Yes, I know, but Derek——'

'Derek is caught in the system. The Earthborns have fallen into a mating pattern for which there is no precedent. The sons of a family marry their mothers, not only to perpetuate their line but because the productive Earthborn female is scarce now that Earth itself is senescent. This is what the Endes have done; this is what Derek Ende has done. His "mistress" is both mother and wife to him. Given the factor of longevity as well—well, naturally, you ensure an excessive emotional rigidity that almost nothing can break. Not even you, my sweet-coated Eva!'

'He was on the point of breaking tonight!'

'I doubt it,' Belix said. 'Ende may want to get away from his claustrophobic home, but the same forces that drive him off will eventually lure him back.'

'I tell you he was on the point of breaking—only I broke first.'

'Well, as Teer Ruche said to me many centuries ago, only a pleasure-hater knows how to shape a pleasure-hater. I would say you were lucky he did not break; you would only have had a baby on your hands.'

Her answering laugh did not ring true.

'My Lady of Endehaaven, then, must be the one to do it. I will never try again—though he seems under too much stress to stand for long. Oh, it's really immoral! He deserves better!'

'A moral judgement from you, Eva!' Jupkey exclaimed amusedly to the fragrant bloom.

'My advice to you, Eva, is to forget all about the poor fellow. Apart from anything else, he is scarcely articulate— which would not suit you for a reason.'

The unseen listener could bear no more. A sudden rage—as much against himself for hearing as against them for speaking—burst over him, freeing him to act. Straightening up, he seized the arm of the couch on which Belix and Jupkey nestled, wildly supposing he could tip them on to the floor.

Too late, his warmsight warned him of the real nature of the couch. Instead of tipping it, it swivelled, sending a wave of liquid over him. The two unglaats were lying in a warm bath scented with ylang-ylang and other essences.

Jupkey squealed in anger and fright. Kicking out, she caught Derek on the shin with a hoof; he slipped in the oily liquid and fell. Belix, unaided by warmsight, jumped out of the bath, entangled himself with Derek's legs, and also fell.

Eva was shouting for lights. Other occupants of the hall cried back that darkness must prevail at all costs.

Picking himself up—leaving only his dignity behind—Derek ran for the exit, abandoning the confusion to sort itself out as it would.

Burningly, disgustedly, he made his way dripping from Eyebright. The hastening footsteps of Jon followed him like an echo all the way to the space field.

Soon he would be back at Endehaaven. Though he would always be a failure in his dealings with other humans, there at least he knew every inch of his bleak allotted territory.

ENVOI

Had there been a spell over all Endehaaven, it could have been no quieter when My Lord Derek Ende arrived home.

I informed My Lady of the moment when his lightpusher arrived and rode at orbit. In the receptor bowl I watched him and Jon come home, cutting north-west across the emaciated wilds of Europe, across Denmark, over the Shetlands, the Faroes, the sea, alighting by the very edge of the island, by the fjord with its silent waters.

All the while the wind lay low as if under some stunning malediction, and none of our tall trees stirred.

'Where is my Mistress, Hols?' Derek asked me, as I went to greet him and assist him out of his suit.

'She asked me to tell you that she is confined to her chambers and cannot see you, My Lord.'

He looked me in the eyes as he did so rarely.

'Is she ill?'

'No. She simply said she would not see you.'

Without waiting to remove his suit, he hurried on into the building.

Over the next two days, he was about but little, preferring to remain in his room while My Lady remained in hers. Once he wandered among the experimental tanks and cages. I saw him net a fish and toss it into the air, watching it while it struggled into new form and flew away until it was lost in a jumbled background of cumulus; but it was plain he was less interested in the riddles of stress and transmutation than in the symbolism of the carp's flight.

Mostly he sat compiling the spools on which he imposed

31

the tale of his life. All one wall was covered with files full of
these spools: the arrested drumbeats of past centuries. From
the later spools I have secretly compiled this record; for all
his unspoken self-pity, he never knew the sickness of merely
observing.

We parthenos will never understand the luxuries of a
divided mind. Surely suffering as much as happiness is a kind
of artistry?

On the day that he received a summons from Star One to
go upon another quest for them, Derek met My Lady in the
Blue Corridor.

'It is good to see you about again, Mistress,' he said, kissing
her cheek. 'Staying confined in your room is bad for you.'

She stroked his hair. On her nervous hand she wore
one ring with an amber stone; her gown was of olive and
umber.

'I was very upset to have you go away from me. The Earth
is dying, Derek, and I fear its loneliness. You have left me
alone too much. However, I have recovered myself and am
glad to see you back.'

'You know I am glad to see you. Smile for me and come
outside for some fresh air. The sun is shining.'

'It's so long since it shone. Do you remember how once it
always shone? I can't bear to quarrel any more. Take my arm
and be kind to me.'

'Mistress, I always wish to be kind to you. And I have all
sorts of things to discuss with you. You'll want to hear what I
have been doing, and——'

'You won't leave me alone any more?'

He felt her hand tighten on his arm. She spoke very loudly.

'That was one of the things I wished to discuss—later,' he
said. 'First let me tell you about the wonderful life form with
which I made contact on Festi.'

As they left the corridor and descended the paragravity
shaft, My Lady said wearily, 'I suppose that's a polite way of
telling me that you are bored here.'

He clutched her hands as they floated down. Then he
released them and clutched her face instead, cupping its
melancholy oval between his palms.

'Understand this, Mistress mine, I love you and want to
serve you. You are in my blood; wherever I go I never can
forget you. My dearest wish is to make you happy—this you
must know. But equally you must know that I have needs of
my own.'

Grumpily she said, withdrawing her face, 'Oh, I know that
all right. And I know those needs will always come first with

you. Whatever you say or pretend, you don't care a rap about me. You make that all too clear.'

She moved ahead of him, shaking off the hand he put on her arm. He had a vision of himself running down a golden staircase and stretching out that same detaining hand to another girl. The indignity of having to repeat oneself, century after century.

'You're lying! You're faking! You're being cruel!' he said.

Gleaming, she turned.

'Am I? Then answer me this—aren't you already planning to leave Endehaaven and me again soon?'

He smote his forehead.

He said inarticulately, 'Look, you must try to stop this recrimination. Yes, yes, it's true I am thinking. . . . But I have to—I reproach myself. I could be kinder. But you shut yourself away when I come back, you don't welcome me——'

'Trust you to find excuses rather than face up to your own nature!' she said contemptuously, walking briskly into the garden. Amber and olive and umber, and sable of hair, she walked down the path, her outlines sharp in the winter air; in the perspectives of his mind she did not dwindle.

For some minutes he stood in the threshold, immobilized by antagonistic emotions.

Finally he pushed himself out into the sunlight.

She was in her favourite spot by the fjord, feeding an old badger from her hand. Only her increased attention to the badger suggested that she heard him approach.

His boscises twitched as he said, 'If you will forgive a cliché, I apologize.'

'I don't mind what you do.'

Walking backwards and forwards behind her, he said, 'When I was away, I heard some people talking. On Pyrylyn this was. They were discussing the mores of our matrimonial system.'

'It's no business of theirs.'

'Perhaps not. But what they said suggested a new line of thought to me.'

She put the old badger back in his cage without comment.

'Are you listening, Mistress?'

'Do go on.'

'Try to listen sympathetically. Consider all the history of galactic exploration—or even before that, consider the explorers of Earth in the pre-space age, men like Shackleton and so on. They were brave men, of course, but wouldn't it be strange if most of them only ventured where they did because the struggle at home was too much for them?'

3   33

He stopped. She had turned to him; the half-smile was whipped off his face by her look of fury.

'And you're trying to tell me that that's how you see yourself—a martyr? Derek, how you must hate me! Not only do you go away, you secretly blame me because you go away. It doesn't matter that I tell you a thousand times I want you here—no, it's all my fault! I drive you away! That's what you tell your charming friends on Pyrylyn, isn't it? Oh, how you must hate me!'

Savagely he grasped her wrists. She screamed to me for aid and struggled. I came near but halted, playing my usual impotent part. He swore at her, bellowed for her to be silent, whereupon she cried the louder, shaking furiously in his arms, both of them tumultuous in their emotions.

He struck her across the face.

At once she was quiet. Her eyes closed, almost it would seem in ecstasy. Standing there, she had the pose of a woman offering herself.

'Go on, hit me! You want to hit me!' she whispered.

With the words, with the look of her, he too was altered. As if realizing for the first time her true nature, he dropped his fists and stepped back, staring at her sick-mouthed. His heel met no resistance. He twisted suddenly, spread out his arms as if to fly, and fell over the cliff edge.

Her scream pursued him down.

Even as his body hit the waters of the fjord, it began to change. A flurry of foam marked some sort of painful struggle beneath the surface. Then a seal plunged into view, dived below the next wave, and swam towards the open sea over which already a freshening breeze blew.

HOW TO BE A SOLDIER

Sergeant Taylor was dreaming.

He was a certain Colonel whose barracks were far below ground. In the mess, the Special Wing was making merry. The place was overcrowded, both with long trestle tables full of food and wine, and with soldiers and the women who had been invited to attend. Despite the Spartan aspect of the mess, the atmosphere was of festival—that especially hectic kind of festival held by men whose motto is the grim old motto: Eat, drink, and be merry, for tomorrow we die.

The Colonel was eating and drinking, but he was not yet merry. Although it pleased him to see his men carousing, he was cut off from them by their merriment. He still knew what they had forgotten, that at any moment the summons might come. And then they would leave, and collect their equipment, and go Above, to face whatever dark things had to be faced.

All this was a part of the Colonel's profession, his life. He did not resent it, nor did he particularly fear it; he felt only a mild attack of something very like stage fright.

The faces around him had receded into a general blur. Now he focused on them, wondering idly who and how many would accompany him on the mission. He glanced too at the women.

Under duress of war, all military had retreated underground. Conditions below were harsh and well nigh intolerable, only mitigated by generous supplies of the new synthetic foods and drinks. After a decade of war, plankton brandy tastes as good as the real thing—when the real thing has ceased to exist. The women were not synthetic. They had forsaken the ruinous towns Above for the comparative safety of the subterranean garrison towns. In so doing, most of them had saved their lives only to lose their humanity. Now they fought and screamed over their men, caring little for what they won.

The Colonel looked at them with both compassion and contempt. Whichever side won the war, women had already lost it.

Then he saw a face that was neither laughing nor shouting.

It belonged to a woman sitting almost opposite him at his table. She was listening to a blurry-eyed, red-faced corporal, whose heavy arm lay over her shoulder as he spun her some rambling tale of woe. Mary, the Colonel thought; she must be called something simple and sweet like Mary.

Her face was ordinary enough, except that it bore none of the marks of viciousness and vulgarity so common in this age. Her hair was light brown, her eyes an enormous blue-grey. Her lips were not thin, though her face was.

Mary turned and saw the Colonel regarding her. She smiled at him.

The moments of revolution in a man's life come silently and unexpectedly. The Colonel had been an ordinary soldier; when Mary smiled, he became something more complex. He saw himself as he was: an old man in his middle thirties who had surrendered everything personal to becoming part of a military machine. This sad, beautiful, ordinary, face told of all he had missed, of all the richer side of life real only to a man and woman who love each other.

It told him more. It told him that even now it was not too late for him. For the face was a promise as well as a reproach.

All this and more ran through the Colonel's mind, and some of it was reflected in his eyes. Mary, it was clear, understood something of his expression.

'Can you get away from him?' the Colonel said, with a note of pleading in his voice.

Without looking at the soldier whose arm lay so heavily over her shoulders, Mary answered something. What she said it was impossible to hear in the general hubbub. Seeing her pale lips move, and in agony at not hearing what she was saying, the Colonel called to her to repeat her sentence.

At that moment the duty siren sounded.

The uproar redoubled. Military police came pouring into the mess, pushing and kicking the drunks on to their feet and marching them out of the door.

Hopelessly, the Colonel rose to his feet. Leaning across the table and touching Mary's hand, he said, 'I must see you again and speak to you. If I survive this mission I will be here tomorrow night. Will you meet me?'

A fleeting smile.

'I'll be here,' she said.

Hope flooded into him. Love, gratitude, all the secret springs of his nature poured forth into his veins. Then he turned towards the doors.

Just outside, a tube truck was waiting. The Special Wing staggered or was pushed into it. When all were accounted for, the doors closed and the tube moved off, snoring into the tunnel on an upward gradient.

It stopped again at Medical Bay, where orderlies with alco-holometers awaited them. Anyone who flipped the needle was instantly given an anti-toxic drug. The Colonel, for all that he had drunk little, had to submit to an injection. The alcohol in his blood was neutralized almost at once. Within five minutes, everyone in the room was stone cold sober again. To wage war in its present form would not have been possible without drugs.

The party, quieter now and with set faces, climbed back into the tube. It rose on an ascending spiral of tunnel, depositing them next at Briefing. They were now near the surface.

Accompanied by a few under-officers and N.C.O.s, the Colonel entered Information Briefing. The rest of his men—or those picked for this particular mission—went to Morale Briefing. Here, film and television would prepare them by direct and subliminal means for the hazards to come.

The Colonel and his party faced a brigadier who began speaking as soon as they sat down.

'We have something fresh for you today. The enemy is try-ing a new move, and we have a new move to counteract it. The six of you will take only eighteen men with you on this mission. You will be lightly armed, and your safety will depend entirely on the element of surprise. When I tell you that if all goes well we expect to have you back here in ten hours, I do not want you to forget that those ten hours may vitally affect the whole outcome of the war.'

He went on to describe their objective. The picture was simple and clear as it built up in the Colonel's mind. He dis-carded all details but the key ones. Half-way round the world, the enemy was gathered in some strength in a forest. In the middle of the forest was an old circular wooden building five stories high. On the top story of this building, looking over the treetops, was a control-room from which fleets of missiles could be launched.

The control-room was also a weather station, and it was for this reason it had been more convenient to situate it above ground. When the right weather prevailed over enemy terri-tory, the missiles would be launched. They contained bacteria.

'We stand to have a major plague on our hands if this set-up is not put out of action at once,' the Brigadier said. 'Another force has been given the task of wiping out the launching site, but it's underground and difficult to locate. First we must put the control-room out of action, and that is your job.

'An anti-cyclone is building up over us now. Reports show that conditions should be ideal for an enemy launching in ten to twelve hours. We have to kill them before that.'

He then described the forces to be met with in the forest. They were heavy, but badly deployed as yet. Only the paths through the forest were defended, since vehicular attack through the trees was impossible.

'This is where you and your men come in, Colonel. Our laboratories, bless 'em, have just turned up with a new wonder drug called Fast-Plus. As far as I can understand, it's a development of the old pep pills. Unfortunately it's still rather in the experimental stage, but desperate situations call for desperate remedies. . . .'

At last the briefing was over, and the officers were joined by the men who had been selected to accompany them. The twenty-four of them then marched to an armoury, where they were equipped with special weapons and combat suits. Then they took one of the big elevators to Above.

On the surface it was still night. In a diesel truck they rode over to a landing strip, ventilator shafts and ruins of an old surface town making no more than vague smudges in the darkness that encompassed them. A plane awaited them. In ten minutes they were all aboard and strapped into position.

A high-ranking medical man entered. In a pouch strapped to his belt he carried the supply of Fast-Plus. This he would administer when they reached the enemy forest; now, he had a preparatory tranquillizer for them which would render the Fast-Plus more effective later. He administered this tranquillizer to them orally just before they took off.

The plane moved upwards with a sickening bound. Twenty-four men subsided into a drugged coma as they hurtled into the stratosphere, as they reached the margins of space, as they glittered in sunlight before turning to fall back like a stone towards Earth. Below them, out of the bowl of night, the enemy forest swam.

Under double parachutes, descending vertically, they braked and landed in an acre of bracken beneath the shadow of the first trees. The sedation period ended as the hatch swung open.

'Let's have you outside quietly, men,' the Colonel said.

He checked his chronometer with the pilot's before leaving. It was 0622 hours, with dawn in the offing and a chill breeze irritating the grass.

The medico came round with the Fast-Plus, which was made into boomerang-shaped capsules that fitted against the bottom teeth, under the tongue.

'Don't bite on them until the Colonel gives the word,' he said. 'And remember, don't worry about yourselves. Just get back to your plane and we'll take care of the after-effects.'

'Famous last words,' someone muttered.

The medico hurried back to his plane. It would be off as soon as they were gone; the special wing had to rendezvous with another one elsewhere when the mission was over. Fast-Plus pills in their mouths, the party set off for the trees in single file. Almost at once, a heavy gun opened fire.

'Keep your heads down. It's after the plane, not us,' the Colonel said. The gun's jerky bursts suggested it was radar-controlled and having trouble from the plane's baffle equipment. He dismissed it from his mind. They would have worries of their own in a moment.

The worries came sooner than he had expected. A strobo-light came on, its nervous blink fluttering across the clearing, washing everything in its path with white. At the same time, the Colonel's helmet beeped, telling him a radio eye had spotted him.

'Down flat!' he roared.

The air crackled with death as they flung themselves down. On their bellies they crawled into a hollow.

'We'll split into our five groups now,' the Colonel said. 'One and two to my left, four and five to my right. Seventy seconds from now on I'll blow my whistle; crunch your pills then and be off. Good luck. Move.'

Twenty men moved. Four stayed with the Colonel. Ignoring the racket in the clearing, he watched the smallest hand on his chronometer, his whistle in his left fist. As he had hoped, the noise had died as he blew his blast. He crunched his capsule and rose, the four men beside him.

They ran for the wood. They were among the trees.

The other four groups of five were among the trees also. Three of them were decoy groups. Only one of the other groups, number four, was actually due to reach the round building, approaching by a different route from the Colonel's.

As they entered the forest, the drug took effect. A slight dizziness seized the Colonel, a singing started in his ears. Against this minor irritation, a vast comfort swept through his limbs. He began to breathe more rapidly, and then to think and move more rapidly. His whole metabolism was accelerating.

Alarm filled him momentarily, although he had been primed on what to expect. The alarm came from some deep and un-plumbed personal core in him, a place that resented this tampering with its personal rhythm. Coupled with it came a vivid picture of Mary's face, as if the Colonel by submitting to this drug was somehow defiling her. Then the image and the alarm were gone, leaving the Colonel clear and superb.

Now he was sprinting, his men beside him. They flicked round dense bush, leaving the clearing behind. A searchlight burst into life, sweeping its narrow beam among the tree trunks in a confusing pattern of light and shade. As it caught group three, the Colonel shot it out.

He had acted fast, hardly realizing he was firing. The guns they carried had special light-touch trigger actions to respond to their new tempo.

A burst of firing answered his shot, but it fell behind them. They were moving faster, already breaking records.

They wove fast among the trees. Dawn gave them light to see by. Opposition, as briefing had forecast, was scattered. Mainly they ran uninterruptedly. They passed caravans, camouflaged vehicles, tanks, tents, some containing sleeping men. All these they skirted. Anything moving they shot. A 50 per cent acceleration of perception and motion turned them into supermen.

Absolute calm ruled in the Colonel's mind. He moved like a deadly machine. Sight and sound came through with ultra-clarity. He seemed to observe movement before it began. Noise played round him. A world of noise surrounded him.

He heard the rapid hammer of his heart, his breathing, the breathing of his fellows, the rustle of their limbs inside their clothes. He heard the crackle of twigs beneath their feet, faint shouts in the forest, distant shots—presumably marking the whereabouts of another group. He seemed to hear everything in the world.

They covered the first mile in five minutes, the second in under four. Occasionally the Colonel glanced at his wrist compass, but a mystic sense seemed to keep him on course.

When an unexpected burst of firing from a flank killed one of the group, the other four raced on without pause. It was as if they could never stop running.

The second mile was easy, and most of the third. Normally, the enemy was prepared for any eventuality: but that did not include a handful of men running. The idea was too laughable to be entertained. The Colonel's group got through only because it was impossible.

Now they were almost at destination. Some sort of warning of their approach had been given. The trees were spaced more widely, anti-tank guns were being rolled up, machine-gun posts manned. Strengthening, the light began to favour the enemy.

'Scatter!' the Colonel shouted, as a gun barked ahead. His voice sounded curiously high in his own ears.

His men swerved apart, keeping each other in sight. They

were moving like shadows now, limbs flickering, brains alight. They ran. They did not fire.

The machine-gun posts opened up. Missing four phantoms, they kept up their chatter in preparation for a main body of men who never arrived. The phantoms plunged on, tormented most by the noise, which bit like acid into their ear-drums.

Again the phantoms grouped in a last dash. Through the trees loomed a round wooden building. They were there!

The four fired together as a section of the enemy burst from a nearby hut. They shot a machine-gunner dead as he swung his barrel at them. They hurled grenades into a sandbagged strong point. Then they were in the control post.

It was as briefing had described it. The Colonel leading, the four bounded up the creaking spiral stair. Doors burst open as they mounted. But the enemy moved with a curious sloth and died without firing a shot. In three seconds flat they were at the top of the building.

Breathing rapidly, the Colonel flung open a door, the only door on this story.

This was the weather- and control-room.

Apparatus had been piled up in disorderly fashion, bearing witness to the fact that the enemy had only moved in here a comparatively few hours ago. But here was no mistaking the big weather charts on the walls—or the control console in the centre of the room. Right here was the point from which the bacteria-carrying missiles took their ultimate orders.

Several of the enemy were in the room. The firing nearby had alarmed them. One spoke into a phone, while except for one other the rest stared out of the windows anxiously. The one other sat at the firing console. He saw the Colonel first.

Astonishment and fear came on to his face, slackening the muscles there, dropping his mouth open. He slid round in his seat, lifting his hand at the same time to reach out for the press buttons. To the Colonel, he appeared to be moving in ultra-slow-motion, just as in ultra-slow-motion the other occupants of the room were turning to face their enemy.

Emitting a high squeal like a bat's the Colonel twitched his right index finger slightly. He saw the bullet speed home to its mark. Raising his hands to his chest, the push-button man toppled off his stool and fell beside the console.

One of the Colonel's men tossed an incendiary grenade into the room. They were running back down the spiral stairs as it roared into life. Again doors burst open on them, again they fired without thought. The grenade thrower squealed and plunged head first down the stairs. His three companions ran past him, out into the wood.

41

Setting his new course, the Colonel led his two men towards their rendezvous. This was the easiest part of their mission; they came on the scattered enemy from an unexpected quarter and were gone before he realized it. Behind them, a wooden building blazed.

They had four miles to go this way. After the first mile, the maximum effect of the drug began to wear off. The Colonel was aware that the abnormal clarity of his brain was changing into deadness. He ran on.

Sunshine broke through in splinters on to the carpet of the forest. Each fragment was incredibly sharp and memorable. Each noise underfoot was unforgettable. A slight breeze in the treetops was a protracted bellow as of an ocean breaking on rock. His own breathing was an adamantine clamour for air. He heard his bones click-click-click in their sockets, his muscles and sinews swishing in the gravies of their blood.

At the end of the third mile, one of the Colonel's two men collapsed without warning. His face was black, and he hit the ground with the sound of a felled tree, utterly burnt out. The others never paused.

The Colonel and his fellow reached the rendezvous. They lay twitching in a ditch until the plane came for them. By then there were twelve twitching men to carry away, all that was left of the original party. Two medical orderlies hustled them rapidly into bunks, sinking needles into their arms to stop their twitching.

Seemingly without interval, it was twelve hours later.

Again the Colonel sat in the mess. Despite the fatigue in his limbs, he had willed himself to come here. He had a date with Mary.

The junketing was getting into full swing about him, the nightly tide of debauchery and drunkenness was rising. Many of these men, like the Colonel himself, had faced death during the day; many more would be facing it tomorrow. Their duty was only to survive: their health was kept in capsules.

The Colonel sat at the end of one long table, close to the wall, keeping an empty chair next to him as the room filled. His ears echoed and ached with the noise about him. Wearily, he looked about for Mary.

Only after half an hour had passed did he feel the first twinge of apprehension. He did not know her real name. The events of the day, the rigours of the mission, had obliterated the memory of her face. She had smiled, yes. She had looked ordinary enough, yes. No . . . he knew not a thing about her except the hope she had stirred in him.

42

An hour passed, and still the chair was empty beside him. He sat on and on, submerged in noise. Probably she was in bed with the drunk who had had his arm round her yesterday. Boom, boom, boom went the meaningless din, and the chair remained empty beside him.

It was after two in the morning. The mess was emptying again. The symbolism of the chair hit the Colonel suddenly. Mary would not come. She would never come. He was just a soldier; there would be an empty chair beside him all his life. No Mary would ever come. Bitterly he pressed his face into his hands, trying to bury himself in those hard palms.

This was Sergeant Taylor's dream, and it woke him crying in his hospital bed.

He wept and shuddered until the shouts of men in nearby beds brought him back to reality. Then he lay back and marvelled about his dream, ignoring the pain of his shattered ear-drums.

The dream was a wonderful mixture of reality and superreality. Every detail concerning the raid had been accurately reconstructed. Just like that, he had led his men to success a very few hours ago. The Fast-Plus pills had behaved in the dream as in real life.

Only in two details had Sergeant Taylor's dream transcended reality——

'Hell, what the hell was you dreaming about?' asked the fellow in the next bed. 'Some dame stand you up or something?'

Sergeant Taylor nodded vaguely, seeing the man's lips move. Well, they had said there might be after-effects. Perhaps even now someone was inventing a drug to grow you new ear-drums. . . .

Only in two details had his dream transcended reality.

He had never seen or consciously looked for any Mary. Yet the authority of the dream was such that he knew that through all the thoughtless debauchery of his life a Mary was what he had been seeking. He knew, too, the dream predicted correctly: given his type of life, given the conditions in the underground barracks, there would never be a Mary for him. Women there were, but not women like Mary.

The other detail fitted with the first one——

'Or maybe the way you was squealing you was Above, playing soldiers again, huh?' suggested the fellow in the next bed.

Sergeant Taylor smiled meaninglessly and nodded at the moving lips. He was in a world of his own at present; and he liked it.

43

Yes, the other detail fitted with the first. In his dream he had promoted himself to colonel. It could be a typical piece of oneiric self-aggrandizement: but more likely it was something deeper than that, another slice of prediction matching the first.

Sergeant Taylor was a soldier. He had been a soldier for a long time, but now he was realizing it all through. That made him soldier-plus. Mary was the softer side of his life, the unfulfilled, the empty chair side; now it was ruled out of being, so that he could only grow harder, tougher, more bitter, more callous. He was going to make a splendid soldier.

No love—but bags of promotion!

Sergeant Taylor saw it all now, clear as a splinter of sunshine. Shakily, he started to laugh, so that the man in the next bed stared at him again.

Heck, they should be able to think up some really bizarre missions for a stone-deaf man. . . .

BASIS FOR NEGOTIATION

THE University College of East Lincoln is a muddle of build-ings. In the centre stands the theatrically baroque pile still called Gransby Manor, while round it lie the pencil-boxes of glass and cedar and cement that are our century's contribution to the treasury of world architecture. John Haines-Roberts and I walked round the grounds in agonized discussion, view-ing our conglomeration of a college from all its meaningless angles.

When I tell you the date was July 1st, 1971, you will know what was the subject under discussion.

'I tell you I cannot just stay here, John, idle, isolated, ignorant,' I said. 'I must go to London and find out what the devil the government is doing.'

Most of the conversations that follow, I feel confident, are word for word what was said at the time. My memory is generally eidetic; in times of stress such as this, it records everything, so that I see John Haines-Roberts now, his head thrust forward from those heavy shoulders, as he replied, 'I will offer you no platitudes about considering your reputation at such a grave time. Nevertheless, Simon, you are a public figure, and were before your knighthood. You have a foot in both worlds, the academic and the world of affairs. Your work on the Humanities Council and the Pilgrim Trust has not been forgotten. You were M.P. for Bedford under Butler. That has not been forgotten. At such a trying time, any untoward move by somebody of your stature may fatally prejudice the course of events, marring——'

'No, no, John, that's not it at all!' I stopped him with a curt movement of my hand. He talked that awful dead language of English newspaper leaders; with his evasions and euphemisms, his 'untoward moves' and 'trying times'. I could not bear to listen to him. He believed as I did on that one fundamental point, that the British Government had made the most fatal error any government could have done; but this apart we could have nothing in common. His woolly language only reflected the numbness of his intellect. At that terrible moment, one more prop fell away. I began to hate John. The man who had been my friend since I took the specially created chair of Moral History two years before suddenly became just another enemy of my country, and of me.

'We cannot discuss the problem in these terms,' I told him. He stopped, peering forward in that intense way of his. In the distance, I saw some undergraduates bunched together in the tepid sunshine and watching us with interest. 'The British have turned basely against their dearest friends and allies. Either this wounds you to the heart or it doesn't——'

'But the Americans can manage alone perfectly well——' he began, with all the patience and reason in the world in his voice. John Haines-Roberts was a saint; nothing in the world could ruffle him in debate. I knew he would be standing reasoning in some quiet corner of University College when the H-bombs fell.

'I'm sorry, John, I'm not prepared to go into it all again. The sands have run out—right out of the bottom of the glass. This is no time for talk. You don't think the Communists are standing talking, do you? I'm going to London.'

He saw I was making to go and laid a placatory hand on my sleeve.

'My dear fellow, you know I wish you well, but you have a reputation for being over-hasty. Never, never let action become a substitute for thought. You'll recall what that great and good man Wilberforce said when——'

'Damn Wilberforce!' I said. Turning away, I strode off. The undergraduates saw me coming and fanned out to intercept me on my way to Manor, pouring out questions.

'Is it true the Americans have cordoned off Holy Loch? Sir Simon, what do you think of the news about the International Brigade? Did you see C. P. Snow on TV, blasting poor old Minnie?' 'Minnie' was their nickname for Sir Alfred Menhennick, the Prime Minister.

Behind my back, John was still calling, 'Simon, my dear fellow. . . .' To my audience, I said, 'Gentlemen, from this week onwards, only shame attaches to the name of England. You know how I feel on this subject. Please let me pass.'

Their faces were before me, troubled, angry, or snivelling. They began bombarding me with preposterous questions— 'Who do you think will win? America or China?' as if it were a boat-race staged for their delight.

'Let me through!' I repeated.

'Why don't you join up, if you feel so strongly?' 'We don't owe the Americans anything.' 'We'll still be here when they're one big hole in the ground.' And so on.

I said: 'You had the police in here last night. Rowdyism will get you nowhere. Why don't you go somewhere quietly and consult your history books if you have no consciences to consult?' I hated them, though I knew they half-sided with me.

'Consult our history books!' one of them exclaimed. 'He'll tell us to cultivate our gardens next!'

Angrily I pushed through them, making my way towards my rooms. That last remark echoed through my head; obviously many of them could not differentiate between my convictions and those of, say, Haines-Roberts. In the final judgement, he and I would be lumped together as men who sat by and let it happen—or, even worse, would be cheered as men who had not interfered.

With distaste I surveyed the comfortable room with Adam fire-place and white panelling that I had chosen in preference to an office in Whitehall, asking myself as I took in—through what a scornfully fresh vision!—the untidy book-cases and neat cocktail cabinet, if there was still time left to do something effective. How terribly often in the past must Englishmen have asked themselves that!

Momentarily I surveyed myself in the looking-glass. Greyhaired, long in the nose, clear of eye, neat in appearance. Not a don. More a retired soldier. Certainly—oh yes, my God, that certainly—a gentleman! A product of Harrow and Balliol and a Wiltshire estate. With the international situation what it was, it sounded more like a heresy than a heritage. Nothing is more vile (or more eloquent of guilt) than to hate everything one has been: to see that you have contaminated the things that have contaminated you.

Taking a deep breath, I began to phone my wife at home. When her voice came over the line, I closed my eyes.

'Jean, I can't bear inaction any longer. I'm going up to London to try and get through to Tertis.'

'Darling, we went over all this last night. You can't help by going to see Tertis—no, don't tell me you can't help by not going either. But it becomes more and more obvious each hour that public opinion here is with Minnie, and that your viewpoint. . . .'

By ceasing to listen to her meaning, I could concentrate on her voice. Her 'all' was pronounced 'arl', her 'either' was an 'eether'; her tone had a soft firmness totally unlike the harshness of so many Englishwomen!—no, comparisons were worthless. It was stupid to think in categories. She was Jean Challington, my beloved wife. When I had first met her in New York, one fine September day in 1942, she had been Jean Gersheim, daughter of a magazine publisher. At twenty-six, I was then playing my first useful role in affairs on the British

Merchant Shipping Mission. Jean was the most anglophile, as well as the most lovely, of creatures; I was the most americanophile and adoring of men. That hasty wartime wedding at least was a success; no better Anglo-American agreement ever existed than our marriage.

This was the woman on whose breast I had wept the night before last, wept long and hard after the bleak TV announcement that in the interests of future world unity the British Government had declared its neutrality in the American–Chinese war. Last night I had wept again, when the U.S.S.R. had come in on the side of the People's Republic and Sir Alfred Menhennick himself had smiled to viewers under his straggling moustache and reaffirmed our neutrality.

Now, with the phone in my hand and Jean's voice in my ear, I could not but recall Menhennick's hatefully assured delivery as he said, 'Let us in this darkest period of civilized history be the nation that stands firm and keeps its lamps alight. It is a difficult—perhaps you will agree that it is the most difficult—role that I and my government have elected to play. But we must never forget that throughout the quarter century of the Cold War, Great Britain's path has been the exacting and unrewarding one of intermediary.

'We must remember, too, that the United States, in facing Communist China, faces an enemy of its own creating. One of the most fatal failures of this century was the failure of the U.S. to participate in world affairs during the twenties and thirties, when Britain and France strove almost single-handedly to preserve the peace. Despite constant warnings, the U.S. at that time allowed their enemy Japan to grow strong on the spoils of an invaded China. As a consequence, the broken Chinese peoples had to restore their position as a world power by what means they could. It is not for us to condemn if in desperation they turned to Communism. That their experiment, their desperate experiment, worked must be its justification. At this fateful hour, it behoves us to think with every sympathy of the Chinese, embroiled yet again in another terrible conflict. . . .'

The hypocrisy! The sheer bloody wicked hypocrisy, the lies, the distortions, the twists of logic, the contortions of history! My God, I could shoot Menhennick!

'Darling, I hadn't mentioned Menhennick,' Jean protested.

'Did I say that aloud?' I asked the phone.

'You weren't listening to a word I said.'

'I'll bet you were telling me to pack a clean shirt!'

'Nothing of the sort. I was saying that here in Lincoln there are some demonstrations in progress.'

'Tell me about them.'

'If you'll listen, honey. The best-organized procession carries a large banner saying "Boot the traitors out of Whitehall".'

'Good for them.'

'My, yes, good for them! The odd thing is, those boys look like exactly the same crowd we used to see marching from Aldermaston to Trafalgar Square shouting, "Ban the Bomb".'

'Probably they are. If you think with your emotions, slight glandular changes are sufficient to revise your entire outlook. In the Aldermaston days, they were afraid of being involved in war; now that Russia has come in on China's side, they're afraid that the U.S. will be defeated, leaving us to be picked off by Big Brother afterwards. Which is precisely what will happen unless we do something positive now. What else goes on in Lincoln?'

Jean's voice became more cautious. 'Some anti-Americanism. The usual rabble with ill-printed posters saying, "Yanks, Go Home" and "Britain for the British". One of them spells Britain "B-R-I-T-I-A-N". So much for the ten thousand million pounds spent on education last year. . . . It feels funny, Simon—to be an alien in what I thought was my own country.'

'It's not my country either till this is all put right. You know that, Jean. There's never been such a time of moral humiliation. I wish I'd been born anything but British.'

'Don't be silly, Simon.'

Foreseeing an argument, I changed the line of discussion.

'You've got Michael and Sheila and Adrian there with you?'

'Oh yes, and Mrs. B. And a platoon or so of sheepish English soldiers drilling opposite the Post Office.'

'Fine. You won't be lonely. I'll be back as soon as I can.'

'Meaning just when?'

'Soonest possible, love. 'Bye. Be good.'

I put the phone down. I looked distractedly round the room. I put pipe and tobacco into one jacket pocket, opened a drawer, selected three clean handkerchiefs, and put them into the other pocket. I wondered if I would ever see the room—or Jean—again, and strove at the same time not to dismiss such speculations as simply dramatic.

London, I knew, could turn into a real trouble centre at any hour. Early news bulletins had spoken of rioting and arrests here and there, but these were mere five-finger exercises for what was to come.

Until now, the sheer momentousness of world events had deadened reactions. After a month of mounting tension, war between the U.S. and China broke out. Then came Menhennick's unexpected tearing up of treaties and declaration of neutrality. Initially, his action came as a relief as well as a surprise; the great bulk of the electorate saw no further than the fact that an Armageddon of nuclear war had been avoided. The U.S.S.R.'s entry into hostilities was more a shock than a surprise, again postponing real thinking.

Now—as I foresaw the situation—a growing mass of people would come to see that if they were to have any hope for a tolerable future, it would be fulfilled only by throwing in our lot heart and soul with our allies, the Americans. We had behaved like vermin, deserting in an hour of need. Even Neville Chamberlain returning from Munich in 1938 to proclaim 'Peace in our time' had not brought the country into such disgrace as Minnie with his 'nation that keeps the lamps alight'.

Soon the English would realize that; and I wanted to be there when trouble broke.

As I was heading for the door, David Woolf entered, quickly and without knocking. David was University Lecturer in Nuclear Physics, with a good but troubled record from Harwell. Three years back, he had run for Parliament, but an ill-timed tariff campaign had spoilt his chances. Though his politics were opposed to mine, his astute and often pungent thinking were undeniably attractive. Tall and very thin, with a crop of unbrushed hair, he was still in his thirties and looked what he undoubtedly was: the sort of man who managed always to be unhappy and spread unhappiness. Despite this—despite our radically different upbringings—his father had been a sagger-magger's bottomer in a Staffordshire pottery—David and I saw much of each other.

'What is it?' I asked. 'I can't stop, David.'

'You're in trouble,' he said, clicking his fingers.

I had not seen him since the Chinese declaration of war forty-eight hours before. His face was drawn, his shirt dirty. If he had slept, clearly it had been in his clothes.

'What sort of trouble?' I asked. 'Aren't we all in trouble?'

'The Dean has you marked down as a dangerous man, and at times like this the Dean's kind can cause a hell of a lot of grief.'

'I know that.'

Dean Burroughs was a cousin of Peter Dawkinson, the reactionary editor of the *Arbiter*, the newspaper as firmly entrenched behind out-dated attitudes as *The Times* had ever been at its worst period—and as powerful. Burroughs and I had been in opposition even before my first day at East Lincoln, back when I edited Garbitt's short-living independent *Zonal*.

'What you don't know is that the Dean has started vetting your phone calls,' David said. 'I was by the exchange just now. You made an outgoing call; Mrs. Ferguson had it plugged through to old Putters, the Dean's fair-haired boy.'

'It was a private call to my wife,' I said furiously.

'Are you leaving or something? Don't mind my asking.'

'Yes, I'm leaving, though by God what you tell me makes me want to go and sort things out with Burroughs first. No, that luxury must wait; time's short. I must leave at once.'

'Then I warn you, Simon, that they may try to stop you.'

'Thanks for telling me.'

He hesitated, knowing I wanted him to move away from the door. For a moment we stood confronting each other. Then he spoke.

'Simon—I want to come with you.'

That did surprise me. The news about the phone did not; in the present tense atmosphere, it merely seemed in character, a small sample of a vast untrustworthiness. I accepted David's words as truth; David, though isolated from the rest of the teaching body by his political and sexual beliefs, had a way of knowing whatever was happening in the college before anyone else.

'Look, David, you don't know what I am doing.'

'Let me guess, then. You are going to drive to London. You have influential friends there. You are going to get in contact with someone like Lord Boulton or Tertis, and you are going to throw in your lot with the group trying to overthrow the government.'

This was so good a guess that he read his answer in my face. I said, with some bitterness, 'Your politics are no secret to me. For years you have preached that we should disarm, that we should cease to behave like a first-rate power, with all the assumptions of a first-rate power, when we are really a second-rate power——'

He seized my arm, only to release it at once. Behind his spectacles, his eyes brimmed with anger.

'Don't be a bloody fool, Simon! We *are* a second-rate power, but now the moment of truth is upon us, isn't it? The bastards who misgovern us would not climb off their silly perches when they had a chance, when we were warning them. Now, *now*, they just *must* honour agreements. You know I've no time for America, but by God we owe it to them to stick by them: we owe it to ourselves! We mustn't behave like a fifth-rate power: that at least we're not.'

'So we've both arrived on the same side?'

From his pocket he produced a revolver.

'You could have worse allies than me, Simon. I don't go to Bisley every year for nothing. I'm prepared to use this when needed.'

'Put it away!'

Savagely he laughed.

'You're a gentleman, Simon! That's your trouble. It's the only really vital difference between us. You don't enjoy force! You're as like Minnie as makes no difference! In the ultimate analysis, his faults are yours—and it's a class fault.'

I grabbed his jacket, clenching a fist in his face and choking with rage.

'You dare say that! Even you've not opposed Minnie as bitterly as I. I hate all he stands for, hate it.'

'No you don't. You both belong to the same league of gentlemen—Balliol and all that. If it wasn't that your wife happened to be American, you'd feel as Minnie does. It's you blasted gentlemen putting the social order before the country that have got us into this bloody disgraceful muddle. . . .' With an effort, he broke off and pushed my hand roughly away, saying, 'And I'm in danger of doing the same thing myself. Sir Simon, my apologies. Our country has disgraced us before the world. Please let me come to London with you. I'm prepared to do anything to boot out the Nationalist party. That's what I came here to say.'

He put out his hand; I shook it.

We were round at the car port getting my Wolseley out when Spinks, the head porter, came thudding up at the double.

'Excuse me, Sir Simon, but the Dean wants you very urgently, sir. Matter of importance, sir.'

'All right, Spinks. I'll just drive the car round to the front of Manor and go in that way. He's in his rooms, I take it?'

His round heavy face was troubled.

'You will go straight in to him *now*, sir, won't you? He did stress as it was urgent.'

'Quite so, Spinks. Thank you for delivering the message.'

I drove round to the front of Manor, accelerated, and in next to no time we were speeding down the drive. David Woolf sat beside me, peering anxiously back at the huddle of buildings.

'Relax,' I said, knowing it would anger him. 'Nobody's going to shoot us.'

'The war's forty-eight hours old—I wonder how many people have been shot already?'

Not answering, I switched on the car radio as we struck

the main road. I tried the three channels, General, Popular, and Motorway. On the first, a theatre organ played *Roses of Picardy*. On the second, a plummy woman's voice said, '. . . when to my bitter disappointment I found that all the jars of strawberry jam had gone mouldy; however, this tragedy——' On the third, a disc jockey announced, 'That was *My Blue Heaven*, and while we're on the subject of colour, here is Reggy Palmer and his Regiment in a colourful arrangement of another old favourite, *Chinatown*.'

'I wonder they didn't censor that one out for reasons of political expediency,' David said sourly.

We stayed with the jocular jockey, hoping to catch a news bulletin, as I drove south. Avoiding Lincoln, we entered the newly opened M 13 at Hykeham and increased speed. Noticing the number of Army vehicles heading south with us, David started to comment when the news came through.

'This morning has been punctuated by disturbances and demonstrations in most of the larger towns throughout Britain. Some arrests have been made. In Norwich, a man was fined twenty pounds for defacing the Town Hall. The Sovereign's visit to Glasgow has been postponed until a later date.'

'Royalty!' David grunted.

'Tautology!' I grunted.

'The Soviet Ambassador to Britain said today that the Soviet peoples greatly sympathized with the wisdom shown by the British in remaining neutral. They themselves had been drawn into the conflict with the deepest reluctance, and then only because vital interests were at stake. M. Kasinferov went on to say that he was sure that guided by our example the rest of Europe would remain neutral, thus saving itself from what could only be complete annihilation.'

'Bloody flatterers,' David growled.

'Concealed threats,' I growled.

'In the United States of America, our neutrality has been generally condemned, although as one Washington correspondent points out, "Had Britain not torn up her treaties with us, she might well have been obliterated by now." Discussions over the immediate evacuation of U.S. air, naval, and military bases in this country are taking place in Whitehall now. A government spokesman said they were proceeding in what he described as "a fairly cordial atmosphere".'

'How English can you get?' David asked.

'They're probably tearing each other's throats out,' I said, instinctively pressing my foot down on the accelerator. I looked at my watch; an idea had occurred to me. From the dashboard, the gentlemanly voice continued in the same tones it had used in happier years to describe the Chelsea flower show.

'Last night saw little aerial activity, though reliable U.S. sources report aerial reconnaissance from points as far apart as the Arctic Circle and Hawaii. Formosa is still under heavy bombardment from shore batteries. Units of the British Fleet stand ready to assume defensive action in Singapore harbour. The fighting between Chinese Airborne forces and units of the Indonesian army in Northern Central Sumatra and near Jakarta in Java still continues. Peking yesterday reported the evacuation of Medan in Sumatra, but Indonesian sources later denied this, while admitting that the city was "almost uninhabitable" by now. The landing of U.S. troops near Palembang continues. So far only conventional weapons are being used on all fronts.'

'So far . . . so far,' David said. 'They're only limbering up yet.'

That was where all the trouble had begun, in Sumatra, little more than a month ago. Peking had protested that the large population of overseas Chinese were being victimized. Jakarta had denied it. A bunch of bandits shot a prominent Indonesian citizen in the Kesawan, Medan. President Molkasto protested. Tempers flared. Fighting broke out. The U.N. were called in. The U.S.S.R. protested against this unwarranted interference in national affairs. A plane full of U.S. experts was shot down near Bali, possibly by accident. The slanging started. Three weeks later, the People's Republic declared 'a crusade of succour': war.

'David, we're going to London via Oxford,' I said.

He looked curiously at me.

'What the hell for? It's a long way round. I thought you were in a hurry?'

'The motorway will take us as far as Bicester. The delay won't be too great. As you know, I'm a Fellow of Saints; I want to call in there and have a word with Norman, if possible.'

His reaction was predictable. Among the less informed on his side of the political arena, Saints had an undeserved reputation for being a sort of shadow Establishment from which the country was governed. This legend had been fostered by the fact that Saints, as a compromise between Princeton's Institute for Advanced Studies and Oxford's own All Souls, naturally contained the influential among its members.

'Who is Norman?' David inquired. 'Do you mean Norman Parmettio, the Contemporary Warfare chap?'

'If you like to put it like that, yes, "the Contemporary Welfare chap". He's in his eighties now, but still active, a sage and lovable man. He drafted the Cultural Agreement of '66 with Russia, you know. He's seen academic and public service, including working as an aide to old Sir Winston at Yalta in the forties.'

'Too old! What do you want to see *him* for?'

'He's an absolutely trustworthy man, David. You forget how out of touch I am. We can't just drive into London knowing absolutely nothing of what is going on behind the scenes. Norman will put us in the picture as to what's happening in the Foreign Office and to who's changed sides in the last forty-eight hours.'

'Touché. Carry on. You know I only came for the ride—but for God's sake let something happen. My stomach's turning over all the time; I have a presentiment of evil. I'm sick!'

'So's the whole confounded country.'

We felt sicker before we reached Bicester. Another news bulletin gave us more details of local events. International news, as I had suspected, was being heavily censored; there was no mention of what was happening in Europe, or of what the Commonwealth was saying or doing.

Several members of the government had resigned—the predictable ones like Hand, Chapman, and Desmond Cooney, with a few unexpecteds such as poor old Vinton and Sep Greene. Martial law had been proclaimed in Liverpool and Glasgow. In the interests of public safety, a curfew would operate tonight and until further notice in the following cities: London, etc. . . . Airline services between Britain and the U.S. and Britain and the U.S.S.R. were temporarily suspended. The L.C.C. were all out at Lords for 114.

At Fogmere Park we ran into trouble. There was a big U.S.A.F. base at Fogmere. You could see the planes and runways from the road at one point. A knot of people perhaps a hundred strong—a fair number for such a country spot—filled the road. Several cars were parked on the verges, some with men standing on top of them. Banners waved, many of them bearing the usual disarmament symbol. One florid individual was haranguing the crowd through a megaphone.

'This'll take your mind off your stomach,' I told David, rolling forward at 20 m.p.h. and sounding my horn. I glanced sideways at him. He sat rigid with his fists clenched in his lap—presumably nursing his presentiment of evil.

The crowd that had been facing the other way turned to look at us, parting instinctively to clear the road. The fellow with the megaphone, a big man with a red face and black moustache, dressed in a loud tweedy suit—how often one saw his type about the country!—bore down on us and tried to open my door.

'It's locked, old fellow,' I said, rolling down my window. 'Looking for a lift to somewhere?'

He got his big fingers over the top of the window and poked the moustache in for me to inspect. His eyes went hotly from me to David and back to me.

'Where do you two think you are going?' he asked.

'Straight down this road. Kindly get your face out of the way. You are being obstructive.'

He was running to keep up with us. I could hear the crowd shouting without being able to grasp what they were saying.

'Don't annoy him,' David said anxiously.

'I want to talk to you,' the heavy man said. 'Slow down, will you. Where are you going? What's the ruddy hurry?'

His head was outside the car door. The window closed electrically, catching his fingers. He roared in anger, dropping the megaphone to clasp his bruised knuckles. As we surged forward, it became apparent why the crowd had gathered. Beyond them had been established a check-point with a black-and-white bar across the road and the legend: 'UNITED STATES AIR COMMANDO. HALT.' Behind sandbags were armed men and a couple of hefty tanks, besides several light vehicles, including a British Army Signals truck. It all appeared very efficient in the colourless sunshine.

As I halted at the barrier, two Americans in uniform stepped forward, a corporal and a sergeant, one on either side of the Wolseley. Again my window came down. The sergeant looked round and amiable. I thrust my face out before he could get his in.

'What's happening here, Sergeant?'

'U.S. Air Commando check-point. Just a formality to check for weapons. We have to stop all vehicles.' This in an East Coast accent: Maine, I guessed.

'Have to? Whose orders?'

'Look, my orders, sir. It's only a formality. We don't want trouble.'

'It's we English, unfortunately, who don't want trouble, Sergeant, but I'm curious to know by whose authority you have closed a main British road.'

The crowd behind, divided in loyalty as in understanding, called 'Lock 'em up!' and 'Let 'em go!' indiscriminately.

The corporal on David's side of the car, a yellow-complexioned fellow I had already marked as a trouble-maker, since his type was prevalent in the British Army, said, 'You Limey copsuckers, you'd always argue rather than act.'

56

'Simon, don't be difficult; tell him what he wants to know and let's get on,' David implored. Turning to the corporal, he added, 'Don't make any mistake, we're really on your side.'

'Oh no you ain't, Mac. You're just a neutral. You ain't on anyone's side.'

'A very apposite answer, if I may say so,' I replied. 'I still wish to know by whose orders you have erected this barrier across the highway.'

'Let's not argue, mister. Let's just say it's necessary, or I wouldn't be here wasting my time,' said the sergeant patiently. A British Army officer, a dapper captain, was coming from behind the barrier towards us. I beckoned to him and repeated my question.

Instinctively he summed me up, just as I summed him up the moment he spoke. Under his Sandhurst veneer I recognized the Birmingham middle-class accent, just as I saw he had identified my Balliol honk, accentuated for the occasion. The moment would be lost on our American sergeant, a breed without many subtleties.

'There's been a spot of trouble, sir,' the captain said, very politely. 'A small private van passed along the road a couple of hours ago and machine-gunned the American planes over on the runway. So we are just taking precautions to see that such a breach of neutrality doesn't happen again.'

'Captain, I am a friend of Lord Waters, the Lord Lieutenant of the county. Who has sanctioned this road block?'

'We naturally have official permission, sir, which I could show you.'

'Get 'em moving, Captain, before we all die of boredom,' urged the sergeant. Two other cars had arrived behind us and were hooting.

'Do you mind me asking, sir, have you any weapons in the car?'

'No, Captain. No bombs, no machine-guns.'

'Splendid. Carry on to the next check-point, sir, and try to keep moving all the time.'

'I will try,' I assured him earnestly, and we rolled under the barrier arm as it lifted. A mile down the road was the other point, stopping vehicles coming from Oxford; it let us through without comment.

'Rather a comic incident that, eh?' I said.

David's face was wooden.

'Your sort loves to make trouble and humiliate people, doesn't it?' he said.

'Not at all. You can't have every Tom, Dick, and Harry

57

blocking the roads, or where would we be? I just asked a question I was perfectly entitled to ask.'

'It comes to the same thing in the end.'

'It's people like you who fail to ask pertinent questions that get misled. Your party, for instance.'

'You dare mention parties after the tragic mistakes *yours* has made this last week?' He was furious. Debate always made his temper rise.

Quietly I said, 'You know I know my party has behaved indefensibly, David—quite indefensibly. But your party's unreal dreams of collective security without armament, of nuclear disarmament in a nuclear age, have hampered the country's striking power so effectively that our shame must also be yours. When you were the ones who pulled our teeth, how could you expect us to bite? What curb could we offer the Red powers? At least these traitors like Minnie and Northleech can plead they had no alternative but to act badly.'

'Christ, you wriggle on the hook as deftly as they do! What about the torn-up treaties? What about the promises? What about the Anglo-American alliance? All hot air, I suppose?'

'Here's Oxford,' I said, as we came on to the top of the Banbury Road.

We were stopped again, this time by an exotic crowd of R.A.F. Regiment, Army, Civil Defence, and police, with a couple of A.A. men for luck. Plus a cheerful bunch of civilians doing good business with an ice-cream man.

'Sorry, sir, can't go through Oxford unless you've got a good reason for it.' This was a well-scrubbed corporal with a tommy-gun over his shoulder, ambling up to the car.

'Such as? I am a fellow of Saints and am on my way there now.'

'Better make it next week instead, sir. There's been a bit of trouble in the town. A fire or two and some hooliganism. We're trying to keep the city centre clear. Try the by-pass, sir, if you were thinking of going through. Keep moving and you won't get into no trouble.'

He wasn't going to be budged.

'There's a phone box over there,' David pointed. 'Try phoning Norman.'

'Good idea. Thanks, Corporal.'

'Thank you, sir. Nice day, anyhow, isn't it?'

'Yes, lovely. Except for the L.C.C., eh?'

'What, sir? Oh yes, quite, sir. They didn't put up much of a show, did they?'

We left him beaming as I drove over to the side of the road. David laughed with an angry face.

'You love playing the decent chap and you love playing the cad, Simon. Which are you really?'

'The common man, David, *l'homme moyen sensuel*. In other words, a bit of both. Buy yourself an ice-cream while I'm phoning.'

I got through to Saints straight away and recognized the head porter's voice at once, strained as it was through thickets of phlegm. Legend has it they built the college round him.

'That you, Dibbs? Challington here. Would you put me through to Professor Norman Parmettio.'

'Hello, sir, nice to hear your voice. We haven't seen you here for months. You used to be so frequent.'

'Pressure of work, I fear. Is the professor there?'

'Well, we had a bit of trouble last night, sir.'

'Trouble? What sort of trouble?'

'Well, sir, we had to have the fire brigade round, sir. Some young hooligans threw petrol bombs over the east wall, sir. Terrible it was, sir. Fortunately I was all right in here. I phoned the police and the fire brigade and anyone I could think of. Proper scaring it was. I've never seen nothing like it.'

'Indeed. Anyone killed?'

'Not to speak of, sir. But the east wing's a ruin. Your old room gone, sir, and part of the chapel. By a miracle of good fortune my lodge was preserved, but——'

'It seems impossible such things could happen in Oxford, Dibbs. The time is out of joint. Where's Professor Parmettio?'

'Those are my feelings exactly, sir. There you have it. Terrible, it was. As for the professor, bless his soul, he committed suicide the day before yesterday an hour or so after the Prime Minister spoke about us British being neutral and keeping the lamps alight. At least he missed the fire and all the fuss——'

'Parmettio dead? Do you say he's dead?'

'No, he committed suicide, sir, up in his bedroom. Left a note to say his country had dishonoured him and that he was taking the only possible course open to him. A fine old fellow he was, sir. . . .'

As I climbed back into the car, David dropped a newspaper he was scanning.

'You're pale as a ghost, Simon. What's the matter?'

'How's your presentiment of evil, David? Norman's dead. Committed suicide—couldn't bear the dishonour. Poor dear old Norman! The porter told me and put me on to the warden.'

'On to Starling? He's a true blue government man. What did he have to say?'

'He's not so true blue as we thought; frankly I feel sorry for him. He sounded like a sick man over the phone. He told me that several of the clearer-thinking younger Fellows, Thorn-Davis, Shell, Geoffrey Alderton, and one or two more, tried to charter a private plane to fly to America. Foolish, I suppose, but quite understandable. They were apparently arrested at the aerodrome and haven't been heard of since. Starling went round and saw the local superintendent of police in person but couldn't get a word out of the man. He was almost weeping as he told me. And then——'

'Then?'

'Starling was cut off.'

We sat in silence.

At last David said, 'I'm sorry if I sounded stupid before. It's all a bit nastier than we thought.'

'No nastier than we had a right to expect. We'd better get to London while we still have the chance.'

'You think all potential trouble-makers are being arrested?'

'What else? And I'd hazard that by now you and I are on the list. Got that gun of yours ready?'

He had bought a local paper from a vendor while I was phoning. As we drove off I caught sight of its headlines: RUSSIAN NUCLEAR SATELLITE IN ORBIT: Ultimate Weapon, Moscow Claims: For Emergency Only.

At one point, David leant over and switched the radio on, but they were playing *Roses of Picardy* again.

We drove into and through the outskirts of London without being stopped. By noon we were crawling through Hammersmith, moving in fits and starts through dense traffic.

'How about stopping for a drink and some sandwiches?' David asked. 'We don't really know when we'll eat again, do we?'

'Good idea. There's a pub over there that looks likely.'

London was far from normal. In the centre of town we would see processions and meetings. Here were only people in small groups, hanging about or strolling. Some of the smaller shops were closed. Never had I seen such a large percentage of the population with their eyes buried in newspapers, not even at the time of the Suez crisis, back in '56—when the Americans had failed to support us, came the treacherous thought to my brain. Momentarily irritated with myself, I ushered David into the pub.

As I ordered drinks, I saw him cast his eye over the men

present. One of them next to him, a man in voluble conversation with his mate, mistaking the intent of David's look, leant towards him and said, 'You agree, don't you, mate?'

I could not be sure what David replied in the general hubbub, but I heard the other fellow say, 'Why should we go to war for a lot of black men in Sumatra? I'd never even heard of Sumatra till last week! I reckon the government did right. Old Minnie has my vote every time. Let the blighters fight their own battles.'

At last I got served. Carrying a tray with a Guinness and a pale ale and expensive chicken sandwiches over to David's table, I was in time to hear David say, 'I can't see that neutrality *is* a way of saving our skins.'

The two men, who worked, or so I surmised, at the big cake factory nearby, were on him with glee.

'You mean you think it would be *safer* to have declared war on the Chinks and Ruskies?'

'I mean that once global war breaks out, safety axiomatically disappears.'

'Never mind axiomatically, mate! As long as we aren't in it, it's not global, is it? 'Ere, Bill, there's a bloke here thinks we ought to be fighting for the bloody Yanks!' They motioned to a couple of their mates, and soon there was a ring of them round our table. David's nervousness increased.

'If they wants a war, let them have it, I say,' Bill opined. His cheeks were heavy with woe and drink-fat. 'It's none of our business.'

'But that's precisely what it is, Bill,' I said. 'You've heard of N.A.T.O., the North Atlantic Treaty Organization, I expect?'

Howls of derision greeted this. The first speaker—Harry, I believe he was—leant over our table and said, 'Are you honestly going to sit there and tell me that you want to see this country blown to bits just because the Americans have come a cropper in Sumatra?'

'That's not a proper question. But if you are trying to ask me whether I support the democratic way of life, then I must answer yes——'

'Democracy! Wrap up!'

'—because I believe, like many another Englishman, that it is better to die fighting than die under Communist bombs or whips.'

'That's all bloody propaganda!'

'Who's he think he is?'

'Go and join the Army!'

'You're a right one,' Bill said to me. 'What have the Yanks done for you to make you so fond of them?'

'You ought to ask yourself that,' David said angrily. 'You're old enough to remember the last war—yes, and the war before that! How do you think we'd have managed without American aid then?'

'Okay then,' Bill said in gloomy triumph. 'Then we'll hang on for three years, and *then* we'll come in to help them, the way they did with us before!'

This sally drew a howl of laughter, and they turned away from us, losing interest and going back to a game of shove-ha'penny.

'Bill certainly averted a nasty moment,' David said with rancour. He drank deeply into his Guinness. 'Thank God for this poisonous British ability to laugh at themselves.'

'And at others.'

We drank up, ate our sandwiches, and rose to go.

'See you on the Russian steppes—scrubbing them!' Harry called. Their laughter followed us into the sunshine.

We drove down the Mall and so to the Foreign Office, where I hoped to see Tertis. We had passed the marchers and the speakers, the ragged and the angry; but the prevalent mood was distastefully light-hearted. Although many of the shops had closed, cafés and pubs were open, and people were treating the whole thing as a grand unplanned holiday, lying in the parks caressing each other or buying each other ice-cream.

All this angered David much more than it did me; he had always been the one with faith in the masses.

I thought of the cities I knew thousands of miles away, their grandeurs and their shortcomings: Washington, New York, San Francisco (my favourite American city), Chicago, Kansas City, and others I had never had the opportunity to visit. Yes, and I thought of Moscow and Leningrad, Baku and Tiflis, each of which I had visited on trade missions in the fifties; and of the teeming cities of the Orient, Canton, Shanghai, Peking with its factories and Ming tombs, Amoy, all cities I had not visited and now never would visit.

What was happening to them now? Were they being crushed to the ground, even while London lazed in the sun? I looked up to the sky, half expecting to see—I knew not what.

'Not yet,' David said grimly, interpreting my look. 'But it will come.'

We parked the car with difficulty and made our way to the F.O.

On the drive down from Oxford, after hearing of Norman Parmettio's death, my mind had become clear. If it were possible to help overthrow Minnie's government, I would help. If I were needed to take part in a new government, in whatsoever capacity, again I would help. Throughout the fifties and the early sixties, when the Cold War had shown signs of thawing (largely because of the then Russian leader Khrushchev's love–hate affair with the West) I had remained convinced that Communism was a declared enemy. Nothing I had written or spoken publicly had wavered from that belief. My record was clean. There were not so very many like me left in Britain. If I were needed, I would serve.

Although I did not know if Tertis was accessible, he was my best line of approach. I had worked with him often; we knew and trusted each other. If he were not available, I would try elsewhere, probably with the Athenaeum as first call.

At the doors of the F.O., David and I were stopped. We had to give our names, after which I was allowed to write a note for a messenger to take up to Tertis. The messenger was gone for a long while; only when fifteen minutes had elapsed did he return and request us to follow him.

Leo Tertis was assistant head of the Military Relations Department formed in the sixties and lately of growing importance. We walked down a corridor I remembered well, with messengers lounging in doorways and chandeliers hanging overhead. Nobody knocks on doors in the F.O., the assumption, I suppose, being that anyone admitted to the building in the first place will be birds of a feather. When our messenger indicated the second room of the Department, I walked straight in.

Tertis was there, five years my junior and at fifty a curiously youthful figure with plump pale cheeks, almost white hair and dark eyebrows. He looked, not unexpectedly, exceedingly grave and very tired. A vacuum flask of coffee stood on his desk; though the window was open, a smell of stale cigarette-smoke pervaded the room.

He had been sitting talking to a short plump man. As David and I entered, he broke off, rose, and came round the desk to shake my hand. I introduced David; Tertis eyed him appraisingly.

'David Woolf; I remember the name. You stood for Fleet-wood in the by-election, didn't you?' he asked.

'I did.'

'Then you're a unilateralist. What are you doing here with Sir Simon?'

Give David his due, he hardly hesitated before replying, 'I've seen the error of my ways.'

'You're too late, my boy,' Tertis said grimly, turning away to add, 'I won't pretend I'm particularly glad to meet either of you just now, but while you're here you'd better be introduced to the Minister of Economic Affairs, Mr. Edgar Northleech.'

I had already recognized the plump man as Northleech. For me he represented one of the country's worst enemies, a crony of Menhennick's, and one of the prime movers for increased appeasement towards the U.S.S.R. since the retirement of Macmillan had allowed his sort to get into power. Northleech moved heavily towards us now, his white hair flowing round his head, paunch well out, beaming through his spectacles as he extended his hand. David took it; I did not.

Moving round to Tertis, I said, 'We don't have to tell each other where we stand. What can I do to help, Leo?'

'I'll give you the true picture in a moment; it's bad. Friend Northleech, like your friend Woolf here, is busy changing sides. These are men of straw, Simon, blowing with the wind. I would rather ditch them than use them.'

Northleech came into the conversation saying, in the rambling manner he maintained even when angry, 'The ability to change should not be despised. I can help you, Tertis. I can get you to Menhennick; he's ready to discuss anything; pressure of events makes him feel he may have been misled.'

'Misled!' David exclaimed. 'We don't want to *talk* to you and Minnie. We want to shoot you. Don't you realize that revolution or civil war are brewing up and down the country? Misled, be damned!'

'Enough of that talk, Mr. Woolf,' said Northleech. 'We have the situation in hand, you know. Anybody can be misled.'

'It's the duty of men in office not to be misled. You've failed in your duty—abysmally. The Communist bloc's intentions have been clear since the forties.'

Red in the face, Northleech pointed a fat and shaking finger at David and said, 'That comes well from a unilateralist and a homosexual!'

'Leave personalities out of this! At least I and my party acted from our convictions. We advocated national disarmament as a first step towards general international disarmament. We advocated neutrality because as a neutral power Britain could weld other neutrals into a powerful enough group to break the deadly *status quo* of Big Two power ideologies that have frozen the world since the close of World War II. But your people, Northleech—yes, and I include you in this, Simon, and you, Mr. Tertis—what were you up to all the time?'

Tertis banged furiously on his desk.

'That's enough,' he said. 'If you wish to remain in here, hold your tongue.'

But David went straight on, levelling one finger like a fire-arm at the three of us.

'Your sort had no real thought for world peace, or even for the country. You were after preserving the social structure to which you belonged, just as Halifax, Baldwin, Chamberlain, and the other hangers-on did in the thirties. You're the damned middle-class powermongers with no knowledge of Russian or Chinese language and culture, or of what goes on in their dangerous skulls. It's your unspoken assumptions that have ruined Britain, not Communism or Socialism or all the other isms put together—your assumption that the best thing that can happen to anyone is that he can become a conformist and a gentleman, your assumption that your own narrow way of life is the only fit way of life. What happened to the workers? Once they got an education—*your* type of education, with a smattering of Shakespeare and a veneer of B.B.C. accent—then they too were hell-bent on becoming gentlemen, poor carbon copy gentlemen.'

'Paranoia!' I exclaimed.

'Why?' he demanded explosively, turning on me. 'Because I don't subscribe to your conventions? Don't worry, you had nearly everyone else subscribing. You fools, you've ended by deluding yourselves. That's why we're all on the brink of disaster: you said to yourselves, "Oh, the Chinese leaders are gentlemen. Treat them like gentlemen and they'll behave like gentlemen!" Look where it's got you.'

'You're a very foolish young man,' Northleech said. 'There is no historical basis for your remarks. If we have in this country a rule by gentlemen, as you claim, then it is simply because the hoi-polloi have proved themselves unfit to rule. Besides, there is no conspiracy. Sir Simon and I went to the same public school, but we never had one opinion in common, then or since.'

'Except the unspoken assumption that you were both of leader material!'

'Bringing you to the F.O. has gone to your head, David,' I said. 'Your speech would have been more effective delivered to rabble in Trafalgar Square.'

'It may be yet. I'd still like to know why Northleech should be here, rather than with Minnie, palling up to the Chinese.'

With a brow of thunder, Tertis said, 'If you'd had the courtesy to keep quiet when you came in here, you would have heard why the Minister is here. It's too late for your type of speechifying, Mr. Woolf, just as it's too late for a lot else. Edgar, you'd better tell them why you came.'

Northleech cleared his throat, glanced anxiously at Tertis,

removed his spectacles to polish them furiously as he said, 'It is no longer possible to keep peace with the People's Republic. Three hours ago—probably at about the time you were leaving your university—the first nuclear weapon of World War III was detonated. A "clean" one-megaton bomb was dropped on Hong Kong. It fell at about six in the evening, local time, when the maximum number of people was about in the streets. We are as yet unable to obtain coherent accounts of the extent of the destruction.'

In the silence that followed, Tertis's internal phone rang. He picked it up, listened, said, 'Bring him in.'

Looking up at us, he said wearily, 'Our country is fatally split, gentlemen. That's the curse of it: when we come to discuss any detail, the opinions on it are infinite, and one man's vote is as good as another's. Perhaps it's the democratic system itself that has brought us to this humiliating position; I don't know. But I must ask you now to put personal considerations aside if you wish to remain here. We are about to be visited by General Schuller, Deputy Supreme Commander of N.A.T.O.'

This I scarcely heard. I was still overwhelmed by the news of the Hong Kong catastrophe and trying to assess its meaning. As a result, I had one of the briefest and most significant exchanges that ever passed between two men.

I asked Northleech, 'Then I suppose we are now actually at war with Communist China?'

Northleech said, 'No. Their Ambassador has apologized. He claims the bomb was dropped by accident.'

There seemed to me no possible reply ever to this, but David asked, 'And you believed him?'

'It seemed politic to do so,' Northleech said stonily.

'Politic! My gods alive, there's a term being used appositely for once!' David broke into ragged laughter.

Hopelessness came up and overwhelmed me. The terrible betrayal all round was at last revealing itself, and not a man in the country was innocent. Faintly, I said to Tertis, 'You were going to put us in the picture. What of the countries of the Commonwealth?'

A deep voice from the door said, 'Canada declared war on the common enemy two hours after the U.S. did so. It was expedient for the defence of the North American continent. Australia entered the war as soon as Sydney got news of the Hong Kong disaster. Your government promptly tore up the S.E.A.T.O. agreement. Seems the one thing it is efficient at is the gagging of news.'

General Schuller did not introduce himself. He marched into the room and planted himself by Tertis. He was brusque and angry and had cut himself shaving with an old-fashioned razor that morning. His German–American accent was thick and nasal. Dark, handsome, very neat and be-medalled, he dominated the room with compressed fury.

'Well, Tertis, here I am. Who are these men? We were to be alone, as I understood it.'

Tertis stood up, listing us without introducing us. I felt like an undergraduate again under that black stare. The General made no comment, save for a snort when Northleech's identity was made known to him. Plainly he dismissed David and me from his calculations. David, with his sensitive nature, would not stand for this. Stepping forward, he produced his revolver and said, 'I am an enemy of your enemies. I'm prepared to shoot any traitors, sir.'

Schuller never paused.

'Shoot Northleech,' he ordered.

As my body seemed to freeze, so the tableau did. Even Northleech only cringed without moving from where he stood. David Woolf remained absolutely immobile. Then he returned the gun to his pocket and spoke contemptuously, in perfect command of himself.

'I kill from conviction, not to pass a personality quiz.'

Schuller grunted again, outwardly unmoved, but from that moment the first impact of his personality was weakened.

'I won't mince matters,' he said, swinging his head so that he spoke directly to Tertis. 'Britain has never added anything to the power of America. Rather, it's been a liability, a weak partner to be helped along, mind without muscle. Get it?'

'There to aid your muscle without mind,' I interposed tartly, but he continued without condescending to notice the interruption.

'We could have done without Britain as a partner once. But because she needed us, we've got bases and personnel and war material over here to defend our friends. Now at the eleventh hour—no, by Jesus, nearer half past midnight!—your Prime Minister announces that Britain is to be neutral. Egged on by Red threats and encouragement, he says America must withdraw from these Isles. Right?

'It so happens it is no longer strategy for us to withdraw. We cannot withdraw. We are not going to withdraw. What's going to happen now, Tertis?'

Without hesitation, Tertis said, 'As things are now, with the present government, we shall fight you to turn you out.'

'Get in the picture, man. You *are* fighting us. Norfolk's a

67

battleground right now. Outside Glasgow, the R.A.F. is bombing our installations.'

'I don't believe it!' I said.

'You'd bloody better believe it, *Sir* Simon, because it's happening right enough.'

'I believe it, General,' Northleech said. 'You presumably want to know what can be done to change the situation?'

'No, I'm going to tell *you* what can be done.'

'You need our help, General. Don't interfere with our offering it to you. What are the alternatives as you see them?'

'The alternatives are brutal. Either you get Minnie Menhennick and his boys out of the way and replace him by a reliable anti-Red government, or—or London is going to be destroyed and this island will become an American forward base. You've got till sundown to act. We can't let you have any further time.'

Put the way he put it, it sounded all wrong. Without American interference, we would have set our house in order anyway. Made to do it under threats, we would become inglorious traitors. After all, what future was there for Britain in a nuclear war? Suddenly before my eyes rose a picture of our cities all in ruins, women and children dying, even as they were dying now in Hong Kong . . . and it could happen in five minutes of our declaration of war. All the same, Schuller's view was understandable, inevitable even. I just wished it could have been put by someone less obviously a gun man.

Dismissing that hopeless argument *ad hominem*, I asked Northleech, 'Where is Minnie? Can you get us to him? Is he at Chequers, or No. 10, or where?'

'He's in London, in an underground H.Q. I could get us there in twenty minutes in my car, if you're sure it's the right thing. . . .'

'It's too late to *talk*. We have to act,' General Schuller said. 'Yes, let's for God's sake go in your car. My Thunderbird might be a little kind of suspicious.'

'I'm staying here,' Tertis said. He was the least ruffled of any of us. 'Though I'm under suspicion, I can be more use by keeping in touch at this end. My boss feels as I do, and there are plenty more in responsible positions who will back a change of government. You're comparatively unknown, Simon, but they'd accept you for P.M. in the emergency. You go with the Minister.'

As the others moved towards the door, I shook Tertis by the hand and said, 'I'll do whatever I can.'

'One word of warning,' he said. 'The country is now under martial law. Conscription for Civil Defence starts tomorrow, and you, Simon, have been officially declared an agitator—by the Dean of your college, so I hear. There's a warrant out for your arrest, so mind how you go.'

'It should improve my reputation if I stand for office,' I said. 'And David?'

Tertis nodded.

'They want him too.'

I turned round just too late to see what happened then. David had evidently gone first into the corridor. Northleech was frozen in the threshold with General Schuller close behind. Shouts came from along the corridor, shouts and the sound of running feet.

David pulled out that wretched revolver and fired twice, backing into the room as he did so. Someone screamed and the running stopped. Belatedly, one shot was fired in reply. It splintered through the door, which David had shut by then.

Gasping, he looked round at me and said, 'They're after us, Simon. Now what the hell do we do?'

'Rubbish,' Schuller growled. 'They're after me: who else? What is this, a trap or something? Northleech, Tertis, get that desk across the door before they rush us.'

He strode across the room as Tertis and Northleech went into action. He wrenched open the side door leading into the third room of Tertis's department. This was the secretaries' room. There were three of them, nice fresh young fellows all looking rather identical with identical suits and their hands raised above their heads. The General had brought two majors and a signalman with him, to wait for him in this outer office. The majors had already attended to the secretaries, while the signalman worked at his walkie-talkie, speaking into it in unhurried code.

'Nice fast work, Farnes and Able,' General Schuller said, striding into the third room and adding to the secretaries, 'Sorry about this, boys, but if I'm in a trap you'll have to play hostage.'

'They're after Woolf and Sir Simon, General, not you,' Tertis said, following Schuller. 'Let me go out into the corridor and explain to them.'

'You'll stay where you are. I'm sorry not to trust you, Tertis, but right now the British aren't my favourite nation. I'm taking no chances with anyone. Farnes and Able, bring those three hostages into the other room. Get the desk in too and barricade the side door with it. Look slippy. Operator, get Green Devil One on the air.'

'Right to hand, sir,' the operator said, looking up and handing a scramblerphone to Schuller.

Both majors carried light machine-guns. The one addressed as Farnes covered Tertis, David, Northleech, and me, while Able directed the three secretaries. The latter worked efficiently, dragging in the desk, even smiling as they did so; for them this seemed just a break in F.O. routine. I wondered whether they were displaying British nonchalance or if they genuinely did not grasp the seriousness of the situation.

For myself, I expected a grenade to come through the door at any moment, until it occurred to me that the guards outside were holding their fire in case they injured the General. Everything happened in such rapid succession that it was difficult to think clearly. Although I did not know in what tone Dean Burroughs had reported my hurried exit from East Lincoln, it seemed likely that he would have exaggerated enough for the group in the corridor to regard me as a potential killer.

The General handed the scramblerphone back to his operator, informing the majors as he did so, 'They're going to have a whirlybird at this window in two minutes minus.'

Instinctively we all glanced over at Tertis's long windows with the balcony looking out across Horseguards' Parade.

Later it occurred to me that here was a moment for clear thought—the first since the General had entered the room. He filled it by striding from one desk to the other with his jaw forward, saying with heavy sarcasm, 'And now, my friend Tertis, we'll test out your theory that the guards outside aren't gunning for me at all. Farnes, throw this guy David Woolf out into the corridor.'

You understand there were ten of us in the room. The place was comparatively crowded. I saw David's face shift as he ducked and moved. He looked rat-like: both frightened and frightening.

'You can't do this, Schuller. I'm on your side. Take me in the helicopter with you!'

He dodged behind Northleech, who whinnied with fright, and behind Schuller, pulling out his gun as he went. The crazy scheme no doubt was to hold Schuller at pistol-point until we were all safe in the copter. Doubtless David fell between self-preservation and patriotism and saw this idea as offering more hope than being pushed out into the corridor.

'Hold still, General, I won't harm——' he began, his voice shrill. But Farnes moved too. He sprang two paces across the room, dropped to one knee, and fired an automatic, one short and deafening burst.

The long window splintered and fell in. Northleech dropped next—through sheer panic reaction. For a second, dazed, I thought David had not been hit. Then dark blood gouted out of three holes in his shirt, spreading fast.

General Schuller swung round on him. David closed his eyes and fired one shot. Schuller blundered forward on to him. The two men fell together, breaking a chair as they went. Appalled, the two majors ran forward.

In moments of extreme crisis, a governing mechanism seems to take over from the rational centres of the brain. Without reflecting at all on what I was doing, I went to the outer door, pushed aside the desk that barricaded it, and threw it open.

Behind an open doorway opposite, armed men watched from cover. I saw their weapons come up. Down the corridor one way, another group had gathered, dark suits mingling with khaki.

'General Schuller has been assassinated! Help!' I called.

Framed in the doorway with smoke drifting past me, I must have looked a wild enough figure. But it was that pregnant cry 'Assassination', echoing down the corridors of the Foreign Office, that brought them all running. As they came, I turned and beckoned Northleech.

In the excitement, the two of us left unnoticed. My last glimpse into the room caught a sudden shadow falling over it. Schuller's helicopter was arriving—on time, but too late. We ran down the corridor, Northleech puffing hard. As we descended the grand staircase, more shots rang out. Another fool had gone trigger-happy. Long bursts of automatic fire indicated that the helicopter was returning as good as it got.

We met several people. To all of them I uttered my formula and they scattered. Even at the door, where a no-nonsense captain in the South Wales Borderers moved to block our escape, I said, 'Captain, General Schuller has been assassinated and you people will have to answer for it. See you get reinforcements and surround the building. Nobody whatsoever must leave until further orders. Clear?'

'I'm not in charge here, sir——'

'Then consider yourself so immediately. Get half a dozen men up on the second floor at once.'

He jumped to it and we were through.

'My car!' Northleech puffed. 'It's got a radio link. I must speak to Whitehall as we go. Over this way.'

He headed towards the Chiefs' Park and I followed, blinking in the sunshine.

'We're going to Menhennick?' I asked.

'Yes.'

His car was one of the new J.C. wagons, with a chauffeur

lounging near who threw open the rear door smartly as we approached.

'The Tower, James—fast,' Northleech ordered.

We climbed in and I asked, 'You mean to say Menhennick's in the Tower of London? How singularly appropriate.'

'Underneath it.'

Northleech was just recovering his breath. As we rolled forward, he opaqued the bullet-proof glass so that we could see out and not be seen. At the press of a button, a small bar slid out at knee level. At the press of another, his radiophone opened before him. We were of course completely sound-proofed off from the driver.

The screen before the Minister lit. A severe matron appeared, with behind her a crowded Whitehall room where people came and went.

'Give me Bawtrey, General Intelligence,' Northleech said, still puffing slightly.

'There may be a moment's delay, Minister. Routine is a little disturbed at present.'

'Fast as you can, miss. Emergency.'

She turned away. Northleech stabbed a finger at the screen.

'I'll give her "routine disturbed". Look, there's some bugger walking round that room with a cup of tea in his hand. Do you wonder the country's going to the dogs!'

I bit off the obvious answer that it was people like him who helped it go. He poured us some drinks, looked more cheerful, and began to grumble, all the while tapping one knee impatiently and staring at the screen before him.

'Sorry we had to leave Leo Tertis with his hands full like that. . . . Expedient, however. Look, Simon, I don't want you to feel disappointed, but Tertis was flannelling you in there.'

'In what way?'

'This incredible stuff about the possibility of your becoming P.M. No offence, but it just shows how far poor old Tertis's judgement is awry. I urged the Foreign Secretary to get him into something safe like Housing years ago. . . . I mean, for P.M. we need a man of experience, a young man, a man in the public eye, a man who knows the ropes, knows where to turn for guidance.'

'To you for instance?'

'I'll serve as long as the public need me, Simon. I'm an old warhorse.'

'You're a bloody pacifist, Edgar. Appeasement's the be-all and end-all of your philosophy.'

He looked broodingly at me, entirely without taking offence.

'You don't really want to see this grand little country blown to bits just to gratify your ambition, do you?'

'My record——'

'Bugger your record! You can't help being what you are, I know. You've never held office and you can't see the reason for being guided by necessity occasionally. There's none of the sticker about you, Simon, that's what's lacking. In my young days, I had the fortune to be guided by the great Lord Halifax——'

'You know what I think of Halifax!'

'I don't care what you think. You don't think enough. That's the world's trouble. Look at Schuller: the action school, as much brain power as a bull. Need never have been killed if he'd spent thirty seconds cogitating instead of emoting. *Non cogitavit ergo fuit.* Same with Woolf—an anarchist and subversive like all his kind. He had no idea he was shooting Schuller; it was simple father-hatred squeezed the trigger.'

'Package reasoning! There was a lifetime's conviction behind that bullet of David's. He had a reasoned hatred of big and noisy men who use their position to make more noise——'

'Putting you through,' said the panel. Simultaneously, a bearded man in shirt sleeves with a cup at his elbow and a pile of flimsies in his fist blinked into being on the screen.

'Hello, Bawtrey,' Northleech said, with a parade of affability. 'What's happening since I called you last?'

'Everything,' Bawtrey said, taking a swig from his cup. 'What do you want to know, Minister?'

'Relevant events of the last two hours. Hong Kong?'

'Nothing fresh. No new H-bombs dropped. First casualty estimate, one hundred fifty thousand dead, wounded, and missing. Singapore on general alert, Aussie fleet engaging Chinese warships off New Guinea. Three Russian nuclear subs detected and destroyed off Alaska coast——'

'What else? Washington?'

'Contact with America is just about defunct,' Bawtrey said, looking at us under his eyebrows. 'They're tearing their hair here, Minister. Not a peep from Washington, New York, Ottawa, Toronto—the whole blessed continent might just as well have disappeared. All cables are reported temporarily out of order, and all wavelengths blanketed with unusually strong interference.'

Northleech and I looked at each other.

'How long has this been the case?' Northleech asked.

Bawtrey glanced at his watch.

'I've been on shift two hours. Two and a half hours, at a

guess. There may be something through in a few minutes. Meanwhile, hang on, here's something else of interest.'

As he was speaking, Bawtrey leafed through his flimsies. 'The first space battle is now in progress. U.S. Orbitters attacking the Red nuclear satellite, meeting opposition from Tsiolkos and China bugs.'

'Europe?'

'Mobilization in France, Italy, and the Scandinavian countries. Every man in Western Germany at the frontier, Reuter reports. Same in Turkey, Greece. Main impression seems to be that they're waiting to see what Great Britain decides.'

As the man talked, I stared out of the window. We moved with unconscionable slowness, though Northleech's driver took short cuts when he could. Trafalgar Square was crowded, and not only with soap-box orators. A figure in a white cassock was holding a service on the steps of St. Martin-in-the-Fields. Down the Strand, traffic was entirely at a standstill. We detoured round Covent Garden, to squeeze into a Fleet Street almost as crowded.

In contrast to the sightseers round the Park, people here looked grave. Outside a Civil Defence recruitment booth, both men and women queued. The military was out in strength: a column of light tanks added to the traffic congestion. I thought of the other grey old capitals of Europe, members of the same dying yet grand order, all teetering on the brink of annihilation.

Bawtrey shuffled up another piece of paper as we approached Ludgate Circus.

'Dame reaffirms Sark's neutrality,' he read disgustedly, screwing it up. 'And here's one more in your line, Minister. Deputy Supreme Commander of N.A.T.O., General Gavin T. Schuller, was assassinated within the last twenty-five minutes by David Woolf, described as a member of the British Communist Party. Members of the Special Police shot Woolf before he could escape. Fighting is still——'

He paused. Someone visible to us only as a torso tapped Bawtrey's shoulder and handed him a fresh communiqué. He read it out slowly, squinting now and again at Northleech as he did so.

'Here's one for the general circuits. Sounds like big stuff. Seems they finally got through to Washington and Ottawa. This one's datelined Washington and reads: "Mr. Martin Mumford, President of the United States, will make a special address to the world at 1500 hours, British Summer Time, today." That's in about twenty-eight minutes' time. "This address will transcend in importance any previous statement ever made by a U.S. President." Hm, some billing. "It is of the utmost importance that the largest possible audience in all countries sees and hears the President speak." Sounds as if the Martians have stepped in, doesn't it?'

'That will be all, thank you, Bawtrey,' Northleech said, obviously disapproving such facetiousness. As he switched off, the bearded man picked up his cup, swigged it and faded into nothing. The set folded neatly back into its compartment.

The traffic thinned; we accelerated along the last stretch of the way, and the Tower swung into sight ahead. The bright dress uniforms had gone. Light tanks had replaced the sentry-boxes. Everything was handled efficiently. Northleech produced a pass for the guard officer, which was okayed. Nevertheless, we and the driver had to climb out and be searched for fire-arms, while two plain-clothes men simultaneously examined our vehicle.

They gave us clearance in about forty-five seconds, saluting us as we drove on under Byward Tower with a guard riding beside the driver.

We drove over to the Queen's House and climbed out. I followed Northleech inside. Another guard stationed by a wooden staircase was replacing the receiver on a handphone as we entered; the main gate had warned him we were about to arrive. He flicked over a switch normally concealed behind oak panelling.

The wooden staircase hinged at the sixth step up, yawning open to reveal a flight of carpeted stone stairs descending underground. Motioning to me, Northleech started down them, his untidy white hair fluttering round his head in the warm updraught of air.

I recognized that smell of canned air, sweet with disinfectant. It reminded me of the underground H.Q. of my department in Hyde Park during World War II. This was a much more elaborate and larger subterranean system. At the bottom of the stairs was a chain of three airlocks giving one on to each other, their indicators all at a neutral green. They opened on to a large circular space, well-lit but almost deserted. Here stood a magazine and paper stall, a tobacconist's, and a café, all open. Piped music played softly. I noticed other stairs leading down into this foyer.

Without hesitation, Northleech led over to a central block of lifts, a row of perhaps a dozen varying sizes, each with an ancient male attendant waiting by the doors. We entered the nearest.

'Level X,' Northleech said crisply.

Glancing at me with a sly humour, he remarked, 'You see

the government hasn't been entirely unprepared for emergencies.'

'Every man for himself,' I replied.

It was an express lift. I climbed out at the bottom feeling slightly sick. For a second we had been in free fall.

Here was a maze of corridors, with many people moving fast with set faces. After some slight confusion and a word or two of barked argument, Northleech got us into an ante-room, where a smartly formidable secretary left us, returning in two minutes.

While he was out of the room, Northleech said, 'I know this man, this secretary. Obviously Menhennick is still in full control. We'll have to watch our step until we see how the land lies. Agreed?'

'It seems inevitable.'

'Keep it that way. We don't want trouble if it can be avoided.'

'Spoken in character, Minister.'

'Don't be a bloody fool, Simon. You're out of your depth and you know it.'

The secretary, returning, said, 'The P.M.'s with the Indian Premier and other Commonwealth gentlemen. You may go in, but don't intrude.'

We went in.

We did not intrude.

The room was impressive. Some fifty men were gathered there, many of them leading diplomats. Waiters with trays unobtrusively served drinks. On the surface it appeared incongruously peaceful. I recognized Mr. Turdilal, the Indian Premier, at once. He stood on a raised platform with Minnie slightly behind him. Minnie looked worn and shrunken; his face reminded me of the ill look I had seen on the face of Sir Anthony Eden at the time of Suez.

Turdilal seemed incongruously cheerful. He was in full spate as we entered, waving a relaxed right hand in time with his phrases.

'. . . and furthermore, gentlemen, you need no reminding from me that India has always stood for the peace of the world. We are an old nation and we have always stood for peace. That is why we are standing now at this terribly black hour of international conflict solidly behind the British government and most of the other members of the Commonwealth for neutrality. We——'

'What about the invasion of Indonesia?' a voice called.

Turdilal smiled a charming smile.

'What about the invasion, indeed, my South American

friend? Carnage added to carnage does not equal peace, my friend. We are not Gadarene swine, may I remind you. Your country is also on friendly terms with Indonesia, but you are not hurrying to bear arms on their behalf. No. You are wise. Instead you are stepping up armament production to sell to China, I guess.'

Ugly murmurs greeted this, but Turdilal flowed on.

'South America must remain neutral. And that is what I am saying also about Britain and the Commonwealth. Someone must rebuild out of the ashes. That is a harder task than creating the ashes. So I for one applaud Mr. Menhennick's stand against the pressure of power politics.'

A hubbub arose as he finished, angry cries mingling with cheers and the odd handclap.

Minnie came forward, clapped Turdilal weakly on the back, and held up his hand for silence. When it came, he rubbed the hand over his moustache and said, 'Thank you for your support, gentlemen. I realize our country is in an invidious position, I realize it only too well. But we have been in an invidious position for a quarter of a century now, ever since the perfection of this deadly nuclear power and the emergence of the two great powers. Rest assured, I have done all in my power to keep our beloved country safe. Rest assured, I shall not stand down——'

'Shame!' I cried.

'—until I feel the nation has no more need for me. . . .'

'Go, in God's name, go!' I shouted.

Two Ghana ministers looked angrily round and said, 'Keep silence while he speaks,' and a waiter pressed a large whisky into my hand.

'I will say no more now,' Minnie continued, looking at his watch. 'In two minutes, the American President, Mr. Mumford, is speaking to the world via Telstar II. We can see it on the wall screen here. I do not know what he is to say, but doubtless it will be of grave import. Just at present our contacts with Washington are disturbed; however, I have been reliably informed that a very few hours ago the American continent was subjected to intense nuclear bombardment on both her seaboards.'

A ripple of amusement that grew with the beginning of his last sentence was killed stone dead by the end of it. A terrible silence, a chill, settled over everyone present—myself, of course, included. Everyone present had their differences with the United States, yet in that moment friction died and love came uppermost. Many faces were full of shame. We all stood motionless.

Not a word was spoken until the big wall screen lit. The time was three o'clock.

The Global Viewing sign came on, a spinning world with the illuminated orbits of the TV reflection stations surrounding it. How long, I wondered, before they were shot down and TV shrank again into a petty national plaything instead of the transnational communication it had become?

A voice said, 'Here is the President of the United States of America, Mr. Martin Wainwright Mumford.'

He sat composedly at a desk bare of everything bar one sheet of paper. He wore a neat suit. Behind him hung the American flag. He looked young, determined, and under enormous strain. He launched into what he had to say without preliminaries; he spoke without rhetoric.

'I invited everyone in the world to see and hear me because what I have to say is of personal importance to you all.

'Only a few hours ago, the enemies of the United States launched their mightiest weapons upon us. Intercontinental ballistic missiles carrying nuclear warheads descended on all our major cities almost simultaneously. Their destructive forces when unleashed on their targets were so great that no nation could have survived the blow.

'Happily, all those missiles were checked some miles up in the atmosphere.

'The United States of America now possesses a sure defence against the hideous and hitherto all-conquering weapon of nuclear bombing.

'This defence is of such a nature that it could only be given thorough trial under actual test conditions. We have had to undergo that test, and we have survived. Had the defence failed, I should not be here talking to you now.

'The defence takes the form of a shield, which we call the geogravitic flux. In theory, this form of defence has been known for some time, but its consumption of energy seemed so vast as to render it impracticable. However, our scientists and technologists have perfected a way whereby the shield—which now covers all of North America, our Canadian allies as well as ourselves—the shield draws its power from the nuclear power it destroys. The greater the force exerted against it, the more greatly the shield is able to resist.

'You will see that we are in consequence impregnable. What is more, we shall remain impregnable for a long time. We have this new defence. Our enemies have new weapons. We were subjected not only to nuclear attack; we were bombarded by a type of anti-matter bomb infinitely more terrible than

78

the nuclear bomb, which must now be regarded as old-fashioned. Our shield effectively repelled all comers.'

Almost furtively, I glanced about me. Every face was fixed in fascination on that grave face looming on the screen. An immense pressure of triumph was building up as the President continued his address.

'I confess that this nation has—as yet—no anti-matter bomb. We have been concentrating on methods of defence rather than offence. But we have literally at our finger-tips the mighty power of the atom. So far we have unleashed no retaliatory bombs in reply to the brutal attack of our enemies.

'It is my hope that retaliation will not be necessary. America and Canada cannot be conquered; but we could bring our enemies to their knees two hours from now. We could destroy them utterly, as they well know. We do not desire to take this ultimate step. The collapse of the two vast Communist countries would involve the rest of the free world in decades of rehabilitation too costly to be visualized. So we are stepping forward, laying our cards on the table, and inviting our enemies to make peace with the Free World at once.

'This is an unprecedented step to take. We live in unprecedented times; God grant us unprecedented courage to meet it.

'Such a step would not have been possible had not our friends the British, and the other North Atlantic countries who look to them for leadership, decided to remain neutral. Had they not so decided, then beyond doubt they would have suffered the same terrible bombardment inflicted on us. Without the geogravitic shield, they would never have survived, and we should have been forced to carry out total war to avenge their destruction.

'So I say again, we whole-heartedly and unreservedly offer a fresh chance to make peace. On behalf of my government and people, I invite the leaders of the Communist bloc to meet me personally on neutral ground in London. I give them forty-eight hours to make a just peace. After that time, if they have not shown themselves more than willing to build a lasting agreement—they know what the consequences will have to be.

'They will be shown no mercy then, as they have shown us no mercy. But United America offers them more than mercy now.'

Mumford's image disappeared. At once a subdued uproar broke out in the hall. Like many of the others, I was weeping with an un-British lack of restraint.

Next to the hall was a canteen. As I was eating there a few minutes later, Northleech approached, talking to a secretary. By his manner, I saw he bubbled with excitement. No doubt he was, in his own phrase, being guided by necessity. He broke off his conversation to speak to me.

'Look here, Sir Simon, this wonderful gesture of Mumford's has put a different complexion on matters. I will see to it personally that the warrant for your arrest is cancelled straightaway.'

'Thank you. Then I can go back to East Lincoln to see how my wife is. Though I shall have to tender my resignation to the Dean.'

'Understandable, quite. Well, that must remain your worry; I can't interfere there, naturally.'

'Naturally.'

'Though the Dean may not accept it. His anti-American views were always too clear. Since you'll no doubt return there as something of a hero, he may feel that by keeping you on he will gain popularity for himself. I'm sure I should feel like that, in his boots.'

I looked down at my plate to conceal my distaste.

'I'm sure you would,' I said, 'But I'm sick of appeasement in all its forms. A new breeze is blowing from now on, and I'm coming back into politics.'

A spark of anger fired in the old boy. He rapped on my table, making my spoon rattle against the plate.

'Before you do that, you'd better learn to distinguish between negotiation and appeasement.'

'I can already. You're a great appeaser, Minister; Mumford is a great negotiator. The difference is in the position from which you talk: a position of weakness or a position of strength. Mumford's is one of strength, yours and Minnie's one of weakness—and chiefly moral weakness.'

He cleared his throat. His wattle had turned a dusky red. In a low voice he said, 'Stop kicking a man when he's down. You saw for yourself how shaken poor old Alfred Menhennick was. He can't resign quickly enough.'

There had never been better news. I only wished Jean—and David Woolf—could have shared it with me. Then, sobering my excitement, came the thought that we would have to turn out all of Minnie's sympathizers before the peace contingent arrived from America. When I spoke, the secretary flinched at the poison in my voice.

'Your own position is none too happy, Edgar. Mumford may have granted Britain a face-saver for general consumption, but you well know how Washington must really be feeling about us. Aren't we revealed, every one of us, as a set of cowardly turncoats—not only to the U.S. but to the world? You might alleviate the situation slightly by resigning with Minnie, as quickly and publicly as possible—or preferably by falling on your sword.'

He gripped the back of his chair.

'I remember this sort of holier-than-thou can from you in the Sixth,' he said. 'I'm a politician, not a Roman. I've no time for your sort of dramatics. It's true the world, and the Americans in particular, are going to need a lot of explanations, but I'm not going to quit now—I'm going to give them those explanations. Now more than ever the country needs experienced leaders.'

Only for a moment did his face grow ugly; then he smiled with his mouth alone. The secretary aped the gesture of ill-omen.

6

SHARDS

THE way of telling the time down here in Mudland was very ingenious. Double A had a row of sticks stuck in the mud in the blackness before his eyes. With his great spongy hands that sometimes would have nothing to do with him, he gripped the sticks one by one, counting as he went, sometimes in numbers, sometimes in such abstractions as lyre birds, rusty screws, pokers, or seaweed.

He would go on grimly, hand over fist against time, until the beastly old comfort of degradation fogged over his brain and he would forget what he was trying to do. The long liverish gouts of mental indigestion that were his thought processes would take over from his counting. And when later he came to think back to the moment when the takeover occurred, he would know that that had been the moment when it had been the present. Then he could guess how far ahead or behind of the present he was, and could give this factor a suitable name—though lately he had decided that all factors could be classified under the generic term Standard, and accordingly he named the present time Standard O'Clock.

Standard O'Clock he pictured as a big Irish guardsman with moustaches sweeping round the roseate blankness of his face. Every so often, say on pay day or on passing out parade, the Lance-Standard would chime, with pretty little cuckoos popping out of all orifices. As an additional touch of humour, Double A would make O'Clock's pendulum wag.

By this genial ruse, he was slowly abolishing time, turning himself into the first professor of a benighted quantum. As yet the experiments were not entirely successful, for ever and anon his groping would communicate itself to his hands, and back they'd come to him, slithering through the mud, tame as you please. Sometimes he bit them; they tasted unpleasant; nor did they respond.

'You are intellect,' he thought they said. 'But we are the tools of intellect. Treat us well.'

II

Another experiment concerned the darkness.

Even sprawling in the mud with his legs amputated unfortunately represented a compromise. Double A had to admit there was nothing final in his degradation, since he had begun to—no, nobody would force him to use the term 'enjoy the mud', but on the other hand nobody could stop him using the term 'ambivelling the finny claws (clause?)' with the understanding that in certain contexts it might be interpreted as approximately synonymous with 'enjoying the mud'.

Anyhow, heretofore, and nutmeggaphonically, it remained to be continued that everywhere was compromise. The darkness compromised with itself and with him. The darkness was sweet and warm and wet.

When Double A realized that the darkness was not utter, that the abstraction utterness was beyond it, he became furious, drumming imaginary heels in the mud, urinating into it with some force and splendour, and calling loudly for dark glasses.

The dark glasses were a failure, for they became covered in mud, so that he could not see through them to observe whether or no the darkness increased. So they came and fitted him with a pair of ebony contact lenses, and with this splendid condescension on their part, Double A hoped he had at last reached a point of non-compromise.

Not so! He had eyelids that pressed on the lenses, drawing merry patterns on the night side of his eyeballs. Pattern and darkness cannot exist together, so again he was defeated by myopic little Lord Compromise, knee-high to a pin and stale as rats' whiskers, but still Big Reeking Lord of Creation. Well, he was not defeated yet. He had filled in Application No. Six Oh Five Bark Oomph Eight Eight Tate Potato Ten in sticks and sandbars and the old presumption factor for the privilege of Person Double A, sir, late of the Standard O'Clock Regiment, sir, to undergo total partial and complete Amputation of Two Vermicularform Appendages in the possession of the aforesaid Double A and known henceforth as his Eyelids.

Meanwhile the application was accepted and the scalpels served, he tried his cruel experiments on the darkness.

He shouted, whispered, spoke, gave voice, uttered, named names, broke wind, cracked jokes, split infinitives, passed participles, and in short and *in toto* interminably talked, orated, chattered, chatted, and generally performed vocal circumbendibusses against the darkness. Soon he had it cowering in a corner. It was less well equipped orally than Double A, and he let it know with a 'Three wise manias came from the Yeast, causing ferment, and bringing with them gifts of gold and Frankenstein and murder' and other such decompositions of a literary-religio-medico-philosophico-nature.

So the powers of darkness had no powers against the powers of screech.

'Loot there be light!' boomed Double A: and there was blight. Through the thundering murk, packed tight with syllables, he could see the dim mud-bound form of Gasm.

'Let there be night!' doomed Double A. But he was too late, had lost his chance, had carried his experiment beyond the pale. For in the pallor and squalor, Gasm remained revoltingly *there*, whether invisible or visible. And his bareness in the thereness made a whereness tight as harness.

III

So began the true history of Mudland. It was now possible to have not only experiments, which belong to the old intellect arpeggio, but character conflict, which pings right out of the middle register of the jolly old emotion chasuble. Amoebas, editors, and lovers are elements in that vast orchestra of classifiable objects to whom or for whom character conflict is ambrosia.

Double A went carefully into the business of having a C.C. with Gasm. To begin with, of course, he did not know whether he himself had a C.: or, of course squared, since we are thinking scientifically, whether Gasm had a C. Without the first C., could there be the second? Could one have a C.-less C.?

Alas for scientific inquiry. During the o'clock sticks that passed while Double A was beating his way patiently through this thicket of thorny questions, jealousy crept up on him unawares.

Despite the shouting and the ebony contact lenses, with which the twin polarities of his counter-negotiations with the pseudo-dark were almost kept a near-maximum in the fairly brave semi-struggle against compromise, Gasm remained ingloriously visible, lolling in the muck no more than a measurable distance away.

Gasm's amputations were identical with Double A's: to wit, the surgical removal under local anaesthetic and two aspirin of that assemblage of ganglions, flesh, blood, bone, toe-nail, hair, and kneecap referred to hereafter as Legs. In this, no cause for jealousy existed. Indeed, They had been scrupulously democratic: one vote, one head; one head, two legs; two heads, four legs. Their surgeons were paragons of the old equality regimen. No cause for Double A's jealousy.

But. It was within his power to *imagine* that Gasm's amputations were other than they were. He could quite easily (and with practice he could perfectly easily) visualize Gasm as having had not two legs but one leg and one arm removed. And that amputation was more interesting than Double A's own amputation, or the fact that he had fins.

So the serpent came even to the muddy paradise of Mudland, writhing between the two bellowing bodies. C.C. became reality.

IV

Double A abandoned all the other experiments to concentrate on beating and catechizing Gasm. Gradually Mudland lost its identity and was transformed into Beating and Catechizing, or B and C. The new regimen was tiring for Double A, physically and especially mentally, since during the entire procedure he was compelled to ask himself why he should be doing what he was, rather than resting contentedly in the mud with his hands.

The catechism was stylized, ranging over several topics and octaves as Double A yelled the questions and Gasm screamed the answers.

'What is your name?'

'My name is Gasm.'

'Name some of the other names you might have been called instead.'

'I might have been called Plus or Shob or Fred or Shit or Droo or Pennyfeather or Harm.'

'And by what strange inheritance does it come about that you house your consciousness among the interstices of lungs, aorta, blood, corpuscles, follicles, sacroiliac, ribs, and prebendary skull?'

'Because I would walk erect if I could walk erect among the glorious company of the Higher Vertebrates, who have grown from mere swamps, dinosaurs and dodos. Those that came before were dirty brates or shirty brates; but we are the vertebrates.'

'What comes after us?'

'After us the deluge.'

'How big is the deluge?'

'Deluge.'

'How deep is the deluge?'

'Ai, deluge.'

'How deluge is the deluge?'

'Deluge, deluger, delugest.'

'Conjugate and decline.'

'I decline to conjuge.'

'Who was that dinosaur I dinna saw you with last night?'

'That was no knight. That was my dinner.'

'And what comes after the vertebrates?'

'Nothing comes after the vertebrates because we are the highest form of civilization.'

'Name the signs whereby the height of our civilization may be determined.'

'The heights whereby the determination of our sign may be civilized are seven in number. The subjugation of the body. The resurrection of the skyscraper. The perpetuation of the species. The annihilation of the species. The glorification of the nates. The somnivolence of the conscience. The omnivorousness of the sex. The conclusion of the Hundred Years War. The condensation of milk. The conversation of muts. The confiscation of monks——'

'Stop, stop! Name next the basic concept upon which this civilization is based.'

'The interests of producer and consumer are identical.'

'What is the justification of war?'

'War is its own justification.'

'What is the desire to feed on justice?'

'A manifestation of opsomania.'

'Let us sing a sesquipedelian love-song in octogenarian voices.'

At this point they humped themselves up in the mud and sang the following tuneless ditty:

No constant factor in beauty is discernible.
Although the road that evolution treads is not returnable,
It has some curious twists in it, as every shape and size
And shade of female breast attestifies.
Pointed, conical, flat or sharp or bonical,
Pendulous or cumulus, pear-shaped, oval, tumulus,
Each one displays its beauty or depravity
In Syncline, incline, outcropping or cavity
Yet from Peru to Timbuctu
The bosom's lines are only signs
Of all the pectoral muscles' tussles
With a fairly constant factor, namely gravity.

They fell back into the mud, each lambasting his mate's nates.

v

Of course for a time it was difficult to be certain of everything or anything. The uncertainties became almost infinite, but among the most noteworthy of the number were the uncertainty as to whether the catechizings actually took place in any wider arena of reality than Double A's mind; the uncertainty as to whether the beatings took place in any wider arena of reality than Double A's mind; the uncertainty as to whether, if the beatings actually took place, they took place with sticks.

For it became increasingly obvious that neither Double A nor Gasm had hands with which to wield sticks. Yet on the other appendage, evidence existed tending to show that some sort of punishment had been undergone. Gasm no longer resembled a human. He had grown positively torpedo-shaped. He possessed fins.

The idea of fins, Double A found to his surprise, was not a surprise to him. Fins had been uppermost in his mind for some while. Fins, indeed, induced in him a whole watery way of thinking; he was flooded with new surmises, while some of the old ones proved themselves a wash-out. The idea, for example, that he had ever worn dark glasses or ebony contact lenses. . . . Absurd!

He groped for an explanation. Yes, he had suffered hallucinations. Yes, the whole progression of thought was unravelling and clarifying itself now. He had suffered from hallucinations. Something had been wrong in his mind. His optic centres had been off-centre. With something like clarity, he became able to map the area of disturbance.

It occurred to him that he might some time investigate this cell or tank in which he and Gasm were. Doors and windows had it none. Perhaps like him it had undergone some vast sea change.

Emitting a long liquid sigh, Double A ascended slowly off the floor. As he rose, he glanced upwards. Two drowned men floated on the ceiling, gazing down at him.

VI

Double A floated back to his former patch of mud only to find his hands gone. Nothing could have compensated him for the loss except the growth of a long strong tail.

His long strong tail induced him to make another experiment; no more nor less than the attempt to foster the illusion that the tail was real by pretending there was a portion of his brain capable of activating the tail. More easily done than thought. With no more than an imaginary flick of the imaginary appendage, he was sailing above Gasm on a controlled course, ducking under but on the whole successfully ignoring the two drownees.

From then on he called himself Doublay and had no more

87

truck with time or hands or ghosts of hands and time. Though the mud was good, being above it was better, especially when Gasm could follow. They grew new talents—or did they find them?

Now the questions were no sooner asked than forgotten, for by a mutual miracle of understanding, Doublay and Gasm began to believe themselves to be fish.

And then they began to dream about hunting down the alien invaders.

VII

The main item in the laboratory was the great tank. It was sixty feet square and twenty feet high; it was half-full of sea-water. A metal cat-walk with rails round it ran along the top edge of the tank; the balcony was reached by a metal stair. Both stair and cat-walk were covered with deep rubber, and the men that walked there wore rubber shoes, to ensure maximum quiet.

The whole place was dimly lit.

Two men, whose names were Roberts and Collison, stood on the cat-walk, looking through infra-red goggles down into the tank. Though they spoke almost in whispers, their voices nevertheless held a note of triumph.

'This time I think we have succeeded, Dr. Collison,' the younger man was saying. 'In the last forty-eight hours, both specimens have shown less lethargy and more awareness of their form and purpose.'

Collison nodded.

'Their recovery has been remarkably fast, all things considered. The surgical techniques have been so many and so varied. . . . Though I played a major part in the operations myself, I am still overcome by wonder to think that it has been possible to transfer at least half of a human brain into such a vastly different metabolic environment.'

He gazed down at the two shadowy forms swimming round the tank.

Compassion moving him, he said, 'Who knows what terrible traumas those two brave souls have had to undergo? What fantasies of amputation, of life, birth and death, of not knowing what species they were.'

Sensing his mood, and disliking it, Roberts said briskly, 'They're over it now. It's obvious they can communicate. The underwater mikes pick up their language. They've adjusted well. Now they're raring to go.'

'Maybe, maybe. I still wonder if we had the right——'

Roberts gestured impatiently, guessing Collison spoke only

to be reassured. He knew how proud the old man secretly was, and answered him in the perfunctory way he might have answered one of the newspaper men who would be round later.

'The security of the world demanded this drastic experiment. The alien ship "landed" a year ago in the North Atlantic, off Bermuda. Our submarines have investigated its remains on the ocean bed. They have found proof that the ship landed where it did *under control*, and was only destroyed when the aliens left it.

'The aliens were fish people, aquatics. The ocean is their element, and undoubtedly they have been responsible for the floods extending along the American and European seaboards and inundating the West Indies. Undoubtedly the popular press is right to claim we are being defeated in an alien invasion.'

'My dear Roberts, I don't doubt they're right, but——'

'There can be no buts, Dr. Collison. We've failed to make any contact with the aliens. They have eluded the most careful submarine probes. Nor is there any "but" about their hostile intent. It seems more than likely that they have killed off all the eel family in some unimaginable slaughter under the Sargasso Sea. Before they upset our entire oceanic ecology, we must find them out and gain the information about them without which they cannot be fought. Here are our spies, here in this tank. They have post-hypnotic training. In a couple more days, when they are fit, they can be released into the sea to go and get that information and return with it to us. There are no buts; only imperatives in this equation.'

Slowly the two men descended the metal stairway, the giant tank on their left, glistening with condensation.

'Yes, it's as you say,' Collison agreed wearily. 'I would so much like to know, though, the insane sensations passing through those shards of human brain embedded in fish bodies.'

'Ethics don't enter into it,' Roberts said firmly.

In the tank, in the twilight, the two giant tunnies swam restlessly back and forth, readying themselves for their mission.

'O MOON OF MY DELIGHT!'

MURRAGH lay on the ground to await consummation. It was now less than five minutes away and it would fall from the air.

The alarms had sounded near and distant. Their echoes had died from the high hills of Region Six. Stretched full length on the edge of a grassy cliff, Murragh Harrison adjusted the plugs in his ears and laid his fume-mask ready by his side.

Everything calm and silent now. The whole world silent. And in him: a growing tension, as strange and ever-delightful as the tensions of love.

He raised his binoculars to his eyes and peered into the valley, where lay the Flange, that wide and forbidden highway down which the starships blazed. Even from his elevation, he could hardly discern the other side of the Flange; it ran East–West right round the equator of Tandy Two, unbroken and unalterable, an undeviating—he'd forgotten the figure—ten, was it, or twelve, or fifteen miles wide. In the sunlight, the innumerable facets of the Flange glittered and moved.

His glasses picked out the mountains on the south side of the Flange. Black and white they were, picked as clear as a dead man's ribs under the abrasion of total vacuum.

'I must bring Fay here before she goes back to Earth,' he said aloud. 'Wonderful, wonderful. . . .' Assuming a different tone, he said, 'There is terror here on Tandy's equator, terror and sublimity. The most awe-full place in the universe. Where vacuum and atmosphere kiss: and the kiss is a kiss of death! Yes. Remember that. "The kiss is a kiss of death." '

In his little leisure time Murragh was writing—and had been ever since I first met him—a book about Tandy Two as he experienced it. Yet he knew, he told me, he knew that the sentences he formed up there on the hill were too coloured, too big, too false. Under his excitement, more truthful images struggled to be born.

While they struggled, while he lay and wished he had brought Fay with him, the starship came in.

This! This was the moment, the fearsome apocalyptic moment! Unthinking, he dropped his glasses and ducked his head to the earth, clinging to it in desperate excitement with all his bones from his toes to his skull.

Tandy Two *lurched*.

The F.T.L. ship burst into normal space on automatic control, invisible and unheard at first. Boring for the world like a metal fist swung at a defenceless heart, it was a gale of force. It was brutality . . . and it skimmed the Flange as gently as lover's cheek brushes lover's cheek.

Yet so mighty was that gentleness, that for an instant a loop of fire was spun completely round Tandy Two. Over the Flange a mirage flickered: a curious elongated blur that only an educated retina could take for the after-image of a Faster Than Light ship chasing to catch up with its object. Then a haze arose, obscuring the Flange. Cerenkov radiations flickered outwards, distorting vision.

The transgravitic screens to the north of the Flange—on Murragh's side of it, and ranged along the valley beneath his perch—buckled but held as they always held. The towering B.G.L. pylons were bathed in amber. Atmosphere and vacuum roared at each other from either side of the invisible screens. But as ever the wafer-thin geogravitics held them apart, held order and chaos separate.

A gale swept up the mountain-sides.

The sun jerked wildly across the sky.

All this happened in one instant.

And in the next instant it was deepest night.

Murragh dug his hands out of the soft earth and stood up. His chest was soaked with sweat, his trousers were damp. Trembling, he clamped his fume-mask over his face, guarding himself against the toxic gases generated by the F.T.L.'s passage.

Tears still ran down his face as limply he turned to make his way back to the highland farm.

'"Kiss of death, embrace of flame . . ."' he muttered to himself as he climbed aboard his tractor; but still the elusive image he really wanted did not come.

In a north-facing fold of hills lay the farmhouse, burrowed deeply into the granite just in case of accidents. Murragh's headlights washed over it. Its outhouses were terraced below it, covered pen after covered pen, all now full of Farmer Doughty's sheep, locked in as always during entry time; not a single animal could be allowed outside when the F.T.L.s came down.

Everything lay still as Murragh drove up in his tractor. Even the sheep were silent, crouching mutely under the jack-in-a-box dark. Not a bird flew, not an insect sparked into the headlights; such life had almost died out during the four hundred years the Flange had been in operation. The toxic gases hardly encouraged fecundity in nature.

Soon Tandy itself might rise to shine down on its earthlike second moon. The planet Tandy was a gas giant as big as Jupiter, a beautiful object when it rose into Tandy Two's skies, but uninhabitable and unapproachable.

Tandy One equally was not a safe place for human beings. But the second satellite, Tandy Two, was a gentle world with mild seasons and an oxygen–nitrogen atmosphere. People lived on Tandy Two, loved, hated, struggled, aspired there as on any of the multitudinous civilized planets in the galaxy, with this difference: that because there was something individual about Tandy Two, there was something individual about its problems.

The southern hemisphere of Tandy Two was lifeless under vacuum; the northern existed mainly for the vast terminal towns of Blerion, Touchdown, and Ma-Gee-Neh. Apart from the cities, there was nothing but grass, grass and lakes and silicone desert stretching to the pole. And by courtesy an occasional sheep farm was allowed on the grasslands.

'What a satellite!' Murragh said, climbing from the tractor. Admiration sounded in his voice. He was a curious man, Murragh Harrison—but I'll stick to fact and let you understand what you will.

He pushed through the spaced double doors that served the Doughty farmstead as a crude airlock when the gases were in the air. In the living-eating-cooking room beyond, Colin Doughty himself stood by the C.V. watching its colours absently. He looked up as Murragh removed his face-mask.

'Good *evening*, Murragh,' he said with heavy jocularity. 'Great to see so nice a morning followed by so nice a night without so much as a bloody sunset in between.'

'You should be used to the system by now,' Murragh murmured, hanging his binoculars with his jacket in the A.-G. cupboard. After being alone in the overwhelming presence of Tandy, it always took him a moment to adjust to people again.

'So I should, so I should. Fourteen years and I still see red to think how men have bollixed about with one of God's worlds. Thank heaven we'll all be off this crazy moon in another three weeks! I can't wait to see Earth now, I'm telling you.'

'You'll miss the green grass and the open space.'

'So you keep telling me. What do you think I am? One of my bloody sheep! Just as soon——'

'But once you get away——'

92

'Just a minute, Murragh!' Doughty held up a brown hand as he cocked his eye at the C.V. 'Here comes Touchdown to tell us if it's bedtime yet.'

Murragh had halted on the way upstairs to his room. Now he came back to peer into the globe with the shepherd. Even Hock the housedog glanced up momentarily at the assured face that appeared in the bright bowl.

'C.V.A. Touchdown talking,' the face said, smiling at its unseen audience. 'The F.T.L. ship "Droffoln-Jingguring-Mapynga-Bill"—and I rehearsed its name beforehand!—has just made a safe and successful entry on the Flange some three hundred and twenty miles outside Touchdown station. As you can see from this live shot, passengers are already being met by helicopter and taken to the S.T.L. port in Touchdown. The "Droffoln-Jingguring-Mapynga-Bill" has come from Pyvries XIII in the Outer Magellans. You are looking at a typical Magellanic now. He is, as you observe, octopedal.

'We hope to bring you news and interviews with passengers and crews in two hours' time, when all the occupants of the F.T.L. have undergone the customary revival. You notice that at present they are still under Light-freeze.

'Now we go over to Chronos-Touchdown for a new time check.'

The assured face gave way to a very shaggy one. Behind it, the untidy computing-room of this astronomical department greeted viewers. The shaggy face smiled and said, 'As yet we have only a rough scheme for you. It will, as usual, take a little while to feed accurate figures into our machines, and some reports have still to come in.

'Meanwhile, here is an approximate time check. The F.T.L. ship—I will not attempt its name—entered Flange influence at roughly 1219 hours 47.66 seconds on today, Seventeenday of Cowl Month. Inertia absorption thrust Tandy through approximately 108.75 degrees axial revolution in approximately 200 milliseconds. So the time at the end of that very short period became roughly 1934 hours 47.66 seconds.

'Since that was about twenty-four and a half minutes ago, the time to which everyone in Touchdown zone should set their watches and clocks is . . . coming up . . . 1959 hours and 18 seconds. . . . Now! I repeat, the time is now 1959 hours, one minute to eight o'clock at night, plus 18 seconds.

'It is still, of course, Seventeenday of Cowl.

'We shall be back to bring you more accurate information on the time in another two hours.'

Doughty snorted and switched the globe off. It slid obediently out of sight into the wall.

'Mucking about with the clocks!' he growled. 'Here I've just had my midday bite and there's Bess upstairs putting the kids to bed!'

'That's what happens on Tandy Two,' Murragh said, edging from the room. Without wishing to seem rude, he was bored with Doughty's complaints which occurred with little variation once a fortnight—whenever, in fact, a F.T.L. ship arrived. He ducked out of the room and almost scuttled up the stairs.

'It may happen on Tandy Two,' Doughty said, not averse to having only Hock to talk to, 'but that don't mean to say Colin Doughty has to like it.' He squared his broad shoulders, thrust out his chest, and stuck his thumbs in his spunsteel jacket. 'I was born on Earth where a man gets twenty-four hours to his day—every day.'

Hock thumped his tail idly twice as if in ironic applause.

As Murragh got upstairs, Tessie marched past him on her way from the washing-room. She was absolutely naked.

'High time the girl was taken to civilization and learnt the common rules of decency,' Murragh thought, good-humouredly. The girl was several months past her thirteenth birthday. Perhaps it was as well the Doughty family were off back to Earth in three weeks; their departure and Tessie's puberty were just about coincident.

'Going to bed at this hour of the day!' Tessie grunted, not deigning to look at her father's help as she thumped past him.

'It's eight o'clock at night. The man on the C.V. has just said so,' Murragh replied.

'Poof!'

With that she disappeared into her bedroom. Murragh did the same into his. He took the time changes in his stride; on Tandy now the changes had to be considered natural, 'for use can almost change the stamp of nature'. Life on the sheep farm was rigorous. Murragh, Doughty, and his wife rose early and slept early. Murragh planned to lie and think for an hour, possibly to write a page more of his book, and then to take a somnolizer and sleep till four the next morning.

His thinking had no time to grow elaborate and deep. The door burst open and Fay rushed in, squealing with exuberance.

'Did you see it? Did you see it?' she asked.

He had no need to ask to what she referred.

'I sat on the top of the cliff and watched it,' he said.

'You are lucky! Gosh!' She did a pirouette, and pulled an ugly grimace at him. 'That's what I call my Life-begins-at-forty face, Murragh; did it scare you? Oh fancy, to see one

94

of those starships actually plonk down in the Flange. Tell me all about it!'

She wore only vest and knickers. A tangle of arms and legs flashed as she jumped on to the bed beside him and began tugging his ears. She was six, gay, primitive, adorable, unpredictable.

'You're supposed to be going to bed. Your mother will be after you, girl.'

'Blow her, she's always after me. Tell me about the starships and how they land and—oh, gummy, you know—all that crap you talk.'

'When you've wrenched my ears off I will.'

He was not easy with her leaning against him. Rising, he pointed out of his little window with its double panes. Since his room was at the front of the farmhouse, he had this view out across the valley. The girls slept in a room considered more safe, at the back of the house, tucked into solid granite ('the living granite', Doughty always called it)' and without windows.

'Outside there now, Fay,' he said as the little girl peered into the dark, 'are vapours that would make you ill if you inhaled them. They are breathed off by the Flange under the stress of absorbing the speed of the F.T.L. ships. The geogravitic screens on this side of the Flange undergo terrific pressures at such times and do very peculiar things. But the beautiful part is that when we wake in the morning the stinks will all have blown away; Tandy itself, this marvellous moon we live on, will absorb them and send us a fresh supply of clean mountain air to breathe.'

'Do the mountains have air?'

'We call the air on the mountains "mountain air". That's all it means.'

As he sat down beside her, she asked, 'Do the vapours make it dark so quickly?'

'No, they don't, Fay, and you know they don't. I've explained that bit before. The Faster-Than-Light ships do that.'

'Are the Vaster-Than-Light ships dark?'

'Faster-Than-Light. No, they're not dark. They come in from deep space so fast—at speeds above that of light, because those are the only speeds they can travel at—that they shoot right round Tandy one and a half times before the Flange can stop them, before its works can absorb the ship's momentum. And in doing that they twirl Tandy round a bit on its axis with them.'

'Like turntables?'

'That's what I told you, didn't I? If you ran very fast on to a light wooden turntable that was not moving, you would stop but your motion would make the turntable turn. Transference of energy, in other words. And this twirling sometimes moves us round from sunshine into darkness.'

'Like today. I get you were scared out on the hillside when it suddenly got dark!'

He tickled her in the ribs.

'No, I wasn't, because I was prepared for it. But that's why we have to get your Daddy's sheep all safely under cover before a ship comes—otherwise *they'd* all be scared and jump over precipices and things, and then your Daddy'd lose all his money and you wouldn't be able to go back to Earth.'

Fay looked meditatively at him.

'Frankly speaking, these Vaster-Than-Light ships are rather a bloody nuisance to us, aren't they?' she said.

Murragh hooted with laughter.

'If you put it like that——' he began, when Mrs. Doughty thrust her head round the door.

'There you are, Fay, you little minx! I thought as much. Come and get into bed at once.'

Bess Doughty was a solid woman in her early forties, very plain, very clean. She of them all was the least at home on Tandy Two, yet she grumbled about it least; among all her many faults one could not include grumbling. She marched into Murragh's room and seized her younger daughter by the wrists.

'You're killing me!' Fay yelled in feigned agony. 'Murragh and I were discussing transparency of energy. Let me kiss him good-night and then I'll come. He is a lovely man and I wish he was coming to Earth with us.'

She gave Murragh an explosive kiss that rocked him backwards. Then she rushed from the room. Bess paused before following; she winked at Murragh.

'Pity you don't like us two to carry on a bit more in that style, Mr. Harrison,' she said, and shut the door after her as she left.

It was something of a relief to him that her crude physical advances were now replaced by nothing more trying than innuendo. Murragh put his feet up on the bed and lay back.

He looked round the room with its sparse plastic furniture. This would be home for only three weeks more: then he would move on to work for Farmer Clay in Region Five. Nothing would he miss—except Fay, Fay who alone among all the people he knew shared his curiosity and his love for Tandy Two.

A phrase of hers floated back to him. 'The Vaster-Than-

Light ships'. Oddly appropriate name for craft existing in 'phase space' where their mass exceeded 'normal' infinity! His mind began to play with the little girl's phrase; reverie overcame him, so that in sinking down into a nest of his own thought he found, even amid the complexity gathered round him, a comforting simplicity, a simplicity he had learnt to look for because it told him that to see clearly into his own inner nature, he had merely to crystallize the attraction Tandy held for him and all would be clear eternally; he would be a man free of shackles, or free at least to unlock them when he wished. So again, as on the cliff and as many times before, he plunged through the receptions of the imagination towards that wished-for truthful image.

Perhaps his search itself was a delusion; but it led him tenderly to sleep.

Murragh and Doughty were out early next morning, going wrapped into the cool hour before dawn. The air, as Murragh had predicted, was sweet to breathe again, although full of a light rain.

Hock and the other dog—Pedro, the yard dog—ran with them as they whistled out the autocollies. Ten of them came pogoing into the open, light machines unfailingly obedient to the instructions from Doughty's throat mike. Although they had their limitations, they could herd sheep twice as quickly as live dogs. Murragh unlocked the doors of the great covered pens. The autocollies went in to get the sheep out as he climbed aboard his tractor. As the sheep poured forth, bleating into the open, he and Doughty revved their engines and followed behind, watching as the flock fanned out towards the choicer grasslands. Then they bumped along in the rear, keeping the autodogs constantly on course.

Dawn seeped through the eastern clouds and the rain stopped. Filmy sun created miracles of chiaroscuro over valley and hill. By then they had the sheep split into four flocks, each of which was established on a separate hillside for pasturing. They returned to the farmland in time to breakfast with the rest of the family.

'Do they get miserable wet days on Earth like this?' Tessie asked.

'Nothing wrong with today. Rain's holding off now,' her father said. Breakfast was not his best meal.

'It depends on what part of Earth you live, just as it does here, you silly girl,' said her mother.

'They haven't got any weather in the south half of Tandy,' Fay volunteered, talking round an epoch-making mouthful of mutton sausage, ''cos it's had to be vacuumized so's the star-ships coming in at such a lick wouldn't hit any molecules of air and get wrecked and without air you don't have weather, isn't that so, Murragh?'

Murragh, who had heard some of this sausage-and-sentence, agreed it was so.

'Shut up talking about the Flange. It's all you seem to think of, these days, young lady,' Doughty growled.

'I never mentioned the Flange, Daddy. You did.'

'I'm not interested in arguing, Fay, so save your energy. You're getting too cheeky these days.'

She put both elbows on the plastic table and said with deliberate devilment, 'The Flange is just a huge device for absorbing F.T.L. momentum, Daddy, as I suppose you know, don't you? Isn't it, Mr. Murragh?'

Her mother leant forward and slapped her hard across the wrist.

'You like to sauce your dad, don't you? Well, take that! And it's no good coming crying to me about it. It's your fault for being so saucy.'

But Fay had no intention of going crying to her mother. Bursting into tears, she flung down her spoon and fork and dashed upstairs howling. A moment later her bedroom door slammed.

'Jolly well serve her *right*!' Tessie said.

'You be quiet too,' her mother said angrily.

'Never get a peaceful meal now,' Doughty said.

Murragh Harrison said nothing.

After the meal, as the two men went out to work again, Doughty said stiffly, 'If you don't mind, Harrison, I'd rather you left young Fay alone till we leave here.'

'Oh? Why's that?'

The older man thrust him a suspicious glance, then looked away.

'Because she's my daughter and I say so.'

'Can't you give me a reason rather than an evasion?'

A dying bird lay in the yard. Birds were as scarce as gold nuggets on Tandy Two. This one had evidently been overcome by the fumes generated in the previous day's entry. Its wings fluttered pitifully as the men approached. Doughty kicked it to one side.

'If you must know—because she's getting mad on the Flange. Flange, Flange, Flange, that's all we hear from the kid! She didn't know or care a thing about it till this year when you keep telling her about it. You're worse than Captain Rogers when he calls, and he has got an excuse because he

98

works on the damn thing. So you keep quiet in future. Bess and me will leave here with no regrets. Tessie doesn't care either way. But we don't want Fay to keep thinking about this place and upsetting herself and thinking Earth isn't her proper home, which it is going to be.'

This was a long speech for Doughty. The reasons he gave were good enough, but irritation made Murragh ask, 'Did Mrs. Doughty get you to speak to me about this?'

Doughty stopped by the garage. He swung round and looked Murragh up and down, anger in his eye.

'You've been with me in Region Six nigh on four years, Harrison. I was the man who gave you work when you wanted it, though I had not much need of you, nor much to pay you with. You've worked hard, I don't deny——'

'I can't see——'

'I'm talking, aren't I? When you came here you said you were—what was it—"in revolt against ultra-urbanized planets"; you said you were a poet or something; you said—heck, you said a lot of stuff, dressed up in fine bloody phrases. Remember you used to keep me and Bess up half the night sometimes, until we saw it was all just blather!'

'Look here, if you're——'

The farmer bunched his fists and stuck out his lower lip.

'You listen to me for a change. I've been wanting to say this for a long time. Poet indeed! We weren't taken in by your blather, you know. And luckily it had no effect on your Tessie either. She's more like me than her sister is—a quite sensible girl. But Fay is a baby. She's silly as yet, and we reckon you're having a bad influence on her——'

'All right then, you've had your say. Now I'll have mine. Leaving aside the question of whether you and your wife can understand any concept you weren't born with——'

'You be careful now, Harrison, what you're saying about Bess. I'm on to you! I'm not so daft as you think. Let me tell you Bess has had about enough of you giving her the glad eye and making passes at her as if she was just some——'

'By God!' Murragh exploded in anger. 'She tells you that? The boot's on the other foot by a long chalk, and you'd better get that clear right away. If you think I'd touch—if I'd lay a hand on that dismal, salacious. . . . No, it'd make me sick.'

The mere thought of it took the edge off Murragh's wrath. It had the opposite effect on Doughty. He swung his left fist hard at Murragh's jaw. Murragh blocked it with his right forearm and counter-attacked in self-defence with his left. He caught Doughty glancingly on the ear as the farmer kicked out at him. Unable to step back in time, Murragh grabbed the steel-studded boot and wrenched it upwards.

Doughty staggered back and fell heavily on to the ground.

Murragh stood over him, all fury gone.

'If I had known how much you resented me all these years,' he said miserably, staring down at his employer's face, 'I'd not have stayed here. Don't worry, I'll say no more to Fay. Now let's go and get the tractors out, unless you want to sack me on the spot—and that's entirely up to you.'

As he helped the older man to his feet, Doughty muttered shamefacedly, 'I've not resented you, man, you know that perfectly well. . . .'

Then they got the tractors out in silence.

The result of Doughty's fall was what he termed 'a bad back'. He was—and when he said it he spoke with an air of surprise more appropriate to a discovery than cliché—'not as young as he was'. For a day or so he sat gloomily indoors by his C.V., letting Murragh do the outside work, and brooding over his lot.

Tandy Two is a harder satellite than it seems at first—I know after two five-year spells of duty on it. Although in size it is only negligibly larger than Earth (its equatorial circumference being one hundred and forty-six miles longer), its composition is denser, so that gravity exacts a noticeably heavier strain than on Earth. And the fortnightly time hop when the F.T.L.s enter takes a psychological toll. In the big towns like Touchdown and Blerion, civilization can compensate for these disadvantages. On the scattered sheep stations there are no compensations.

Moreover, Colin Doughty had found his farming far less profitable than it had looked on paper from Earth fourteen years ago. Tandy Two offered the best grazing in a stellar region full of ready-made mutton markets: twenty hundred over-urbanized planets within twice twenty light years. But his costs had been stiff, the costs of transport above all, and now he counted himself lucky to be able to get away with enough brass saved to buy a small shop, a butcher's, Earthside. As it was, margins were narrow: he was reckoning on the sale of farm and stock to buy passages home for himself and his family.

Much of this I heard on my periodic tours through Region Six, when I generally managed a visit to the Doughtys. I heard it all again the next time I called, thirteen days after the scuffle between Doughty and Murragh.

I looked in to see Bess, and found Doughty himself, sitting

by a fire, looking surly. Having returned to work, he had again wrenched his back and was having to rest it.

'It's the first time I've ever known you to be off work. Cheer up, you've only got a week to go before you're making tracks for home,' I said, removing my coat.

My truck was outside. Though only half a mile away by hill paths, the unit to which I was attached was at least ten miles off by the circuitous track round the mountains.

'Look how long the flaming journey back to Earth takes when we do get off from Touchdown,' he complained. 'Pity we can't get an F.T.L. ship to Earth—there are enough of them around.'

He spoke as if the F.T.L. ships were my responsibility, which in a sense they were.

'You know by their nature they're only fit for trans-galactic distances,' I said, speaking as though to a child. 'Earth's too near—you have to catch a S.T.L. to get there. And even S.T.L.s are fast enough to make the subjective time of the journey no more than three or four months.'

'Don't start explaining,' he said. He waved his hand dismissively. 'You know I'm only a simple farmer. I don't grasp all that technical stuff.'

That is what I love about simple farmers. They practically invite you to give them explanations, they swallow them, then they say they do not want them. I often found it hard not to despise Doughty.

The two girls Fay and Tessie were there, having just finished their C.V. lessons. Tessie was preparing lunch; eyeing me warily—she was a mistrustful creature—she told me that her mother was out helping Murragh with the flocks while Doughty was laid up. Both girls came over to the farmer to join in the discussion; I coaxed Fay up on to my knee.

She wanted the whole business of how they got home explained to her.

'You're a Flange Maintenance Officer, Captain Rogers,' she said. 'Tell *me* all about it and then I'll tell Daddy so's he can understand.'

'You don't have to understand,' her father said. 'We just take a ship and it'll get us there eventually and that's all there is to it, thank God. The likes of us don't need to bother our heads about the technicalities.'

'*I'm* going to be educated,' Fay replied.

'It's *good* for us to listen,' Tessie said, '—though I understand it all already. A child could understand it.'

'I'm a child and I don't understand it,' her sister said.

'The universe is full of civilized planets, and in a week's time

101

you're all going to hop from one such to another such,' I began. And as I sought for the simple words and the vivid pictures with which to put my explanation across to them, the wonder of the universe overcame me as if for a moment I too was a child.

For the galaxy had grown up into a great and peaceful unit. War existed, but it remained planet-bound and never spread between planets. Crime survived, but did not flourish. Evil lived, but knowledge kept pace with it and fought it. Man prospered and grew kindlier rather than otherwise. Certainly his old vices were as green as ever, but he had devised sociological systems that contained them better than had been the case in earlier epochs.

The galaxy worked something like a clock, its parts interdependent. Space ships formed its connecting links.

Because of the varying distances that had to be covered between planets, some of them colossal, some relatively small, two main classes of space ships had been developed.

Bridging all but the lesser distances were the F.T.L. ships, travelling in super-universes at multiple-light velocities. Bridging the lesser distances went the S.T.L., the Slower-Than-Light ships. And the two sorts of travel were, like the planetary economies themselves, interdependent.

The F.T.L. ship, that ultimate miracle of technology, has one disadvantage: it moves—as far as the 'normal' universe is concerned—at only two speeds, faster than light and stationary.

An F.T.L. ship has to stop directly it comes out of phase space and enters the quantitative fields of the normal universe. Hence bodies such as Tandy Two, spread throughout the galaxy; they are the Braking Planets or Satellites.

An F.T.L. cannot 'stop' in space (a meaningless expression). Instead, its velocities are absorbed by the braking planets or, more accurately, by the inertial absorbers of the flanges which girdle such planets. The F.T.L.s burst in and are reduced to zero velocity within a time limit of about 200 milliseconds—in which time they have circuited the flange, gone completely round the planet, one and a half times.

S.T.L.s then disperse the passengers to local star systems, much in the way that stratoliners land travellers who then disperse to nearby points by helicab.

Though S.T.L.s are slow, relativistic time contractions shorten the subjective journeys in them to tolerable limits of months or weeks.

So the universe ticks, not perfectly (or I'll be accused of smugness!) but workably.

And this is what I told Doughty and his daughters, as Fay snuggled against me, and Tessie kept her distance.

'Well, I'd better go and finish your dinner, Daddy,' Tessie said, after a pause.

He patted her bottom and chuckled with approval.

'That's it, girl,' he said. 'Food's more in our line than all this relativistic stuff. Give me a lamb cutlet any day.'

I had no answer. Nor had Fay, though I saw by her face that she was still thinking over what I had said, as she slid off my knee to go and help Tessie. How much did it mean to her? How much does it all mean to any of us? Though Doughty had little time for theory, I also relished the thought of the lamb cutlet.

Before the food was ready, I took a turn outside with the farmer, who used his stick as support.

'You'll miss this view,' I said, gazing over the great mysterious body of Tandy whose contours were clad in green and freckled here and there with sheep. I must admit it, I am fonder of the beauties of women than of landscape; for all that, the prospect was fine. In the voluptuous downward curve between two hills, Tandy the primary was setting. Even by daylight the banded and beautiful reds swirling over its oblate surface were impressive.

Doughty looked about him, sniffing, admitting nothing. He appeared not to have heard what I said.

'Rain coming up from somewhere,' he observed.

In my turn I ignored him.

'You'll miss this view back on Earth,' I repeated.

'Bugger the view!' Doughty exclaimed and laughed. 'I'm not a clever man like you and young Murragh, Captain; I get simple satisfaction out of simple things, like being in the place where I was born.'

Although I happened to know he was born eight layers under the sky-port in Birmingham, where they still had slot meters for your ration of fresh air, I made no answer. All he meant was that he valued his personal illusions, and there I was with him every time. Convictions or illusions: what matter if all conviction is illusion, so long as we hang on to it? You would never shift Doughty from his, fool though he was in many ways.

I could never get under his skin as surely as I could with some people—Murragh, for instance, a more complicated creature altogether; but often the simplest person has a sort of characterless opacity about him. So it seemed with Doughty, and if I have drawn him flat and lumpy here, that was how I experienced him then.

To produce talk between us, for his silence made me uneasy, I asked after Murragh.

Doughty had little to say on that subject. Instead he pointed with his stick to a tracked vehicle bumping southwards towards us.

'That'll be Murragh with Bess now, coming home for a bit of grub,' he said.

He was mistaken. When the tractor drew nearer, we saw that only Bess was inside it.

As we strolled forward, she drove round the covered pens and pulled up beside us. Her face was flushed, and—I thought—angry-looking, but she smiled when she saw me.

'Hullo, Captain Rogers!' She climbed down and clasped my hand briefly. 'I was forgetting we'd be having your company today. Nice to see a strange face, though I'd hardly call yours that.' She turned straight to her husband and said, 'We got trouble up on Pike's Brow. Two autocollies plunged straight down a crevasse. Murragh's up there with them now trying to get them out.'

'What were you doing up on Pike's Brow?' he demanded. 'I told you to keep number three flock over the other side while I was off—you know it's tricky on Pike's with all that faulting, you silly woman. Why didn't you do as I told you?'

'It wouldn't have happened if my throat mike hadn't jammed. I couldn't call the collies off before they went down the hole.'

'Don't make excuses. I can't take a day off without something going wrong. I——'

'You've had six days off already, Colin Doughty, so shut your trapper——'

'How's Harrison managing?' I asked, thinking an interruption was necessary.

Mrs. Doughty flashed me a look of gratitude.

'I tell you, he's trying to get down the crevasse after the autocollies. Trouble is, they're still going and won't answer to orders, so they're working themselves down deeper and deeper. That's why I came back here, to switch off the juice; they work on beamed power, you know.'

I heard Doughty's teeth grind.

'Then buck up and switch off, woman, before the creatures ruin themselves! You know they cost money. What you waiting for?'

'What? For some old fool to stop arguing with me, of course. Let me by.'

She marched past us, an aggressive woman, rather ugly, and yet still to my taste pleasing, as though the thickness of her body bore some direct if mysterious relationship to the adversities of life. Going into the control shed, she killed the power and then came back to where we stood.

'I'll come with you, Mrs. Doughty, and see what I can do to help,' I said. 'I don't need to get back to my outfit for another hour.'

A look of understanding moved across her face and I climbed on to the tractor with her after a brief nod to Doughty.

There was some justification for this. If the situation was as she said it was, then the matter was one of urgency—for the next F.T.L. ship was due in under four hours and forty thousand sheep had to be herded under lock and key before that. *Had to be:* or darkness would be on them, they would stampede and kill or injure themselves on the rocky slopes, and Doughty's hard-earned savings would be down to nil. If, that is, the situation was as Bess said it was.

When we were out of sight of old Doughty and the farm, Bess stopped the tractor. We looked at each other. My whole system changed gear as we saw the greed in each other's eyes.

'How much of this story is a lie to get me alone and at your mercy?' I asked.

She put her hard broad hand over mine.

'None of it, Vasco. We'll have to shift back to Murragh as soon as possible, if he hasn't already broken his neck down that crevasse. But with Colin hanging about the house I couldn't have seen you alone if this opportunity hadn't turned up—and this'll be our last meeting, won't it?'

'Unless you change your mind and don't go to Earth with him next week.'

'You know I can't do that, Vasco.'

I did know. I was safe. Not to put too fine a point on it, she'd have been a nuisance if she had stayed for my sake. There were dozens of women like Bessy Doughty—one on nearly every hill farm I visited, bored, lonely, willing, only too happy to indulge in an affair with a Flange Maintenance Official. It was not as if I loved her.

'Then we'll make it really good this last time,' I said.

And there was the greed again, plain and undisguised and sweet. We almost fell out on to the grass. That's how these things should be: raw, unglamourized. That's the way it must be for me. Bess and I never made love. We coupled.

Afterwards, when we came to our ordinary senses, we were aware that we had been longer than we should have been.

Scrambling back into the tractor, we headed fast and bumpy for Pike's Brow.

'I hope Murragh's all right,' I muttered, glancing at my arm watch.

She neither liked nor understood my perpetual interest in Murragh Harrison.

'He's queer!' she sneered.

I didn't ask her to elaborate her crudity. I had heard it before, and the pattern behind it was obvious enough: Murragh disliked her hungry advances—and why not? She was plain, solid, coarse . . . no, I do myself no justice saying all this—for though she was all that, Bess also had a pure peasant honesty that in my eyes excused everything—or so I told myself to justify the circumstances. There you are: I'm the kind that prefers bread to cake.

At first when Murragh arrived at Doughty's farm, I had been jealous, afraid that he would spoil my innocent little game. When it was clear he would do no such thing, that he was not a bread man, I grew interested in him for his own sake. Sometimes this had caused trouble between Bess and me—but enough of this; I am trying to tell Murragh's tale, not mine. If I deviate, well, one life is very much tangled with the next man's.

We must have created some sort of speed record to the foot of Pike's Brow. Then the terrain became so steep that we had to halt, leave the tractor, and climb on our own two feet.

Bending our backs, we climbed. Sheep moved reluctantly out of our path, eyeing us with that asinine division of feature that marks a Tandy sheep's face: all rabbity and timid about the eyes and nose, and as arrogant as a camel about the lower lip.

Rain came on us with the unexpectedness it reserves for Region Six, as if a giant over the hump of the mountains had suddenly emptied his biggest bucket across our path. I remembered Doughty's forecast as I turned up my collar. Still we climbed, watching little rivulets form among the short blades under our boots. After my recent exertions, I began to wish I hadn't volunteered for this.

At last we reached the crevasse. We scrambled along by its side towards the point where Murragh had climbed over into it, a point marked by the two live dogs, Hock and Pedro, who sat patiently in the rain, barking at our approach.

The downpour was dying by now. We stood, pulled our backbones painfully upright, and breathed the damp air deep before bothering about Murragh.

He was some twenty feet down into the crack, where it was

106

so narrow that he could rest with his back to one side of it and his feet to the other. He was drenched from the water pouring over the edge; it splashed past him and gargled down into a ribbon of a stream a further thirty feet beneath his boots.

One of the autocollies was wedged beside him, covered in mud, The other lay a little way and some feet lower down, upside down but seemingly unharmed.

I noted the expression on Murragh's face. It was blank, while he seemed to gaze into nothing, ignoring the rivulets that splashed round him.

'Murragh!' Bess called sharply. 'Wake up. We're back at last.'

He looked up at us.

'Hello,' he said. 'Hello, Vasco! I was just communing with the great earth mother. She's really swallowed me. . . . It's funny, stuck down here in a fissure . . . like climbing between the lips of a whale.'

And there would have been more like that! Generally I had patience with his curious fancies, enjoyed them even, but not at such a moment, not with Bess standing there sneering, and the water running down my back, and a stitch in my side, and the time against us.

'It's raining, Dreamer Boy,' I reminded him. 'In case you didn't notice, we're all wet through. For God's sake, stir yourself.'

He seemed to pull himself together, dashing wet hair back from his face. Peering upwards rather stupidly, as if he were a fish regarding from a ditch his first humans, he said, 'Fine day for mountaineering, isn't it? If we're not careful, the earth under this autocollie will crumble and the machine may get wedged or damaged. As it is, it is still in working order. Fling me the rope down, Bess. You and Vasco can haul it up while I steady it.'

She stared blankly into my face.

'Damn it to hell, I left the bloody rope back in the tractor,' she said.

I remembered then. She'd unhooked it from her waist when we lay on the grass and later had not bothered in her haste to tie it on again, tossing it instead into the back of the vehicle.

'For God's sake go and get it then!' Murragh shouted impatiently, as if suddenly realizing how long he had waited. 'I can't stay down here much longer.'

Again Bess looked at me. I gazed away down at my muddy boots.

'Go and get it for me, Vasco,' she urged.

'I'm out of breath,' I said. 'I've got the stitch.'

'—you!' she said. She started off down the hillside again without another word.

Murragh looked sharply at me; I did not return his stare.

It took her twenty-five minutes to return with the rope. In that time, the rain cleared entirely. I squatted by Pedro and Hock, gazing over the dull and tumbled terrain. Murragh and I did not speak to each other.

The best part of another hour passed before we three bedraggled creatures had managed to haul the autocollies up safely. We could have done the job in half the time, had we not been so careful to preserve them from harm; we all knew the balance of the Doughty finances, and an autocollie can cost anything from twenty percentages to five parapounds.

Panting, I looked at my arm watch.

In two hours less six minutes the next F.T.L. was due for entry on Tandy Two. It was past the time I should have reported back to my unit for duty.

I told Murragh and Bess that I must be going—told them curtly, for after missing my lunch, getting a soaking, and nearly wrenching my arms off rescuing the dogs, I was none too sweet-humoured.

'You can't leave us *now*, Vasco,' Murragh said. 'The whole flock's in jeopardy, and not only this lot on the Brow. We've *got* to have every sheep under cover in two hours—and first of all someone must go back to the farm and switch the beam on again to get the dogs going. We want your help still.'

His eyes were as appealing as Bess's.

God, I thought, the way some people need people! He has his emotional requirements the way she has her physical ones. Whereas hers are crashingly simple, his I don't understand; once these auto-dogs are running again, they will see the sheep home in no time, without help.

Right then, I could not think of two people I would less like to be stuck on a mountain with. But all I said was, 'I'm a maintenance officer, Murragh, not a shepherd. I've made my-self late for duty as it is. Since my truck's at the farm, I'll have to go back to collect it, so when I get there I'll tell Colin to beam the juice to you—but from then on you're on your own.'

As I turned to go, Bess put her hand round my wrist. When I swung round on her, I saw her flinch from my expression.

'You can't just ditch us like this, Vasco,' she said.

'I'm ditching nobody. I helped you drag the collies out, didn't I? I've got a job to do, and I'll be in the shit for reporting back late as it is. Now let me go.'

She dropped my hand.

I made off down the slope at a slow trot, digging in my heels as I went. Now and again I slipped, falling back on the wet grass. Before I got to the level, I saw another tractor approaching.

Doughty was in it. He yelled at me as we drew nearer.

'I came to see what you lot were doing all this time. You've been taking so long I thought you'd all fallen down the hole with the collies.'

Briefly I told him what was happening, while he climbed slowly out of the tractor, clutching his back.

'So I'm borrowing Bess's tractor to go back and switch on the juice, so that the autos can start herding as soon as possible,' I finished.

He fell to cursing, saying he was going to lose all his live-stock, that they could never be driven under cover before the F.T.L. arrived. I tried to reassure him before going over to the other vehicle.

As I climbed in he said, 'When you get there, tell Tessie to come back here with the tractor. She can drive well enough, and we'll need her help. The more hands here the better. And tell her to bring the signal pistols. They'll get the sheep moving.'

'And Fay?'

'She'd only be in the damned way here.'

Giving him a wave, I stood on the acceleration and rattled back to the farm. By now the sun was bright and the sky free of cloud, which did not stop my boots squelching or my clothes from clinging to me like wet wallpaper.

Directly I reached the farm buildings, I marched into the control shed, crossed to the appropriate board, and pushed the rheostat over. Power began its ancient song, that hum of content that sounds perpetually as if it is ascending the scale. Up on the pastures, the electronic dogs would be leaping into activity.

Everything appeared in order, though Colin Doughty was not a man to keep his equipment spotless—and I reflected, not for the first time that day, that if he had cared to lay out an extra twenty parapounds or so he could have had switchboard-to-flock communication, which would have saved him valu-able time on a day like this.

Well, it was not my concern.

In the living-eating-cooking room, Tessie was alone. She stood in her slip, cutting out a dress for Earthside, and I sur-veyed her; she was developing well.

As usual, she seemed displeased to see me—baffling

creatures, adolescent girls; you never know whether they are acting or not. I gave her her father's orders and told her to get out to Pike's Brow as soon as she could.

'And where's Fay?' I asked.

'It's none of your business, Captain Rogers.'

As if she felt this was a bit too sharp, she added, 'and anyhow I don't know. This is one of my great not-knowing days.'

I sniffed. I was in a hurry and anyhow it was, as she said, none of my business now, although I would dearly have liked a farewell word with the younger girl. Nodding to Tessie, I squelched out of the building, collected the maintenance truck, and drove fast back to my unit round the other side of the mountains. To perdition with all Doughtys!

Murragh used to say that there wasn't a more interesting job than mine on all Tandy. Though he was prepared to talk for hours about his feelings—'my Tandian tenebrosities', he sometimes called them—he was equally prepared to listen for hours while I explained in minute detail the working of the Flange and the problems of repair it posed. He learnt from me any facts he filtered on to Fay.

Maintaining the Flange is a costly and complicated business, and would be even more so had we not costly and complicated machines with which to operate. Between F.T.L. arrivals, my unit is working ceaselessly over the Region Six strip, testing, checking, replacing, making good.

The complex nature of the Flange necessitates this.

To start with, there is the Bonfiglioli Geogravitic Layer, marked by tall pylons, along the north of the Flange, which maintains all of Tandy Two's atmosphere within its stress; were this to contract more than a minimum leakage, the lives of everyone on the planet would be in jeopardy.

Before the B.G.L. comes the 'fence', which prevents any creature from entering the Flange zone, while after it come our equipment stores, bunkers, etc., before you get to the actual twelve-mile width of the Flange itself.

If you want to learn how the beast works, you must mug it up in a technical publication. All I will say here is that the Flange is a huge shock absorber, three stories deep and girdling the planet. It has to absorb the biggest man-made shock of all time, though it is a delicate instrument with an upper surface of free-grooved pyr-glass needles. Its functioning depends first and foremost on the taubesi thermocouple, of which there is one to every square millimetre of surface; these detect an F.T.L. ship before it re-enters normal space and activate the rest of the system immediately. The rest of the system is, briefly, an inertia vacuum. The F.T.L. ship never actually makes contact with the Flange surface, of course, but its detectors mesh with the inertials and transfer velocities, stopping it, as was explained earlier, in milliseconds—the figure varies according to planetary and ship's mass, but for Tandy Two is generally in the order of 201·5 milliseconds.

The whole Flange is activated—switched on metre by metre of its entire twenty-five thousand miles length—two hours before an F.T.L. ship arrives (only the computers beneath the strip know precisely when the starship will materialize from phase space). At that time the various maintenance units give the whole system a final check-over, and the needle-like surface of the Flange looks first one way and then another, like stroked fur, as it searches for breakthrough point. I should have been back for that event.

I had come down to the valleys by now. Over to my left ran the graceful B.G.L. pylons, with the Flange itself behind, already stretching itself like a self-activated rubber sheet; beyond it burned the dead half of Tandy, sealed off in vacuum, bleached dust-white in the sun. Less than a mile remained between me and the unit post. Then I saw Fay.

Her blue dress shone clearly against the tawny ground. She was several hundred yards ahead of me, not looking in my direction and running directly towards the electrified 'fence' that guards the B.G.L. and the Flange itself.

'Fay!' I yelled. 'Come back!'

Instinctive stuff! I was enclosed in the truck; had she heard my cry it would only have speeded her on her way.

This was her last chance to see an F.T.L. ship enter before she went back to Earth. The absence of her father and mother had given her the chance to slip out, so she had taken it.

In my head as I gunned my vehicle sharply forward, I heard again some of the silly sweet inquisitive questions she had asked me on my visits.

'Can you *see* the ships when they land?'

'You do get an image of them, but it's after they've passed because they're moving fractionally faster than light.'

'Gosh, Captain Rogers, light is funny stuff when you come to think. Everything's funny stuff when you come to think.'

And now she was darting towards the electrified fence, and that was not funny.

'Fay!' I yelled as I drove, letting my lungs shout because in my fear I could not stop them.

The fence was built of two components, an ordinary strand fence with a mild shock to keep sheep away, and then, some yards beyond that, a trellis of high voltage designed simply and crudely to kill. Warning notices ran all the way between

111

the two fences, one every three hundred and fifty yards, 125,714 of them right round the planet—and this kid in a blue frock ignoring every one.

She dived through the strand fence without touching it.

Now I was level with her. Seeing me, she began running parallel between the two fences. Beyond her the eyes of the needles of the Flange turned first this way then that, restless and expectant.

I jumped from the truck before it stopped moving.

'You'll get killed, Fay!' I bellowed.

She turned then, her face half mischievous, half scared. She was running off course towards the second fence as she turned. Something she called out to me—I could not make out, still cannot make out what.

As I ducked under the sheep strand after her, she hit the other fence.

Fay! Ah, my Fay, my own sweet free-born daughter! She was outlined in bright light, she was black as a cinder, the universe screamed and yapped like a dying dog. My face hit the dust shrieking as I fell. Noise, death, heat, slapped me down.

Then there was mind-devouring silence.

Peace rolled down like a steam-roller, flattening everything, the eternal hush of damnation into which I wept as if the universe were a pocket handkerchief for my grief.

Fay, oh Fay, my own child!

Beyond the B.G.L., safe in vacuum, the Flange peered towards the heavens, twisting its spiked eyes. I rolled in the blistered dust without comprehension.

How long I lay there I have no idea.

Eventually the alarms roused me. They washed round me and through me until they too were gone and the silence came back. When my hearing returned, I heard a throbbing in the silence. At first I could not place it, had no wish to place it, but at last I sat up and realized that the motor of my truck was still patiently turning over. I stood up shakily on my two legs. The ill-co-ordinated action brought a measure of intelligence back to my system.

All that presented itself to me was that I had to return to the farm and tell Bess what had happened. Everything else was forgotten, even that the F.T.L. ship was due at any time.

I got back somehow under the sheep fence, and into the cab. Somehow I kicked in the gears and we lurched into action. Fay, Fay, Fay, my blood kept saying.

As I steered away from the Flange, from the burnt ground to grass again, a figure presented itself before me. Blankly I stopped and climbed out to meet it, hardly knowing what I did.

It was Murragh, waving his arms like one possessed.

'Thanks to your aid we got the flocks under cover in time,' he said. 'So I came down here to see the F.T.L. entry. You know for me to see an entry—well, it's like watching the creation.'

He stopped, eyeing me, his face full of a private emotion.

'It's like the creation, is it?' I said dumbly. My mouth felt puffy. Fay, Fay, Fay . . . okay, I was all kinds of a cur, but I didn't deserve that, that actually before my eyes——

'And Vasco, we've always been close friends, I don't have to mind what I say to you, you know that this event once a fortnight—it's the excitement of all excitements for me. I mean . . . well, it's just that even something like sex palls beside watching an F.T.L. entry——'

In the state I was in, I could not grasp what he was saying or meaning. It came back to me long after, like finding a private letter behind the wainscoting of an empty house: titillating, but all old history.

'And I've got the image of Tandy Two I was after, Vasco. . . .' His eyes were alight. Full of that divine inner fire of a poet: it lit him too well inside for him to see me. 'Tandy's a woman——'

There was no warning.

The F.T.L. ship entered.

Cerenkov radiations belched outwards, distorting our vision. For a second, Murragh and I were embedded in amber. Tandy was girdled in a noose of flame, most of which expanded south safely into vacuum. Then the giant fist of inertial reaction struck us.

The sun plunged across the sky like a frightened horse.

As we fell, day turned to night.

For one of those long minutes that under their own weight can iron themselves into a small eternity, I lay on the ground with Murragh half on top of me.

He moved before I did. Vaguely I realized he was fumbling round doing something. When it penetrated my mind that he was slipping a fume-mask on, I automatically did the same, without thinking, I had carried my mask from the vehicle with me.

He had switched on a torch. It lay on the ground as we sprouted bug-eyed jumbo faces, and splashed a great carica-ture of us up the mountain-side. In the sky, Tandy had appeared, near full and bright, a phantom. As ever it was impossible to believe it was not our moon rather than vice versa; facts have no power against the imagination.

Sitting there stupidly, I heard the words of an old poet scatter through my head, half of his verse missing.

> *O, moon of my delight who know'st no wane,*
> *Something, something once again.*
> *How oft hereafter rising shall she look*
> *Through this same garden after me—in vain!*

But I had no time to connect up the missing words; if I had thought of it, I preferred them missing to emphasize my sense of loss. But no rational thought came.

All that came was the clash of two nightmares, Murragh's and mine. It seemed that I kept crying 'Fay is dead!' that he kept crying 'Tandy Two's a woman!' And we were fighting, struggling together while the ground steamed, I hating him because he did not care where I had expected him to care, he hating me because I had spoilt his vigil, ruined his climax.

My mind ran in shapes, not thoughts, until I realized that I had begun to fight. When I went limp, Murragh's fist caught me between the eyes.

I do not have to say what I felt then, slumped on the ground—the place I hated and Murragh loved—for this is supposed to be his story, not mine, although I have become tangled up in it in the same directionless bindweedy way I became entangled in Bess's life.

Murragh—you have to say it—could not feel like ordinary people. When I heard from him again, he never even mentioned Fay; he had only used her to talk about his real obsession.

When, a week later, the S.T.L. ship *Monteith* lit out for Earth from Tandy, Colin, Bess, and Tessie Doughty travelled in it. So did I. I lay in a bunk in the medical bay, classified under some obscure technical label that meant I was dull of mind and unfit for further service.

The Doughtys came to see me.

They were as cheerful as crickets. After all, they had made their packet and were about to begin life anew. Even Bess never referred to Fay; I always said she was hard and coarse.

They brought me a letter from Murragh. It was elaborately overwritten. Wrapped in his own discoveries, he clearly mourned as little for Fay as did the Doughtys. His letter, in fact, displayed his usual sensitivity and his blindness where other humans were concerned. I had no patience with it, thought I later re-read the final passages (which he has since used in his successful book *To my Undeniable Tandy*).

114

'. . . Yilmoff's twenty-third century *Theory of Images* reveals how places can hold for men deep psychic significances; we inherit an Experience of place as we do of (say) women. So when a planet exists with as distinct a personality—for the term in context is no exaggeration—as Tandy Two's, the significance is increased, the effect on the psyche deepened.

'I declare myself to be in love, in the true psychological sense of the word, with Tandy. She is my needful feminine, dwelling in my psyche, filling it to the exclusion of other needs.

'So I give you my true portrait image of her: the planet-head of a girl, all sweet rich hair north, but the south face a skull, and bound round her brow a ribbon of flame. This is the portrait of my terrible lover.'

You may make of this what you will. Crazy, was he?

Only Murragh of all mankind has his mistress perpetually beneath him.

THE INTERNATIONAL SMILE

THE room, with its Spy cartoons and the oil of Chequers hanging on the chimney-breast like the promise of a better world, held a cluttered comfort. So did the two men slumped in easy chairs; they were tired. The woman also was tired, but her straight back and splendid *coiffure* did not admit the fact. She could have poured their tea with no more command had she been before the TV cameras.

As if aware of reason for guilt, both men straightened in their chairs when a tap sounded at the door and Tarver peered in.

The Prime Minister glowered from behind his cup and said, 'What is it, Tarver? Can't we have five minutes in peace?'

The butler of No. 10 said apologetically, 'It's Colonel Quadroon to see you, sir.'

'The Governor of Pentonville Prison. More escapes, I suppose—more questions in the House. Better show him in.'

The P.M. turned to Lady Elizabeth and the Foreign Secretary in mock-resignation.

'You remember you did make an appointment for him yesterday, Herbert,' Lady Elizabeth said. She managed men as easily and gracefully as she managed herself. 'The Colonel said it was of great national importance.'

'I don't doubt he did. Quadroon presumes too much, my dear. Just because I've been on his shoots a couple of—Oh, Colonel, good afternoon. Come in.'

The P.M. wiped his moustache and gestured irritably to a free armchair as Quadroon moved into the room. The Governor of Pentonville was a tall, sharp-featured man, Haileybury and Queen's, O.B.E. He bowed stiffly to Lady Elizabeth and shook hands perfunctorily with Ralph Watts-Clinton, the Foreign Secretary.

'I wouldn't bother you, Prime Minister, if this was not a matter of the highest moment,' he said.

'I should hope not. No more rioting, I trust?'

'The Opposition gave you a pretty stiff time in the House this afternoon, I hear.'

At that, the P.M. had the grace to smile.

116

'Sorry, Colonel. Give the Colonel a cup of tea, will you, my dear? Well, what can we do for you?'

'No sugar, thank you, Lady Elizabeth. In this instance, sir, it's a matter of what we can do for you. I mentioned the Opposition just now. Has it ever occurred to you that the Opposition consists of unhappy men?'

Watts-Clinton guffawed.

'It's often occurred to us, Colonel. Take the debate on the Immigration Restriction Bill this afternoon—they were frankly miserable. Harold Gaskin almost wept crocodile tears over what he calls "the overworked and under-privileged in less fortunate lands".'

'Precisely.' The Colonel balanced Lady Elizabeth's Spode cup and saucer on his angular knee and said, 'All that can be changed tomorrow.'

The P.M. made a noise he had been heard to make more than once in the House.

'I have no idea what sort of political chicanery you have up your sleeve, Colonel, but let me put it to you beforehand that nothing can alter Gaskin's jaundiced view of the enlightened measures we are proposing.'

'Polyannamine could,' said the Colonel.

After a cold and curious pause, Lady Elizabeth said, 'I'm sure we are all three very impressed by your air of mystery and indeed, certainty—oh, mind you don't upset your tea, Colonel. Perhaps you'd better put your case to us. I'm sure Herbert can spare you five minutes before he goes to prepare his Berlin speech.'

She embodied all the qualities needful in a Prime Minister's wife: directness, indirectness, tact, and insolence.

Blowing his nose lustily, the Colonel said by way of pre-amble, 'You know I have always been a staunch party man. There can be few people in this country who do not recall the famous recruiting speech I made at East Moulton, when I was so narrowly defeated in the '45 election. This is why I have come straight to you, Prime Minister, as a staunch party man, to lay polyannamine at your feet.'

'I know your record,' said the P.M. testily. 'Proceed.'

'Well, to come straight to the point, you probably remember the unfortunate riots we had in Pentonville a couple of years back. The Beaverbrook Press made a lot of fuss about it— they love a prison story. Two convicts were killed, and three severely injured. One of the injured men was Joseph Branksome. Remember the name?'

'We must all remember the name,' said Watts-Clinton. 'He was the member for Dogsthorpe East in Eden's time.'

'That's it. Seven years for embezzling party funds—but a good man, all the same. A good party man. You'd never shake him. I know at the time of Suez he——'

'Yes, yes, you were saying he was injured, Colonel.'

'So I was. So he was. Injured in the kidney—nasty business. It was touch and go for several days; I had to have him transferred to Bart's. They put a patch on his kidney; first time that particular op had been done at Bart's, so they were telling me. Anyhow, it seemed to do the trick, and in a fortnight we were able to bring Branksome back to the prison hospital. He was still very feeble, but extremely cheerful. I went to visit him. Never met a man more full of happiness and optimism. He was the life and soul of that ward. Why, when Christmas came round——'

'Branksome's dead now, isn't he?' the P.M. said.

'Eh? Dead? Oh yes. I was coming to that. His general air of cheer deceived us all. We thought he was fit again, although he lost a deal of weight. He was back at his old job—I had him on a pretty soft number in the prison library. Then one morning—this would be just over a year ago now—he collapsed in the Do-It-Yourself section and was dead within an hour. Poor Branksome, he died laughing!'

Overcome by the tragedy of his tale, Quadroon sat in the chair, nodding his head sorrowfully. Lady Elizabeth rescued his cup.

With a touch, not to say load, of finality in his voice, the P.M. said, 'Thank you very much, Colonel Quadroon, for coming along and——'

The Colonel held up a long and stringy hand, at which the others gazed with curiosity.

'At the inquest, a remarkable fact emerged. Owing to the injury it had sustained, Branksome's kidney had been—what d'you call it?—malfunctioning. As far as I could make out from our prison specialist, Mark Miller—very capable chap—instead of making new tissue or whatever it was supposed to do, this kidney had been secreting a substance hitherto unknown to science. Miller christened this secretion Polyannamine. Apparently it had circulated to Branksome's endo—ah, endocrine glands and there had set up a sort of permanent imbalance if that's not a contradiction in terms. Anyhow, this imbalance had the effect of keeping him happy even when he was dying painfully by inches.'

'Hmm.' The P.M., with a gesture familiar to millions of TV viewers, lit a briar pipe and sat with his nose almost hanging into the bowl. 'And has this stuff been synthesized, Colonel?'

For answer, the Colonel drew from an inner pocket a small plastic tube. He performed the gesture with what, in a better actor, would have been a grand flourish.

'There's enough synthesized polyannamine in here, Miller informs me, to keep all your opposition happy for the rest of their lives.'

The P.M. cast an eyebrow at Watts-Clinton who, never at a loss, cast one back.

'I think the Berlin speech might be given a miss till we've seen Miller. My old constituency wouldn't like to think I let grass grow under my feet, eh, Ralph? Elizabeth, my dear, do you think——'

'Oh, Herbert, I really can't, not again! I wouldn't know what to put.'

'Nonsense, pet. Usual stuff about standing fast, backing Adenauer to the hilt, Western solidarity, and all that, with the safety clause about striving for peace by all means within our power, and so on. By now you can do it as easily as I can. Tarver, the Bentley, please.'

Traffic was thick about the gloomy façade of Pentonville Prison.

'Visitors' night tonight,' Quadroon said gloomily. 'Always draws the crowds.'

'I must tell you how much I admire all your far-reaching reforms; the Home Sec. was telling me about them only the other day,' Watts-Clinton said ingratiatingly; he had no special liking for the Colonel, but to be included on one of his shoots would be no bad thing.

'Got Johnny Earthquake and the Four Corners playing tonight. Keeps the men happy.'

The P.M. looked shocked.

'But the M.I. Massacre Man—what's his name, McNoose, is due to be executed tomorrow. Surely——'

'That's what's drawn all this crowd tonight. Dodge in after that confounded Volkswagen, Chauffeur. We're letting McNoose have a last request from Johnny Earthquake, for his mum and dad and all at 78 Montpelier Road, Camden Town.'

'Very doubtful taste,' the P.M. said.

'You were the one who wanted the prisons to pay their way, sir.'

'This is really no time to bring up old election promises.'

The three men lapsed into moody silence. At last a clear way showed itself, and the car swept into the front square and round beyond the bright lights and marquees to the

Governor's house. As they hurried up the steps, blaring loud-speakers carried music and a nasal voice droned

> *Eva Bardy's doin' it, doin' it, doin' it,*
> *Eva Bardy's doin' it . . .*

It was good to get inside. Quadroon showed them into his study and summoned a servant to fetch Mark Miller.

Impatiently, the P.M. looked about the solid dingy room. Trophies, lowering photographs, handcuffs, an amateur pencil portrait of John Reginald Halliday Christie, certificates, maps, a death-mask, and a pokerwork legend bearing the words 'Stone walls do not a prison make', surrounded them on all sides. The smell was one of tapioca with vegetable additives. Reluctantly, the P.M. selected the less horsy-looking of two horsehair chairs and gave it the benefit of his posterior.

'Interesting place,' Watts-Clinton said, in the manner of one volunteering information.

The Colonel himself looked shrunken by his surroundings.

'I could put the fire on,' he said. He coughed, rubbed his hands together, and added, 'I ought to warn you, gentlemen, that Miller has injected himself with his own prescription; at first you may find him a little—ah, ha ha, ah, Miller, there you, ah, are! Come in.'

Miller was in. He swept in with his arms wide, smiling broadly, and shook hands with them all before he was introduced.

'So, gentlemen, you're in at the birth of a new nation, in on the ground floor, eh? In fact, you're in before the birth—on the underground floor, you might say. We're all set to go into production, ready to transform the country, thanks to poly-annamine, the new wonder drug that makes your body work for you instead of against you.'

Introductions were belatedly performed. Miller shook hands again exuberantly, remarked how tired the P.M. looked, and admired the quality of Watts-Clinton's suiting. He was a tall thin man—almost as given to bony protuberances as the Colonel—with tufts of hair on his fingers and hands. In his late forties, he gazed cadaverously at the world from beneath the sheltering foliage of his eyebrows. Not, one would have estimated, a man given to mirth; yet his geniality flowed through the room like champagne into a footsore slipper.

'The Government is very interested in your formula, Mr. Miller,' the P.M. said, 'but we should naturally require a con-clusive test, under proper surveillance, of your discovery.'

Miller winked conspiratorially.

'It's in the bag. You're laughing—or you will be. Why don't

you let me give *you* an injection? How about going down in history as Sir Herbert Macclesfield, the Smiling Prime Minister—no, the Primed Prime Minister? Don't mind me, I'm only being funny. Believe me, I've never felt so good. Fallen arches? I've still got them; they don't bother me. Bills, income-tax demands? They still pile up; they don't bother me. I just don't let the worries worry me, thanks to polyannamine.'

'Can you control your obvious ebullience enough to tell us roughly how the stuff works?'

'Tell you roughly? Nay sire, as I hope for an O.B.E., I will tell you gently. My prescription may be applied orally or intravenously or by inhalation; 10 c.c. only needed. Infallible! Guaranteed to cheer up even a TV comedian. No harmful side effects. No dimming of intelligence—I always looked this stupid, ha ha!'

'I have a question to put to you, Mr. Miller,' said Watts-Clinton, seeming to offer it transfixed on one stabbing finger. 'You make large claims for this—er, medicament. Personally, I should be grateful if you would explain how it differs in any appreciable way from the tranquillizers and euphorics which have been on the market for some years.'

Miller squeezed his cheeks and mouth into a lemon face that aped the Foreign Secretary's features with considerable success.

'I have an answer to put to you, Mr. Clotts-Winton—er, Witts-Clunt——, er, Watts-Clinton, that I trust will answer your question. Polyannamine is permanent! It does not act directly on the endocrines. It goes straight to the kidney and there establishes a receptive area which begins immediately to secrete its own supply of polyannamine. From then on, the process is irreversible. It becomes part of the natural function of the kidney. Without impairing its other functions to any noticeable extent, the kidney will continue to secrete polyannamine until death does its part, and that polyannamine does its part in the endocrines from then on without stopping. In other words, one injection only of the synthetic solution is needed—for life.'

'I see,' said Watts-Clinton. Then his face burst into a slow smile. 'By God, Herbert, if this is true. . . .'

'Just what I was thinking . . .' said the P.M. 'We've got to face the House with this second reading of the Capital Punishment Bill in the morning. If only. . . .'

Bowing low, Miller produced a small object from a waistcoat pocket. It looked like an anemone bulb, a cushion with a small spike on it. It was made of glass and contained a clear liquid.

'If I catch your meaning, sir, you need a few dozen of these. If you sit on this, you get an injection of polyannamine—no trouble.'

The P.M. looked at Watts-Clinton. He looked at Quadroon. He looked at the pencil portrait of Christie. Then he looked back at Miller.

'It's worth a knighthood,' he breathed.

Quadroon moved restlessly.

'Two knighthoods,' he corrected.

'*Two* knighthoods,' the P.M. agreed.

They all walked back together to the car. A bevy of convicts in evening dress were writhing to the voice of Johnny Earthquake.

> *In the big wide world I'm all alone,*
> *They gone and left me on my own,*
> *I'm shedding tears on tears to be*
> *A Teenage Divorcee.*

The P.M. looked up at the slow-moving grey smog of London overhead.

'Beautiful evening,' he said. 'Beautiful evening. The prospect is distinctly rosy.'

Next day, Lady Elizabeth—wearing a tailored Italian costume that fitted her with mathematical exactitude—stood in her cosy room in Downing Street looking down pensively at the TV announcer.

The announcer, whose eyes were of an irreproachable blue, looked pensively back at Lady Elizabeth and said, '. . . case of horse-doping at Newmarket this month. Scotland Yard has been called in. This morning, the so-called M.I. Massacre Man, Gulliver McNoose, was executed at Pentonville Prison. Under the new dispensation, his girl friend was allowed to be with him in the condemned cell; she held his hand till the last, singing "Rock of Ages Rock", the new religious pop song which was McNoose's favourite tune. We hope to have pictures on our later bulletin. Meanwhile, capital punishment was the subject of debate in the House of Commons this morning.'

A view of Parliament came on to the screen as the announcer's head dissolved; this did not prevent his continuing, 'The Government were seeking to make unofficial strikers liable to the death penalty, and it was expected that they would meet lively opposition. Mr. Gaskin, however, who was to have spoken against the motion, appeared to be in exceptionally genial mood, says our Westminster correspondent, Geoffrey Dee. He rose and said that he felt compelled to

122

admit unofficial strikes were a bit of a nuisance; he added that if the country was to get ahead it had better lose a few. The laughter, particularly on Mr. Gaskin's side of the House, lasted for many minutes, after which the government measure was carried through without further discussion. Her Majesty the Queen, who is on a goodwill visit to the Isle of Man——'

Lady Elizabeth switched the set off. Her face did not relax into a smile.

'You don't look very pleased,' her sister Nancy, the Honourable Mrs. Lyon-Bowater, said, pouting prettily. 'Sounds jolly good to me. Of course, I know I'm only an old silly.'

'Of course,' Lady Elizabeth agreed. She did not enjoy her pretty younger sister's visits. Since a certain nursery-days quarrel over a palomino pony, the sisters had never entirely seen eye to eye. 'The passing of this Bill is a triumph for Herbert—a vindication of all he has been working for. Unfortunately, it must be counted as a minor triumph. Perhaps you don't realize it, Nancy, but we stand on the brink of a third world war.'

'Oh yes, isn't it terrible? Still, we have for years, haven't we? It's all Towin ever talks about—that and his mouldy old shares.'

Lady Elizabeth sat down in the most graceful way on the very edge of her chaise-longue and said, 'Nancy dear, this time it is rather different. There was a serious border incident in Berlin in the early hours of this morning.'

'Politics is your business, darling, not mine; I prefer chihuahuas.'

'This is everyone's business, darling. You will remember the East Germans built a wall round their sector four or five years ago—or perhaps you won't. Then in the American sector a huge tower was built, the New Brandenburg tower. We claimed it was for the new U.N. office; the East Germans claimed it was to spy into their territory. In retaliation they built huge screens behind their wall, so that nobody could see into their sector.'

'As though anyone would want to see into their sector,' said Nancy, lighting a cigarette with the elaborate ritual gesture of a waiter about to scorch a crêpe suzette in an expense account restaurant.

'Be that as it may, Nancy, the screens were built. The Western Powers agreed in finding this an aggressive gesture; accordingly, they prepared a warning.'

'Oh yes, if *they* do it, it's a threat; if *we* do it, it's a warning. I do know that much about politics.'

'Well, our warning took the form of a big statue, two hundred and five feet high and thus the highest in the world——'

'Oh, you mean Buster!'

'It's official name is The Statue of Freedom. It is so large that even the poor East Germans can see it, especially as its eyes light up at night.'

'It's lovely, Elizabeth. Towin and I saw it when we were over there last year; they had some sort of a crisis on then, as I recall. It looked lovely—much more fun than the dreary old Eiffel Tower, and with this rather absurd crown on its head saying "Coca-Cola".'

'Yes. The Western Powers had some trouble among themselves about that. The crisis to which you refer was of course caused by the Russian insistence on regarding Buster—mm, the Statue of Freedom as a provocative act. We should have had a war then but for Herbert's personal intervention. He flew over to speak to the Russian Premier, Nikita Molochev. Instead of declaring war, the East Germans built a statue themselves.'

Nancy burst into bored laughter and coughed over her cigarette.

'Even I know about *that*, darling. It made me pro-Communist on the spot. Such a delightful sense of humour!'

'Really, Nancy, you are too frivolous. Not only is it a statue representing a very ugly worker, but it is *higher* than Buster; *and* it is thumbing its nose at Buster. As President Kennedson said, quite rightly, it is an aggressive act—as well as a threat to Western air space.'

'At least it was his idea to call it Nikko.'

'Last night, Nancy, at three o'clock Central European Time, a daring gang of West Berliners blew Nikko's head off with explosive shells.'

'Good heavens, I shouldn't have thought it possible!'

'Well, Nikko lost his nose, anyway. The full extent of the damage is not clear yet; there are conflicting reports. Unfortunately the East Germans and Russians have chosen to regard this innocent prank as a threat to their security.'

'So—we're on the brink of war again. Ho hum. And what is dear Herbert doing about it?'

'He's making a conciliatory speech in the Guildhall, at the bi-annual luncheon of the Ancient Order of Swan-Uppers and Down-Pluckers,' said Lady Elizabeth. She stood up with a grace that rested on a firm foundation and began pacing the room daintily. 'The unfortunate part is, that he is reading a speech I wrote for him. At least, I put in bits from several of his old speeches, but it is mainly my work. I feel the future of the world rests in my hands—the Russians and Americans seem so eager to have this war.'

'Perhaps they feel it would be best to get it over with. It is awkward for us, being in the middle, so to speak. Well, darling, I must go. I hope the Swan-Uppers give Herbert a good lunch, anyhow.'

'I hope I haven't bored you. Being a woman in a position of responsibility can be so difficult.' Lady Elizabeth took her younger sister's hands and gazed into her eyes.

'How fortunate then that you are a woman of determination,' Nancy said, disengaging herself to assume her gloves, 'as you proved long ago over the palomino.'

The noise of voices in the hall made them both pause. Lady Elizabeth raised a humorously quizzical eyebrow.

'Sounds like a regiment out there.'

'A regiment plus Herbert!'

Lady Elizabeth went to see. The P.M. was being abstracted from his coat by Tarver; from his flushed look she could tell at once that the luncheon had been (a) good and (b) televised. Knowing the quality and extent of the Guildhall cellars, Lady Elizabeth resolved to get black coffee to him as soon as possible. Struggling with their own coats were Ralph Watts-Clinton and Lord Andaway, the Home Secretary; they too bore the Swan-Upping insignia in their cheeks.

Surprisingly, Miller was also there, grinning broadly at all that went on. Balancing a large carton on one hip, he waved cordially to Lady Elizabeth.

'Here's your wandering boy, Your Ladyship,' he called. 'I met him on the doorstep as I was about to deliver the goods.'

'Who's he? Did he lose his way to the tradesmen's entrance?' the Hon. Mrs. Lyon-Bowater asked, in a steamily *sotto* sort of *voce* in her sister's ear.

Behind Miller, lined up like discarded gravestones, were three dark and solemn men. One she recognized as Bernard Brotherhope, the secretary of the Transit and Gradual Workers' Union. By their air of non-denominational piety and their collars, Brotherhope's companions were recognizable as union leaders. They stood patient, strong, unblinking, with their hats in the on-guard position; as Brotherhope nodded curtly over the heads of the others to Lady Elizabeth, a line of Hilaire Belloc's about hating the Midlands which are sodden and unkind rose impertinently to her mind.

'Take these gentlemen into the visitors' room, Tarver,' the P.M. said. 'If you will excuse me, gentlemen, I will join you in a minute. Oh, Miller, I want you.'

'What *sweet* men, Herbert!' Nancy exclaimed from her corner as the others filed into the front room, each anxiously offering precedence to his companion.

125

'Oh, you're here, Nancy,' the P.M. said glumly.

'It must be such fun being P.M. You meet all sorts of people you wouldn't otherwise, don't you?'

'You remind me to inquire after your husband.'

Unabashed, Nancy said, 'Still living, I suppose.'

The P.M. pushed past her into the cosy room and subsided slowly into the chaise-longue, letting his heavy lids fall as he went.

'Coffee's coming, my darling,' Lady Elizabeth said. 'You'll have some too, Mr. Miller, or are you not stopping?'

She successfully outstared him. Miller's eyes retreated like little wet animals under his eyebrows and he laughed in admission of defeat.

'Don't want to intrude on the old family circle, you know. That is one circle of which there's never enough to go round! Anyhow, here's a supply of polyannamine as promised. Why not give your husband a shot? He looks as if he needs it.'

'Thank you for your advice. Tarver will show you the door.'

'That's very good of him. I must say I admire that door more every time I see it. You must come up and see mine some day, Lady Elizabeth.'

As he was passing her, she thought for a dreadful moment that he was reaching out to kiss her. Instead, he whispered something in her ear. Her features relaxed; she smiled and nodded. When he had tiptoed, all comically conspiratorial, from the room, she went over and knelt by Herbert. Unnoticed, Nancy moved to look into Miller's carton.

'How did the speech go, Herbert?' Lady Elizabeth asked tenderly.

The P.M. patted his brow and groaned.

'That confounded port. . . . Either I'm getting too old for it or it's getting too old for me. And then I arrive back here to find a delegation from the T.U.C. awaiting me; I shall have to go and see them. Where's that coffee?'

'It's coming. . . . Here it is. Thank you, Jane, I'll take it here. How did the speech go, darling?'

As she took the coffee tray and began to pour, Nancy said, 'It's none of my business, Herbert, but can't you put the T.U.C. chappies off? What's the fun in being P.M. if you have no power?'

'There's no fun. . . .' He took the cup in trembling hands and sipped through his moustache. 'We're in trouble there, Elizabeth. I can't think how I can have been so short-sighted. We romped home with the Capital Punishment Bill this morning, thanks to Miller's polyannamide, but of course the trade

126

unions are on to us now like a ton of nationalized bricks. They've threatened a general strike if we don't retract. . . . I must go and see Brotherhope. The coffee was lovely.'

Wiping his moustache, he rose and squeezed her upper arm. Having long ago trained herself not to respond with disgust to this old man's gesture, Lady Elizabeth merely said, 'Take this polyannamide capsule in with you; Miller advised it in case you had any trouble. How's the head now?'

'Better for your coffee, my dear. Have some yourself.' He pocketed the capsule, adjusted his tie, and shuffled out of the room.

Elizabeth sighed deeply, passed a hand over her forehead, and turned towards her sister.

'Nancy, I fear I must turn you out now, unles you came for anything in particular?'

'Can you tell me what polyannamine is?'

'Just a sort of tranquillizer; nothing to be curious about. Shall I get Tarver to let you out?' She turned her back on Nancy and commenced to pour herself coffee.

'Damn your conceit, no, Elizabeth! I came for something in particular and you may as well hear it. I want—I need—a divorce from Towin.'

Lady Elizabeth forgot her coffee.

'But Towin is Secretary of State for Air!'

'You don't have to remind me of the dangers of nepotism.'

'Spite always did improve your repartee. You know you *can't* have any fuss in public at present, Nancy. The General Election is only two years away.'

'The Last Trump may precede it.'

'The Last Trump will scandalize the British public less than a ministerial *decree nisi*. You're in some sort of a *mess*, aren't you?'

'How you adore your euphemisms and your clichés! Yet how else could you bear to be married to Herbert? You'll be talking next about washing dirty linen in public.'

Lady Elizabeth rose and said, with the glacial courtesy of anger, 'You're in some sort of a mess, aren't you?'

'Yes, I am, if you must know. I am having, ducky, a rather hot affair with a pop singer called Johnny Earthquake.'

They faced each other lividly, hate and love running together like a spilt Irish coffee. Finally Lady Elizabeth turned away and marched over to the door saying, 'The Prime Minister's sister-in-law involved with a pop singer. . . . Governments have fallen for less.'

Deftly, while her sister's back was turned, Nancy knocked the nipple off one of the polyannamine capsules she had pocketed, and poured the contents into Lady Elizabeth's coffee. Then she marched towards the door. Again the two were face to face.

'A pop singer!'

'He makes me feel horribly democratic!' With an angry leer, Nancy swaggered out.

For some minutes, Lady Elizabeth stood inside the cosy room, clutching her temples.

Then the phone rang.

Her voice when she answered gave no hint of her feelings.

It was an agitated young secretary to an under-secretary, Rupert Peters, phoning from Whitehall. Lady Elizabeth knew him well, and admired him; the feeling was reciprocated—as she had perceived.

'This is a horribly informal way to come through to you, as Your Ladyship knows; I can only plead in extenuation a grave emergency. Would it be at all practicable for me to have a word with Sir Herbert?'

'He has the T.U.C. on his back at present.'

'Jolly! Well, look, we've got the Ambassador to Russia speaking on a scramble call from Moscow. He has just had an extremely abusive note handed to him from Nikita Molochev. We're going to be at war before morning unless something happens fast.'

'Rupert! But this is unprovoked!'

'Within the contemporary usage of the term, not entirely.' Rupert paused. She sensed his embarrassment down the other end of the line.

'What do you mean, "not entirely"?'

'I'm afraid it was that remark of Sir Herbert's in his Guildhall speech.'

A cold hand with ill-manicured nails wrapped itself round Lady Elizabeth's heart. She sat down on the chaise-longue. Her coffee stared coolly up at her.

'*What* remark?' she managed to ask.

'Sir Herbert said—and Your Ladyship must realize I quote from memory—that after prolonged consideration he had concluded that President Molochev was a disagreeable sight that should be abolished.'

She made an inarticulate noise in her throat.

'Not, one must admit, the year's most tactful political utterance,' Rupert said. 'As I say, it seems in the present inflamed state of world affairs that it may precipitate hostilities, unless speedily retracted or ameliorated. I would like to ask Sir Herbert if we should offer the Russians a complete denial.

Would you, Lady Elizabeth, in view of the emergency, detach him from the embrace of the T.U.C.?'

Lady Elizabeth sat back, pale with horror. Clearly before her mind's eye floated the typescript pages of the speech she had prepared for the Guildhall. Page five, dealing with the Berlin question, had had the P.M. saying that after prolonged consideration he had concluded that President Molochev had historical logic but not contemporary logic on his side in his demand for an East German peace treaty. Such little meaning as this statement possessed had then been obliterated in succeeding paragraphs, into which, by the bottom of the page, a reference to the statues Buster and Nikko had been introduced. Of these, the speech only said that the two figures confronting each other formed—and here one turned to page seven—a disagreeable sight that should be abolished.

Beyond a doubt, Lady Elizabeth knew what had happened. In the jocular hurly-burly of Guildhall wine and food, Sir Herbert had dropped page six, and read on without noticing the omission.

'Lady Elizabeth, could you get him?'

The tinny voice of Rupert recalled her.

'Just a minute,' she said.

Limply she rose and went to fetch her husband. As she passed the hideous daguerrotype of Gladstone, she heard singing—singing at 10 Downing Street!—but Lady Elizabeth was beyond surprise. Opening the front study door, she discovered Bernard Brotherhope with his arms round his two supporters. Their hats were on their heads at a rakish angle, and with verve they executed a few lively unison steps to their own version of 'Rule, Britannia!'

Not only that. The Foreign and Home Secretaries were conducting the trio, singing heartily with them as they did so.

> Rule, Britannia, two tanners make a bob;
> Three makes one and six, and four two bob.
> No Common Market shall rule the Common Man
> While two bob buys us booze throughout the lan'—
> I don't mean maybe—
> Buys us booze throughout the la-a-a-n'.

They went smartly into a reprise; no attention was paid to Lady Elizabeth, beyond a suggestively raised eyebrow from Watts-Clinton. The P.M. sat feebly by the drinks cupboard, emitting an inconstant smile; here, thought Lady Elizabeth with a gush of sympathy, was a man who had had greatness thrust upon him. She beckoned and he came at once.

'Strike's off,' he said, as they went into the corridor, closing the door behind them. 'Do you know what Brotherhope said to me? "Between you and me, I'm more interested in the power than the glory." Slipping polyannamine into the sherry did the trick.'

'But Herbert, you've given it to Andaway and Watts-Clinton too!'

'Couldn't be helped—emergency. I had to pour the stuff into the decanter. Of course I refrained from drinking it myself. It's a pity about Ralph, but after all he is happy; he's got no worries, whereas we've got plenty.'

'You don't know how many, my dear.'

'It occurred to me that by spraying polyannamine over London and other big cities, we could face the next election with equanimity; I instructed Miller accordingly. Has the fellow gone?'

'Yes, and we are in trouble, Herbert. The British Embassy in Moscow is on the line.' And she told him what had happened.

'My God!' he said. They were into the cosy room by now; the jazz version of 'Rule, Britannia!' was silenced as Lady Elizabeth closed the door. The P.M. sank down on the nearest chair and stared unseeingly at Lady Elizabeth's coffee. 'How absolutely ghastly! You know, now you mention it I recall thinking that something dropped just as I rose to make my speech. It must have been page six. It must have gone under the table.'

'If only you'd read the speech through first!'

'I didn't have time.'

'Didn't you notice what you were saying?'

He hid his face in his hands. She saw, through his thinning grey hair, freckles on his skull.

'You know how it is after a heavy lunch. . . . I just read in a stupor, I'm afraid—though I do remember everyone clapping and laughing unexpectedly. . . . Oh, my country!'

Feeling only compassion, Lady Elizabeth patted his shoulders.

'You'd better speak to Rupert Peters. All is not lost yet.'

'How can I face anyone, after making such a fool of myself?'

'Because it is your duty to,' she said composedly to his bowed head. She picked up the phone from the side table.

'Rupert, are you there? . . . Hello, Rupert? . . . Whitehall? I think we're cut off. Oh, hello, Rupert; I thought we were cut off.'

The young secretary's voice had a new note of tension in it.

'Lady Elizabeth, I'm afraid the situation is more desperate

than we at first thought. We've been cut off from the British Embassy in Moscow; that line is dead. The last word we had was that it was surrounded by an angry mob who were trying to break in. Meanwhile, the Kremlin has come through to us on another line. Is Sir Herbert there?'

'He's here and he will speak.'

'Praise be. Tell him I am in a position to switch him straight through to Zagravov, Molochev's Deputy. The man is in a flaming temper and claims that Sir Herbert has committed an act of personal persiflage that is tantamount to a declaration of war. Impress on Sir Herbert that Zagravov will need very delicate handling.'

'I understand.'

Her face was pale as she turned to Sir Herbert. He had just finished draining her cold cup of coffee.

'I feel a bit more cheerful for that,' he said.

'You have need to be.' Gravely she told him what Rupert had said. The P.M. got up and paced the room as he listened. When she had finished, she added, 'You'll have to explain to Zagravov about page six as tactfully as possible.'

To her astonishment, the P.M. burst into laughter.

'It's all so terribly funny, when you think of it,' he said. 'And after all, President Molochev *is* a disagreeable sight that should be abolished! These miserable diplomats have no sense of humour. Give me that phone. Let me try and make old Zagravov see the joke.'

'Herbert!'

Lady Elizabeth backed away in horror as the P.M., smiling broadly, seized the phone and began to tell Moscow exactly what he thought of Russian statesmen.

Nancy, the Hon. Mrs. Lyon-Bowater, second wife of Towin, the Rt. Hon. Lord Lyon-Bowater, Secretary of State for Air, vigorously embraced Johnny Earthquake as their taxi carried them south through the patchily-lit streets of London after dark.

'How was the show, Honey?' he asked at last, gasping for breath.

'You were great, Johnny. "Teenage Divorcee" was an absolute gas, if I have the phrase right.'

'They were really rolling! Think that new number, "Everlovin' Friendship" is going to be a winner?'

'It'll be a stampede, Johnny, with the pushing you give it. At one point I thought you were going to crack the echo chamber.'

Thus discoursing on matters of art, they arrived at one of

the more drearily respectable sectors of Croydon. Johnny hopped out and dealt the taxi driver two notes from the pack of pounds he carried. Nancy was still thrilled by the way he never thought to hold a door open for her; how wonderful, she reflected, it must be to be so *natural*.

Johnny Earthquake's father, Mr. Ian Quaker, owned a small chemist's shop specializing almost entirely, if the evidence of its one window was to be believed, in very large bottles and very small packets. Glancing through the window, they could see Mr. Quaker's tonsure bobbing about in his tiny dispensary.

Pushing through the back door, they entered the living-room, the centre of which was at present filled by a piebald wardrobe. Mrs. Quaker, secure behind the fortress of her embonpoint, entered from the kitchen and raised an eyebrow at them, though she greeted them civilly enough.

'First time we've seen you this week,' she said.

'You know how it is, Mum. My publicity agent insists I keep up this pretence of being the son of a sea cook who lives in the East End. It's good for sales. If my fans found out I was really respectable middle class, I'd be out of the running.'

'What's all that to do with coming home?'

'I have to watch my chance. I can only come when nobody's looking.'

Mrs. Quaker sniffed.

'He went over very well tonight, Mrs. Quaker,' Nancy said.

'Well, I'm pleased to hear that, I must say. We'd better have a sherry. Ian! Ian! Your father's about somewhere.'

Manoeuvring round the wardrobe, she stooped to the side-board and began to rifle through a selection of bottles, each of which was thrust in turn between her squinting eye and the light. Their net alcoholic yield, judging by Mrs. Quaker's expression, was dismally slight.

'What we came for really was to have Mr. Quaker analyse a liquid for us,' Nancy said. 'Don't worry too much about the drink, thank you.'

The conversation, if that is not too grand a word for the exchange, was cut short by a steaming sheet of formica. It issued from the shop at a run and was slapped against one of the panels of the wardrobe, revealing a gasping Mr. Quaker, who began to thump against the edges of the panel as if his life depended on it.

'I don't know what I'll do if it doesn't stick this time,' he said gloomily. His face was well-equipped to express gloom. The scanty hair motif given such generous play about his scalp was echoed lower down by his features: his mouth, his moustache, his nose, and his eyes were the scantiest available. These features congregated now in the centre of his face, in an expression of gloom that was not mitigated by the sight of Johnny and Nancy.

'You're here, are you? Still chasing married women, a kid your age? You ought to be learning a trade, young man, same as I did, not singing pop records. You can't imagine me singing in front of a mike, can you?'

'No, I can't,' Mrs. Quaker said genially, splashing sherry. 'And don't nag the poor boy directly he comes in.'

'What're you doing, Mr. Quaker?' Nancy asked.

'Doing? I'm veneering this wardrobe, that's what I'm doing. Nobody wants these old walnut suites these days. I don't know if you've an eye for this sort of thing, but it will look good, if I can get the veneers to stick. The glue's my own mixture.'

'We wondered if you could analyse something for us. A liquid.' Nancy produced one of the bulbs of polyannamine she had taken when her sister's back was turned.

'What is it? Where did you get it?' Mr. Quaker's eyes came together as he lifted it to the light.

'We don't know what it is, but it's called polyannamine and I found it at 10 Downing Street.'

Father and Mother stared suspiciously at her. If there was one thing they regretted more than Johnny's connection with Nancy, it was Nancy's connection with the Government.

'It's all right, it's harmless,' Nancy said, smiling. 'It was suggested that some be given to the P.M. to cheer him up, but they were so odd about it that I thought I'd like to know what was going on.'

'Ten Downing Street!' said Mr. Quaker, in what the Press would have referred to as a hushed whisper. Still bearing the bulb at eye level, he backed away in the direction of the shop. Taking advantage of his departure, the gay tartan veneer began to peel off the wardrobe.

'Well, at least we do see life,' Mrs. Quaker commented. 'Ten Downing Street! I like that!' She brought the sherry forward, and for the next quarter of an hour regaled them with it and an account of the matrimonial misadventures of her dentist. But Nancy's regaleability was at what, for want of a worse phrase, might be termed a new all-time low; throughout life she had enjoyed being perverse, and it was not that she intended to blot her record with regret this late in the day; but she saw that by being spiteful to her sister, Lady Elizabeth, she was only stirring up trouble for herself later . . . and there was the thought that she did not know quite how Elizabeth's coffee might have taken her. Excusing herself, she slipped into the back of the chemist's shop to the phone, and dialled No. 10 on a private line.

It was a long time before a distraught Tarver managed to bring a distraught Lady Elizabeth to speak.

'I can't talk to you now, Nancy. Poor Herbert's in a terrible state.'

'Dying?'

'No, I've never seen him more cheerful, unfortunately. Somehow he has taken a ghastly drug called polyannamine, and nobody can get——'

'Are *you* all right?'

'Of course I am, but I'm distraught, Nancy, absolutely distraught! I can't stay talking. Herbert has insulted Molochev, and unless they get a full apology from him by 2 a.m. to-morrow morning—that's 6 a.m., Moscow time—they are going to declare a state of war with Britain.'

'Elizabeth!'

'The world's gone mad! I *can't* stand talking. God bless you, Nancy, whatever happens.'

The line went dead.

It was just after ten o'clock. The pubs would be closing.

With the blood drained from her face, Nancy stood where she was, staring into the dark shop. Slowly she replaced the receiver on its cradle. Slowly, her face still pale, she walked back into the living-room—to be confronted by her husband, Lord Lyon-Bowater.

Accompanying him, standing by the wardrobe like a sentry by his box, was a small man in a tightly belted mac.

'There she is, sir. That's her,' this individual told Lord Lyon-Bowater.

'Do you think I doubt it? Nancy, we have followed you: we saw you through the window. What have you to say for yourself?'

'Oh, Towin!' She burst into tears. Even as she did so, she saw to her shame that Johnny was attempting to hide from the intruders; the tail of his bright satin jacket protruded from the wardrobe.

Five minutes later, Nancy had controlled herself enough to tell her story to a shocked audience, her husband, the private detective, Mrs. Quaker, and Johnny. They received her news in silence; Mrs. Quaker was the first to speak.

'War! So it's come at last—what us innocent people have been dreading ever since the last one!' exclaimed Mrs. Quaker.

'England don't stand a chance this time,' the detective said, lugging at his belt to gird himself against an invisible foe. 'It'll be the end of most of us.'

'Nonsense,' said Lord Lyon-Bowater, but a roar of laughter had greeted the detective's remark. They turned to see Mr. Quaker cackling helplessly by the door. He pointed at Nancy, his finger shaking with his mirth, his tiny features huddling in the centre of a convulsed area of cheek.

'That's the funniest thing I heard for years, Nancy. Really funny. I don't know when I laughed so much. For years, we've all been saying we'd like to tell Molochev what we thought of him; it's only fitting it should be the P.M. who finally does it. By gosh, really funny! Really—Worth a few H-bombs, I'd say. Long live free speech!'

Johnny grasped him by the shoulders and shook him.

'Pull yourself together, Dad. This isn't a laughing matter and you know it. You're hysterical.'

'Oh, no, I'm not, my little teenage divorcee. I just tasted that solution your fancy woman gave me to analyse, and believe me it's a real cure for any sort of misery.'

He went into a fresh peal of laughter. Johnny smacked him across the face.

The laughter stopped, but Mr. Quaker said amiably, 'You only did that because you're unhappy and frightened——'

' 'Course I'm frightened——'

Meanwhile, Lord Lyon-Bowater had come to life. He rammed his hat on to his head, seized his stick and gloves, and thrust his chin forward.

'I can't wait about here any longer. My post is at the Air Ministry. The country's full defensive forces must be mobilized immediately. Nancy, you'd better come with me.'

But it was Johnny Earthquake who stepped forward.

'If you want to defend the country, sir, here's the ideal way,' he said excitedly. 'Drop this stuff over Russia, over Moscow, and you'll have 'em all as merry as crickets in no time. It would save anyone bashing anyone.'

'Oh, the boy's got a lovely idea!' exclaimed his mother.

'It's a wonderful idea!' exclaimed Nancy. 'What do you say, Towin?'

The Secretary of State for Air looked at his watch.

'Where do we get hold of this stuff?'

'From a man called Miller,' Nancy said. 'He lives—well, according to the label on his box, he lives in Pentonville Prison.'

'Mark Miller!' exclaimed Johnny. 'I was introduced to him when we played at Pentonville last night. I know where his lab is. Come on! What are we waiting for?'

His Lordship looked him straight in the eyes. Then he grasped his shoulder.

'Why not, by George? Johnny, my boy, you're on. You and Nancy go and collect as much of this drug as you can lay your hands on and bring it round to me at the Air Ministry. I'll be seeing that a ground-to-air missile is readied. We can pack the solution into a warhead and explode it over the Kremlin. On your way!'

'Be seeing you!' Johnny said, grabbing Nancy's hand; he dragged her towards the door, with a farewell wave at his mother. His Lordship, the detective still keeping him company, followed close behind. In a minute, Mr. and Mrs. Quaker were left alone.

'If only they can make it in time!' Mrs. Quaker said. Her hands were shaking. She turned eagerly to the sherry.

'Old wardrobe looks as if an H-bomb's hit it already!' Mr. Quaker said. He began to laugh again.

It was a week later that Joseph Kennedson, President of the U.S.A., paid his historic visit to Great Britain. During his two-day stay at Chequers, he and Lady Elizabeth Macclesfield sat in the Green Lounge and watched on a monitor screen while Sir Herbert, in the room next door, had an unscripted exchange of insults before the TV cameras with Nikita Molochev in Moscow. The show was a partial failure: it had to be stopped before the end because both Molochev and Sir Herbert were laughing too much to go on.

'Oh, that was wonderful' exclaimed Lady Elizabeth. 'You can see now, Joseph, why the war collapsed. Once our missile exploded over Moscow, the Russians were too busy being happy to care about war.'

'Too bad that young Johnny Earthquake set fire to Miller's lab, though, so that all his notes were destroyed. Now we may never be able to synthesize polyannamine again.'

Lady Elizabeth started laughing once more.

'Who cares? It did the trick. And they had a wonderful blaze at Pentonville.'

The P.M. entered. He wore only vest and trousers, and was towelling himself.

'Phew, it was hot under the searchlights,' he exclaimed, grinning at the President. 'Talk about sweated labour, what price sweated Tory?'

'You were marvellous, darling,' Lady Elizabeth said, laughing and kissing him. 'You ought to be on TV.'

'I'll think about it, sweetie. We'd better see how the election goes first, eh, Joseph!'

When the Macclesfields had somewhat lapsed into sobriety, the President said, 'One point about this affair that interests me. Happiness is naturally a highly desirable state, yet nobody had taken polyannamine voluntarily; curious, isn't it?'

'None of us wants change—except small change.'

'I mean that I didn't know—well, the rest of the world doesn't know—whether or not to envy you.'

The P.M.'s eyebrows rose towards his thinning hair.

'You soon will.'

'How's that?'

Both the P.M. and his wife began to laugh again.

'Of course you wouldn't have heard—we only discovered it yesterday,' Lady Elizabeth said. 'The effects of polyannamine are not only irreversible: they're contagious and infectious.'

The President stared at her open-mouthed. He scratched his head. Then he began to smile.

Then he too began to laugh.

THE GAME OF GOD

IN the afternoon they brought him entrails.

At other times of day, the pygmies brought the old man fish from the river, or the watercress which he loved, but in the afternoon they brought him two bowls of entrails.

He stood to receive them, staring over their heads through the open door, looking at the blue jungle without seeing it. He was in pain. He dared not let his subjects see that he suffered or was weak; the pygmies had a short way with weakness. Before they entered his room, he forced himself to stand erect, using his stick for support.

The two bearers stopped before him, bowing their heads until their snouts were almost in the still steaming bowls.

'Your God gives you thanks. Your offering is received,' the old man said.

Whether or not they really comprehended his clicking attempt to reproduce their tongue, he could not tell. Shaking slightly, he patted their scaly heads. They rose and departed with their rapid, slithering walk. In the bowls, oily highlights glistened, reflected from the sunshine outside.

Sinking back on to his bed, the old man fell into his usual fantasy: the pygmies came to him, and he treated them not with forbearance but hatred. He poured over them the weight of his long-repressed loathing and despisal, striking them over the heads with his stick and finally driving them and all their race for ever from this planet. They were gone. The azure sun and the blue jungles were his alone; he could live where nobody would ever find or worry him. He could die at last as simply as a leaf falls from a tree.

The reverie faded, and he recognized it for what it was. He knotted his hands together till the knuckles stood out like cobble-stones, coughing a little blood. The bowl of intestines would have to be disposed of.

Next day, the rocket ship landed a mile away.

The overlander lumbered along the devious forest tract. It was losing as little time as possible with Barney Brangwyn's expert hand at the wheel. On either side of the vehicle, the vegetation was thick, presenting that sombre blue-green hue which characterized most of the living things on the planet Kakakakaxo.

'You neither of you look in the pink of health!' Barney observed, flicking his eyes from the track to glance at the azure lights on the faces of his companions.

The three members of the Planetary Ecological Survey Team had blue shadows shading every plane of their countenances. The shadows gave an illusion of chill, yet in this equatorial zone, and with the sun Cassivelaunus shining at zenith, it was comfortably warm, if not hot. The surrounding jungle grew thickly, with an almost tropical luxuriance, the bushes sagged under the weight of their own foliage. It was strange to recall that they were heading for a man who had lived in these un-inviting surroundings for almost twenty years. Now they were here, it became easier to see why he was universally regarded as a hero.

'There's plenty of cover here for any green pygmies who may be watching us,' Tim Anderson said, peering at the passing thickets. 'I was hoping to see one or two.'

Barney chuckled at the worried note in the younger man's voice.

'The pygmies are probably still getting over the racket we made in landing,' he said, 'we'll be seeing them soon enough. When you get as ancient as I am, Tim, you'll become less keen to meet the local bigwigs. The top dogs of any planet are generally the most obstreperous—*ipso facto*, as the lawyers say.'

He lapsed into silence as he negotiated a gulley, swinging the big vehicle expertly up the far slope.

'By the evidence, the most obstreperous factor on Kakakakaxo is the climate,' Tim said. 'Only six or seven hundred miles north and south of here, the glaciers begin, and go right on up to the poles. I'm glad our job is just to vet the planet to see that it's safe for colonists—I shouldn't want to live here myself, pygmies or no pygmies. I've seen enough already to tell you that.'

'It's not a question of choice for the colonists,' Craig Hodges, leader of the team, remarked. 'They'll come because of some kind of pressure on them: economic factors, oppression, destitution, or the need for *liebensraum*—the sort of grim necessities which keep us all on the hop.'

'You're a cheerful couple!' Barney exclaimed. 'At least Daddy Dangerfield likes it here! He has faced Kakakakaxo for nineteen years, playing God, wet-nursing the pygmies!'

'He crashed here accidentally in the first place; he's had to adjust,' Craig said, unwilling to be shaken out of a melancholy which always descended on him when the P.E.S.T. first confronted the mystery of a new planet.

'What a magnificent adjustment!' Tim exclaimed. 'Daddy Dangerfield, God of the Great Beyond! He was one of my childhood heroes. I can hardly believe we're going to meet him.'

'Most of the legends built around him originate on Droxy,' Craig said, 'where half the ballyhoo in the universe comes from. I am chary about the blighter myself, but he could prove informative—don't forget we're not on an autograph hunt, Tim.'

'He'll be informative,' Barney said, skirting a thicket of rhododendron. 'He'll save us a whack of field work. In nineteen years—if he's anything like the man he's cracked up to be—he should have accumulated a mass of material of inestimable value to us.'

The P.E.S.T. task was seldom simple. When a three-man team landed on an unexplored planet like Kakakakaxo, they had to categorize its possible dangers and determine exactly the nature of the opposition any superior species might offer colonizing man. The superior species in a galaxy tumbling with diversity, might be mammal, reptile, insect, vegetable, mineral, or virus. Frequently it was so obstreperous that it had to be exterminated entirely before man could move in—and exterminated so that the ecological balance of the planet was disturbed as little as possible.

Their journey ended unexpectedly. They were only a mile from their ship when the jungle on one side of the overlander gave way to a cliff, which formed the base of a steep and afforested mountain. Rounding a high spur of rock, they saw the pygmies' village ahead of them. When Barney braked and cut out the power, the three of them sat for a minute in silence, taking in the scene.

Rapid movement under the trees followed their arrival.

'Here comes the welcoming committee,' Craig said. 'We'd better climb down and look agreeable, as far as that is possible; Heaven knows what they are going to make of your beard, Barney. Get your blaster on, Tim, just in case it's needed.'

The trio was surrounded as soon as it jumped to the ground. The pygmies moved like jerky lightning, enclosing the ecologists. Though they appeared from all quarters, apparently without prearranged plan, it took them only a few seconds to form a wall round the intruders. And for all their speed, there was a quality of stealth about them; there was something menacing about their haste; they were ugly creatures.

They moved like lizards, and their skin was like lizard-skin, green and mottled, except where it broke into coarse scales down their backs. Pygmy-sized, none of them stood more than four feet high. They were four-legged and two-armed. Their heads, perched above their bodies with no visible neck, were like cayman-heads, fitted with long, cruel jaws and serrated teeth. These heads now swivelled from side to side, like gun-turrets on tanks seeking sight of the enemy.

Once they had surrounded the ecologists, the pygmies made no further move. The initiative had passed from them. In their baggy throats, heavy pulses beat.

Craig pointed at a cayman-head in front of him and said, 'Greetings! Where is Daddy Dangerfield? We intend you no harm. We merely wish to see Dangerfield. Please take us to him.'

He repeated his words in Galingua.

The pygmies stirred, opening their jaws and croaking. An excited clack-clack-clackering broke out on all sides. Over-poweringly, an odour of fish rose from the creatures. None of them volunteered anything which might be construed as a reply. The wave of excitement, if it was that, which passed over them emphasized their more formidable features. Their stocky bodies might have been ludicrous, but their two pairs of sturdy legs and their armoured jaws would deter anyone from regarding them as figures of fun.

'These are only animals!' Tim exclaimed. 'Look at them—they relieve themselves as they stand, like cattle. They possess none of the personal pride you'd expect in a primitive savage. They wear absolutely nothing in the way of clothes. Why, they aren't even armed!'

'Don't say that until you've had a good look at their claws and teeth,' Barney said cheerfully. He had caught the loathing in the youngster's voice, and knew how loathing cloaks fear. He himself felt curious, dry tension, originating less from thought of the pygmies than from the reflection that the three of them were in an unknown world, without precedents to guide them; when he ceased to feel that tension, he would be due for retirement.

'Move forward slowly with me,' Craig said. 'We are doing no good standing here. Dangerfield must be about somewhere, heaven help him.'

Thigh-deep in clacking cayman-heads, who kept them en-circled, the P.E.S.T. men advanced towards the settlement, which lay in patchy tones of blue sunshine and blue shade.

This manoeuvre was resented by the pygmies, whose noise redoubled, though they backed away without offering opposition. When they spoke, their grey tongues wagged up and down in their long mouths. Following Craig's lead, Barney and Tim kept their hands at their sidearms, ready for trouble.

So they moved slowly into the village. Bounded on one side by the cliff face, it stood under trees. In the foliage of these trees, a colony of gay-coloured birds, evidently a sort of weavers, had plaited a continuous roof out of lianas, climbers, leaves, and twigs. Under this cover, on the dropping-bespattered ground, the pygmies had their rude huts, which were no more than squares of woven reed propped at an angle by sticks, to allow an entrance. They looked like collapsed bivouacs.

Tied outside these dismal dwellings were furry animals, walking in the small circles allowed by their leashes and calling to each other. Their mewing cries, the staccato calls of the birds, and the croaking of the cayman-heads, made a babel of sound. And over everything lay the stench of decaying fish.

'Plenty of local colour,' Barney remarked. 'These tethered animals are an odd touch, aren't they?'

In contrast to this squalid scene was the cliff face, which had been ornately carved with stylized representations of foliage mingled with intricate geometrical forms. The decoration rose to a height of some twelve metres and was inventive and well-proportioned. Later, the ecologists were to find this work crude in detail, but from a distance its superiority to the village was marked. As they came nearer, they saw that the decorated area was the façade of a building hewn in the living rock, complete with doors, passages, rooms, and windows, from which pygmies watched their progress with unblinking curiosity.

'I begin to be impressed,' Tim observed, eyeing the patterns in the rock. 'If these little horrors can create something as elaborate as that, there is hope for them yet.'

'Dangerfield!' Craig called, when another attempt to communicate with the pygmies had failed. Only the whooping birds answered him.

Already the pygmies were losing interest in the men. They pressed less closely; several scuttled with lizard speed back into their shelters. Looking over the knobby heads of the crowd, Barney pointed to the far side of the clearing. There, leaning against the dun-coloured rock of the cliff, was a sizeable hut, built of the same flimsy material as the pygmy dwellings, but constructed with more care and of less uncouth design.

142

While the ecologists were looking at it, an emaciated figure appeared in the doorway. It was human. It made its way towards them, aiding itself with a stout stick.

'That's Dangerfield!' Barney exclaimed. 'It must be Dangerfield. As far as we know, there's no other human being on the whole benighted planet.'

A warming stream of excitement ran through Tim. Daddy Dangerfield was a legend in this region of the inhabited galaxy. Crash-landing on Kakakakaxo nineteen years ago, he had been the first man to visit this uninviting little world.

Although only fifteen light years from Droxy, one of the great interstellar centres of commerce and pleasure, Kakakakaxo was off the trade lanes. So Dangerfield had lived alone with the pygmies for ten standard years before someone had chanced to arrive with an offer of rescue.

By then it was too late: the poison of loneliness had become its own antidote. The stubborn man refused to leave. He claimed that the native tribes, the pygmies, had need of him. So he remained where he was, King of the Crocodile People, Daddy to the Little Folk—as the Droxy tabloids phrased it, with their affection for capital letters and absurd titles.

As Dangerfield approached the team now, the pygmies fell back before him, maintaining their clacking chorus. Many of them slid away, indifferent to affairs beyond their comprehension.

It was hard to recognize, in the bent figure peering anxiously at them, the young, bronzed giant by which Dangerfield was represented in the comic strips on Droxy. The thin, sardonic face with its powerful hook of nose had become a caricature of itself. The grey hair was long and dirty. The lumpy hands which grasped the stick were bespattered with liver marks. This was Dangerfield, but appearances suggested that the legend would outlive the man.

'You're from Droxy?' he asked eagerly, speaking in Galingua. 'You've come to make another solid about me? I'm very pleased to see you here. Welcome to the untamed planet of Kakakakaxo.'

Craig Hodges put out his hand.

'We're not from Droxy,' he said. 'We're based on Earth, although most of our days are spent far from it. Nor are we a film unit about to make a solid; our mission is rather more practical than that.'

'You ought to shoot a solid—you'd make your fortune. What are you doing here, then?'

As Craig introduced himself and his team, Dangerfield's

manner became noticeably less cordial. He muttered angrily to himself about invaders of his privacy.

'Come over and have a drink with us in our wagon,' Barney said. 'We've got a nice little Aldebaran wine you might like to sample. You must be glad to see someone to talk to.'

'This is my place,' the old man said pugnaciously, waving his stick over the tawdry clearing. 'I don't know what you people are doing here. I'm the man who beat Kakakakaxo. The God of the Crocodile Folk, that's what they call me.' As if Barney's suggestion about the wine had just sunk in, he began moving towards the overlander, talking as he went. 'If you had pushed your way in here twenty years ago as you did just now, the pygmies would have torn you to bits—right to little bits. I tamed 'em! No living man has ever done what I've done. They've made films about my life on Droxy—that's how important I am. Didn't you know that?'

His sunken eyes rested on Tim Anderson. 'Didn't you know that, young man?'

Tim evaded the stare.

'I was brought up on those films, sir. They were made by the old Melmoth Solid Studios.'

'Yes, yes, that was the name. You don't belong to them? Why don't they come back here any more, eh, why don't they?'

'I believe I read somewhere they went bankrupt a couple of years ago.'

Tim wanted to tell this gaunt relic that Dangerfield, the Far-Flung Father, the Cosmic Schweitzer, had been one of his boyhood heroes, a giant through whom he had first felt the ineluctable lure of space travel; he wanted to tell him that it hurt to have the legend outfaced by the reality. Here was the giant himself—bragging of his past, and bragging, moreover, in a supplicatory whine.

They came up to the overlander. Dangerfield stared at the neat shield on the side, under which the words Planetary Ecological Survey were inscribed in grey. After a moment, he turned pugnaciously to Craig.

'Who are you people? What do you want here? I've got troubles enough.'

'We're a fact-finding team, Mr. Dangerfield,' Craig said levelly. 'Our business is to gather data on this planet. Next to nothing is known about ecological or living conditions here; the planet has never even been properly surveyed. We are naturally keen to secure your help; you should be a treasury of information——'

'I can't answer any questions! I never answer questions.

144

You'll have to find out anything you want to know for yourselves. I'm a sick man—I'm in pain. It's all I can do to walk. I need a doctor, drugs. . . . Are you a doctor?'

'I can administer an analgesic,' Craig said. 'And if you will let me examine you, I will try to find out what you are suffering from.'

Dangerfield waved a hand angrily in the air.

'I don't need telling what's wrong with me,' he snapped. 'I know every disease that's going on this cursed planet. I've got fiffins, that's my trouble, and all I'm asking you for is something to relieve the pain. If you haven't come to be helpful, you'd best get out altogether!'

'Just what is or are fiffins?' Barney asked.

'None of your business. They're not infectious, if that's what's worrying you. If you have only come to ask questions, clear out. The pygmies will look after me, just as I've always looked after them.'

As he turned to go, Dangerfield staggered and would have fallen, had not Tim moved fast enough to catch his arm. The old fellow shook off the supporting hand and hurried back across the clearing in a shuffle that sent the captive animals squeaking to the far end of their tethers.

Catching him up, Tim laid a hand on his arm.

'We can help you,' he said pleadingly. 'Please be reasonable. You look as if you need medical treatment, which we can give you.'

'I never had help, and I don't need it now. And what's more, I've made it a rule never to be reasonable.'

Full of conflicting emotion, Tim turned back. He caught sight of Craig's impassive face.

'We should help him,' he said.

'He doesn't want help, from you or anyone,' Craig replied, not moving.

'But he's in pain!'

'No doubt, and the pain clouds his judgement. That may account for his uneasy mixture of insult and abasement. But he is still his own self, with his own ways. We have no right to take him over against his expressed wishes.'

'He may be dying,' Tim said. 'You've no right to be so damned indifferent.' He looked defiantly at Craig, who returned his gaze. Then he walked rapidly away, pushing past the few cayman-heads who still remained on the scene. Dangerfield, on the other side of the clearing, glanced back once and then disappeared into his hut. Barney made to follow Tim, but Craig stopped him.

'Leave him,' he said quietly. 'Let him have his temper out.'

Barney looked straight at his friend.

'Don't force the boy,' he said. 'He hasn't got your complicated outlook on life. Just go easy on him, Craig.'

'We all have to learn, and it is easier to learn fast,' Craig observed, almost sadly. Then, changing his tone, he said, 'For a reason we have yet to discover, Dangerfield is un-co-operative. From first impressions, he is unbalanced, which means he may soon swing the other way and offer us help: that we should wait for; I'd be interested to get a straight record of his nineteen years here. It would make a useful psychological document, if nothing else.'

'He's a stubborn old blighter, to my way of thinking,' Barney said, shaking his head.

'Which is the sign of a weak man. That's why Tim was unwise to coax him; it would merely make him more obdurate. Ignore Dangerfield and he will come to us. Until he does, we shall work on our own here, completing the usual ground sample survey. First, we must establish the intelligence status of the pygmies, with a view to finding out how much opposition they will offer the colonists when they arrive. One or two other odd features may also prove interesting.'

Thrusting his hands in his pockets, Barney surveyed the shabby settlement. Now that it was quieter, he could hear a river flowing nearby. The pygmies had dispersed; some lay motionless in their crude shelters, only their snouts showing, the blue light lying like a mist along their scales.

'Speaking off the cuff, I'd say the pygmies are infra-human,' Barney remarked, picking from his beard an insect which had tumbled out of the thatched trees above them. 'I'd also hazard they have got as far, evolutionwise, as they're ever going to get. They have restricted cranial development, no opposed thumb, and no form of clothing—which means the lack of any sexual inhibition, such as one would expect to find in this Y-type culture. I should rate them as Y gamma stasis, Craig, at first blush.'

Craig nodded, smiling, as if with a secret pleasure.

'Which means you feel as I do about the cliff temple,' he said, indicating with his grey eyes the wealth of carving visible through the trees.

'You mean—the pygmies couldn't have built it?' Barney said. Craig nodded his large head.

'These cayman-heads are far below the cultural level implicit in the architecture. They are its caretakers, not its creators. Which means, of course, that there is—or was—another species, a superior species, on Kakakakaxo, which may prove more elusive than the pygmies.'

Craig was solid and stolid; he spoke unemphatically. But Barney, who knew something of what went on inside that megacephalous skull, knew that Craig's habit of throwing away an important point, revealed that he was chewing over a problem which excited his intellectual curiosity.

Understanding enough not to probe on the subject, Barney filed it away for later and switched to another topic. For such a bulky specimen of manhood, he possessed surprising delicacy; but the confines of a small spaceship make a good schoolroom for the sensibilities.

'I'm just going to look at these furry pets the cayman-heads keep tied up outside their shelters,' he said, 'they're intriguing little creatures. We might make a pet of one ourselves.'

'Go carefully,' Craig cautioned. 'I have a suspicion the cayman-heads may not appreciate your interference. Those pets may not be pets at all; the pygmies don't look like a race of animal-lovers.'

'Well, if they aren't pets, they certainly aren't livestock. Doesn't smell as if the cayman-heads eat anything but fish, does it?'

Barney walked slowly among the crude shelters. He was careful to avoid any protruding pygmy snouts, which lay along the ground like fallen branches; they remained motionless as he passed; only the big pulse throbbed in their throats.

Outside most of the shelters, two different animals were tethered, generally by their hind legs. One animal, a grey, furry creature with a pushed-in face like a Pekinese dog, stood almost as high as the pygmies; the other animal, a pudgy-snouted little creature with brown fur and a gay yellow crest, was half the size of the 'peke', and resembled a miniature bear. Both pekes and bears had little black monkey-like paws, many of which were now raised as if in supplication as the ecologists approached.

'They're a deal more cuddlesome than their owners,' Craig said. Stooping, he extended a hand cautiously to one of the little bears. It leapt forward and clutched his hand, chattering in appealing fashion.

'Do you suppose the two species, the pekes and the bears, fight together?' Barney asked. 'You notice they are kept tied just far enough apart so that they can't touch each other. We may have found the local variation on cock-fighting.'

'Blood-sports may be in accord with the looks of the pygmies,' Craig said, 'but not with the character of these creatures. Look at them—as pugnacious as bunny rabbits! Even their incisors are blunt. They have no natural weapons at all.'

'Talking of teeth, they exist on the same diet as their

147

masters,' Barney commented. 'Though whether from choice or necessity we'll have to discover.'

He pointed to decaying piles of fish-bones, fish-heads, and scales, on which the little animals were sitting disconsolately. Iridescent beetles scuttled among the debris, busy almost beneath Barney's feet.

'I'm going to try taking one of these pekes back to the overlander,' he announced. 'It should be well worth examining.'

From the corner of his eye, he could see a pygmy snout sticking out of its shelter not three yards away; keeping it under observation, he bent over one of the pekes and tried to loosen the tightly-drawn thong that kept it captive. The tethered creatures nearby, large and small, set up an excited chatter as they saw what Barney was doing. At the same time, the watching pygmy moved.

Its speed was astonishing. One second, it was scarcely visble in its shelter, its nose extended along the ground; the next, it confronted Barney with its claws resting over his hand, its ferocious teeth bared in his face. Small though the reptile was, undoubtedly it could have snapped his neck through. Its yellow eyes glared unblinkingly up at Barney.

'Don't fire, or you'll have the lot on us!' Craig said, for Barney's free hand had gone for his blaster.

They were surrounded almost immediately by pygmies, all scuttling up and clacking excitedly. The reptiles made their typical noises by waggling their tongues without moving their jaws. Though they crowded in, apparently hostile, they made no attempt to attack Craig and Barney. Then one of them thrust himself forward. Waving his small upper arms he commenced to harangue them.

'Some traces of primitive speech pattern,' Craig observed coolly. 'Let's try a little barter for your pet, Barney, while we have their attention.'

Dipping into one of the pouches of his duty equipment, he produced a necklace, in whose marble-sized stones spirals of colour danced, delicate internal springs ensuring that their hues changed continually as long as their wearer moved. It was the sort of bauble to be picked up for a few minicredits on almost any civilized planet. Craig held it out to the pygmy who had delivered the speech.

The pygmy leader scrutinized it briefly, then resumed his harangue. The necklace meant nothing to him. With signs, Craig explained the function of the necklace, and indicated that he would exchange it for one of the little bears. Abundant though these animals were, their owners showed no sign of wishing to part with one. Pocketing the necklace, Craig produced a mirror.

Mirrors unfailingly excite the interest of primitive tribes—yet the pygmies remained unmoved. Many of them began to disappear now the crisis was over, speeding off with their nervous, lizard movements. Putting the mirror away, Craig brought out a whistle.

It was an elaborate toy, shaped like a silver fish with an open mouth. The pygmy leader snatched it from Craig's hand, leaving the red track of its claws across his open palm. It popped the whistle into its mouth.

'Here, that's not edible!' Craig said, instinctively stepping forward with his hand out. Without warning, the pygmy struck. Perhaps it misinterpreted Craig's gesture and acted unthinkingly in self-defence. Snapping its jaws, it lunged out at Craig's leg. The ecologist fell instantly. Hardly had he struck the ground when a blue shaft flashed from Barney's blaster. As the noise of the thermonuclear blast rattled round the clearing, the pygmy toppled over and fell flat, its hide smoking.

Into the ensuing silence broke the terrified clatter of a thousand weaver birds, winging from their homes and circling high above the tree tops. Barney bent down, seized Craig round the shoulders, and raised him with one powerful arm, keeping the blaster levelled in his free hand. Over Craig's thigh, soaking through his torn trousers, grew a ragged patch of blood.

'Thanks, Barney,' he said. 'Trade seems to be bad today. Let's get back to the overlander.'

They retreated, Craig limping painfully. The pygmies made no attempt to attack. They mostly stood still, crouching over the smoking body and either staring fixedly or waving their snouts helplessly from side to side. It was impossible to determine whether they were frightened by the show of force or had decided that the brief quarrel was no affair of theirs. At last they bent over their dead comrade, seized him by his hind feet, and dragged him briskly off in the direction of the river.

When Barney got Craig on to his bunk, he stripped his trousers off, cleansed the wound, and dressed it with antiseptic and restorative powder. Although Craig had lost blood, little serious damage had been done; his leg would be entirely healed by morning.

'You got off lightly,' Barney said, straightening up. 'It's a deep flesh wound, but that baby could have chewed your knees off if he had been trying.'

Craig sat up and accepted a mescahale.

'One thing about the incident particularly interested me,' he said. 'The cayman-heads wanted the whistle because they mistook it for food; fish, as we gather from the stink outside, is a main item of diet. The mirror and necklace meant nothing to them; I have never met a backward tribe so lacking in simple, elementary vanity. Does it connect with the absence of any sexual inhibitions which you mentioned?'

'What have they to be vain about?' Barney asked, stripping off and heading for the shower. 'After five minutes out there, I feel as if the stench of fish has been painted on me with a brush.'

It was not long before they realized Tim Anderson was nowhere in the overlander. Craig pursed his lips.

'Go and see if you can find him, Barney,' he said. 'He isn't safe wandering about on his own. He'll have to learn to enjoy freedom of thought without freedom of action.'

The afternoon was stretching its blue shadows across the ground. In the quiet, you could almost hear the planet turn on its cold, hard axis. The birds had returned to their tight-knit home and made occasional bright darting forays to the ground. They would be picking up the beetles in the piles of fish debris, Barney thought. He saw one of the raiders fall victim—in a flurry of motion—to a cayman-head. It killed and did not eat.

Barney was familiar with the pattern of nature. He did not pause, except to take his bearings. He set out towards the distant murmur of water, thinking that a river would hold as much attraction for Tim as for himself. He turned down a narrow track among the trees, then stopped, unsure which way to go. He called Tim's name once.

An answer came almost at once, unexpectedly. In a minute, Tim emerged from the bushes ahead and waved cheerfully to Barney.

'You had me worried,' Barney confessed, catching up with him. 'It's wiser not to stroll off like that without telling us where you are going. What have you been doing?'

'I'm quite capable of looking after myself, you know,' Tim said. 'There's a river just beyond these bushes, wide and deep and fast-flowing. I suppose these cayman-heads are cold-blooded?'

'They are,' Barney confided. 'I should know. I had one holding hands with me a while back.'

'Just as well for them,' Tim remarked. 'There's a bunch of them in the water now and it's ice cold. It must flow straight down off the glaciers. The pygmies are superb swimmers, very fast, very sure; they look altogether more graceful in the water than they do on land. I watched them diving and coming up with fish the size of a big salmon in their jaws.'

Barney told him about the incident with the fish-whistle.

'I'm sorry about Craig's leg,' Tim said, 'but while we're on the subject, perhaps you can tell me why he's got his knife into me, and why he jumped down my throat when I went after Dangerfield?'

'He hasn't got his knife into you, and he didn't jump down your throat. When you've been on this team a little longer, Tim, you'll see that Craig Hodges doesn't work like that at all. He's a neutral man. At present he's worried because he smells a mystery, but is undecided where to turn for a key to it. He probably regards Dangerfield as that key; certainly he respects the knowledge the man must have, yet I think that inwardly he would prefer to tackle the whole problem with a clean slate, leaving Dangerfield out of it altogether.'

'Why should Craig feel like that? P.E.S.T. H.Q. instructed us to contact Dangerfield.'

'Quite. And H.Q. being a tidy few light years away is often out of touch with realities. But Craig probably thinks that old Dangerfield might be—well, misleading, ill-informed. . . . Craig's a man who likes to work things out for himself—and he likes other people to work things out for themselves.'

They turned and began to make their way back to the settlement, walking slowly, enjoying the mild air uncontaminated by fish.

'Surely that wasn't why Craig was so ragged about helping Daddy Dangerfield?' Tim asked.

Barney sighed and tugged at his beard.

'No, that was something else,' he said. 'You develop a certain outlook to things when you've been on the P.E.S.T. run for some years, because a way of life induces an attitude to life. P.E.S. Teams are the precursors of change, remember. Before we arrive, the planets are in their natural state—that is, unspoiled or undeveloped, whichever way you care to phrase it. After we leave, they are going to be taken over and altered, on our recommendation. However cheery you feel about man's position in the galaxy, you can't help a part of you regretting that this inevitable mutilation is necessary.'

'It's not our business to care,' Tim said, impatiently.

'But Craig cares, Tim. The more planets we survey, the more he feels that some mysterious—divine—balance is being overthrown. I feel it myself; you'll grow to feel it in time; directly you land on an unmanned planet, an occult sense of *secrecy* comes up and hits you. . . . You can't avoid the idea that you are confronting an individual entity—and your sworn duty is to destroy it, and the enigma behind it, and turn out yet another assembly-line world for assembly-line man.

'That's how Craig feels about planets and people. For him, a man's character is sacrosanct; anything that has *accumulated* has his respect. It may be simpler to work with people who are mere ciphers, but an individual is of greater ultimate value.'

'You mean that's what he meant when he said Dangerfield was still his own self?'

'More or less,' Barney agreed.

'Hm.'

'Sound sceptical if you like. It'll hit you one day. Look at this place! Now think of it in fifty years, if we give it a clean bill of health. Do you think your river will run as it does now? It may be dammed to provide hydro-electric power, it may be widened and made navigable, it may be a sewer. These birds overhead'll be extinct or roosting on factory roofs. Everything'll be changed—and we take much of the credit and blame for it.'

'I shan't miss the stink of fish,' Tim said.

'Even a stink of fish has——' Barney began, and broke off. The silence was torn right down the middle by piercing screams. The two ecologists looked at each other and then ran down the trail, bursting full tilt into the clearing.

Beneath the spreading thatch of the treetops, a peke creature was being killed. A rabble of pygmies milled everywhere, converging on a large decayed tree stump, upon which two of their kind stood in full view, the screaming peke held tightly between them.

The furry prisoner struggled and squealed, while to its cries were added those of all the others tethered nearby. The cries stopped abruptly. Without fuss, cruel talons came up and ripped its stomach open. Its entrails were then scooped, steaming, into a crudely shaped clay bowl, after which the ravaged body was tossed to the crowd. With delighted cries, the pygmies scrambled for it.

Before the hubbub had died down, another captive was handed up to the two executioners, kicking and crying as it went. The crowd paused briefly to watch the fun. This time, the victim was one of the bear-like animals. Its body was gouged open, its insides turned into a second bowl. It, too, was tossed to the cayman-headed throng.

'Horrible!' Tim exclaimed. 'Horrible!'

'Good old Mother Nature!' Barney said angrily. 'How many more of the little blighters do they intend to slaughter?'

But the killing was over. The two executioner pygmies,

bearing the bowls of entrails clumsily in their paws, climbed from the tree stump and made their way through the crowd, which ceased its squabbling to fall back for them. The vessels were carried towards the rear of the village.

'It almost looks like some sort of a religious ceremony,' Craig said. Barney and Tim turned to find him standing close behind them. The screaming had drawn him from his bed; in the tumult, he had limped over to them unobserved.

'How's the leg?' Tim asked him.

'It'll be better by morning, Tim.'

'The creature that bit you—the one Barney killed—was thrown into the river,' Tim said. 'I was there watching from the bank when the others turned up with his carcass and slung him in.'

'They're taking those bowls of guts into Dangerfield's hut,' Barney said, pointing across the clearing. The two cayman-headed bearers disappeared through the doorway; a minute later they emerged empty-handed from the hut by the cliff, and mingled with the throng.

'I wonder what he wants guts for,' Tim said. 'Don't say he eats them.'

'There's smoke!' Craig exclaimed. 'His hut's caught fire! Tim, quick and fetch a foam extinguisher from the overlander. Run!'

A cloud of smoke, followed by a licking flame, had shown through Dangerfield's window. It died, then sprang up again. Craig and Barney ran forward as Tim dashed back to the overlander. The pygmies, some of whom were still quarrelling over the pelts of the dead peke and bear, took no notice of them or the fire as the men pelted past.

Arriving at the hut first, Barney burst in. The interior of the first room was full of smoke. Flame crawled among the dry rushes on the floor. A crude oil-lamp had been upset; it lay on its side among the flames. Only a few feet beyond it, Dangerfield sprawled on his bed, his eyes closed.

Without wasting words, Craig pulled a rug from the other side of the room, flung it on to the fire and stamped on it. When Tim arrived with the extinguisher, it was hardly needed, but they soused the smouldering ashes with chemicals to make doubly sure.

'There might be an opportunity to talk to the old boy when he pulls out of his faint,' Craig said. 'Leave me here with him, will you, and I'll see what I can do. Keep an eye on the cayman-heads.'

As Tim and Barney left, Craig noticed the two bowls of

entrails standing on a side table. They were still gently steaming.

On the bed, Dangerfield stirred. His eyelids flickered, one frail hand went up to his throat.

'No mercy from me,' he muttered, 'you'll get no mercy from me.'

As Craig bent over him, his eyes opened. He lay looking up at the ecologist. Blue shadows crept like faded ink-stains over the planes of his face.

'I must have passed out,' he said tonelessly. . . . 'Felt so weak.'

'You knocked over your oil-lamp as you collapsed,' Craig said. 'I was just in time to save a nasty blaze.'

The old man made no comment, unless the closing of his eyes was to be interpreted as an indifference to death.

'Every afternoon they bring me the bowls of entrails,' he muttered. 'It's a . . . rite—they're touchy about it. I wouldn't like to disappoint them. . . . But this afternoon it was such an effort to stand. It quite exhausted me. You people coming here exhausted me. If you aren't making a solid, you'd better stay. . . .'

Craig fetched him a mug of water. Dangerfield accepted it, drinking without raising his head, allowing half the liquid to trickle across his withered cheeks. After a minute, he groaned and sat up, propping himself against the wall. Without comment, Craig produced a hypodermic from his emergency pack and filled it from a plastic phial.

'You're in pain,' he said. 'This will stop the pain but leave your head clear. It won't hurt you; let's have a look at your arm, can I?'

Dangerfield's eyes rested on the syringe as if fascinated. He began to shake slowly, until the rickety bed creaked.

'I don't need your help, mister,' he said, his face crinkling.

'We need yours,' replied Craig indifferently, swabbing the thin palsied arm. 'What are these unappetizing offerings? Some sort of religious tribute?'

Unexpectedly, the old man began to laugh, his eyes filling with tears.

'Perhaps it's to placate me,' he said. 'Every day for years, for longer than I can remember, they've been bringing me these guts. You wouldn't believe me if I told you, Hodges—your name is Hodges, isn't it?—that one of the chief problems of my life is hiding guts, getting rid of guts. . . . The pygmies must think I swallow them, and I don't like to disillusion them, in case—well, in case I lost my power over them.'

154

He laughed and groaned then at the same time, hiding his gaunt, beaky face in his hands; the paper-thin skin on his forehead was suddenly showered with sweat. Craig steadied his arm, injected the needle deftly, and massaged the stringy flesh.

Standing away from the bed, he said deliberately, 'It's strange the way you stay here on Kakakakaxo when you fear these pygmies so much.'

Dangerfield looked sharply up, a scarecrow of a man with a shock of hair and a sucked-in mouth. Staring at Craig, his eyes became very clear, as if he realized for the first time that he was confronted by someone with an awareness of his own. Something like relief crept into his expression. He made no attempt to evade Craig's statement.

'Everyone who goes into space has a good reason driving them,' he said. 'You don't only need escape velocity, you need a private dream—or a private nightmare.' As always he spoke in Galingua, using it stiffly and unemphatically. 'Me, I could never deal with people; it's always been one of my troubles; perhaps that was one of the reasons why I was touchy when you arrived. Human beings—you never know where you stand with them. I'd rather face death with the pygmies than life with humanity. There's a confession for you, Hodges, coming from Far-Flung Father Dangerfield. . . . Maybe all heroes are just escapees, if you could see into them, right into the core of them.'

The injection was taking effect. His words were coming more slowly.

'You have it entirely wrong. Though it may be that all escapees pose as heroes,' Craig said, but the old man continued to mutter to himself.

'. . . so I stay on here, God of the Guts,' he said. 'That's what I am, God of the Guts.' His laugh wrecked itself on a shoal of wheezes; clutching his chest, he lay back.

He hunched himself up in the foetal position, breathing heavily. The bed creaked, and in a moment he was asleep. Craig sat quite still, his face expressionless, integrating all he had learnt or guessed about Dangerfield. At last he shrugged, rose, and slipped the P.E.S.T. harness from his shoulders; unzipping a pouch, he extracted two specimen jars. Standing them on the table, he poured the bloody contents of the clay bowls into one jar, one into the other. He set down the bowls, stoppered up the jars, and returned them to his pack.

'That solves his worry about disposing of the tribute for today,' Craig said aloud. 'And now, I think, a little helminthology.'

As he returned through the village, he noticed that several

155

pygmies lay motionless on the ground, glaring unwinkingly at each other over the two lacerated heaps of fur that were all remaining from the recent sacrifice. Circling them, he entered the overlander. It was unexpectedly good to breathe air free from the taint of fish and corruption.

'I think I've broken the ice with Dangerfield,' he announced to Barney and Tim. 'He's sleeping now. I'll go back over there in a couple of hours, to try and treat his "fiffin", and get him in a proper frame of mind for talking. Before that, let's eat; my stomach grows vociferous.'

'How about exploring the temple in the cliff, Craig?' Tim asked.

Craig smiled. 'If it *is* a temple,' he said. 'We'll let it keep till the morning. We don't want to upset the locals more than possible: though I admit they're a pretty phlegmatic lot, they might well take umbrage at our barging in there. And by morning I'm hoping Dangerfield will have given us more to go on.'

Over the meal, Barney told Craig of two weaver birds that he and Tim had snared while Craig was with Dangerfield.

'The younger one had about one thousand six hundred lice on it,' he said. 'Not an unusually large number for a bird living in a colony, and a youngster at that, not yet expert at preening. It goes to show that the usual complex ecological echelons are in full swing on Kakakakaxo.'

With their meal, they drank some of Barney's excellent Aldebaran wine—only the wine of heavy-gravity planets will travel happily through space. As they were lingering over the coffee, Tim volunteered to go over and sit with Dangerfield.

'Excellent idea,' Craig agreed, gratefully. 'I'll be over to relieve you when I've done some work here. On your way, take a look at what the pygmies in the clearing are up to. They appeared to be enjoying a motionless fight when I passed them. And be careful—night's coming down fast.'

Collecting his kit and a torch, Tim went out. Barney returned to his birds. Craig closeted himself in the tiny lab with his jars of entrails.

Outside, the curtains of night drew across the sky with sad finality. A chill moved in the dusk. Tim zipped up his jacket and looked about. Striking through the grass a yard away from him passed a lithe serpent resembling the *fer-de-lance*, that deadly snake with the beautiful name. Intent on its own affairs, it ignored Tim.

Cassivelaunus was sinking below the western horizon. Beneath the sheltering trees, darkness was already dominant;

a fish-scale gleamed here and there like a muddy star. In the treetops, where the weavers were settling to roost, making a perpetual uneasy noise, an entanglement of light and shade moved. Kept apart by their tethers, peke and bear lay staring at each other in disconsolate pairs, indifferent to day and night. Hardly a cayman-head moved; joylessly they sprawled beneath their crude shelters, not sleeping, not watching.

Five of them lay in the open. These were the ones Craig had noticed earlier. They waited with their heads raised. In the gloom, only their yellow-white throats, where a pulse beat like a slow drum, were clearly distinguishable. As he made his way across the clearing, giving them a wide berth, Tim saw that they were waiting, two round one body, three round the other body of the two creatures who had been sacrificed. They crouched tensely about the two little bundles of battered fur, glaring at one another, unmoving as Tim skirted them.

In Dangerfield's hut, he found the overturned oil-lamp and a jar of fish-oil with which to refill it. He trimmed the wick and lit it. Though it gave off a reek of fish, he preferred it to the glare of his solar torch.

Dangerfield slept peacefully. Tim covered the old man with a blanket and settled down beside him.

The silence came down. In the chill air moving through the hut, Tim thought he caught a breath of the glaciers only a few hundred miles away, north or south.

Over him moved a feeling of wonder, or perhaps it was what Barney had called 'the occult sense of secrecy' emanating from an unknown planet. Tim experienced it with the strange sense man still does not officially recognize; and the vast barriers of space, the forests of Kakakakaxo, and the old hermit sleeping with a head stuffed full of untapped knowledge were all part of it. He felt nothing of Craig's dislike of altering the nature of a planet, but suddenly he was impatient for the morning, when they would integrate and interpret the riddles they glimpsed around them.

A succession of leathery blows sounded outside. Jumping up, seizing his blaster, Tim stared out into the fishy shadows of the clearing. In the thick silence, the noises were crude and startling.

The three cayman-heads that had crouched over one of the mutilated pelts were fighting. They fought voicelessly, with a terrible skill. Though they were small, they battled like giants. Their main weapons were their long jaws, which they wielded as deftly as rapiers, parrying, thrusting, slashing, biting. When their jaws became wedged together in temporary deadlock, they used their claws as well. Each fought against the other two.

157

After some five minutes of this murderous activity, the three fell apart. Collapsing with their jaws along the ground they eyed each other motionlessly once more over the body of the sacrificed bear.

Later, the two pygmies crouching over the dead peke rose and also did battle, their ferocious duel ending with a sudden reversion into immobility. The deep sudden evening light made the battles more terrible. However much the five pygmies suffered from any wounds they received, they gave no sign of pain.

'They are fighting over the gutted bodies of their slaves. It's a point of honour with them.'

Tim turned from the window. Dangerfield had roused, woken by the thumping outside. He spoke tiredly, without opening his eyes. By a quirk of the dim lighting, his eye sockets and the hollows of his cheeks looked like deep holes.

'What are they fighting for?' Tim asked, instinctively dropping his voice.

'Every sunset they fight in the same way.'

'But *why*?'

'Tenacity . . . fight to the death. . . . Sometimes goes on all night,' the old man muttered. His voice trailed off.

'What does it all mean?' Tim asked, but Dangerfield had drifted back into sleep. The question faded unanswered into the darkness.

For an hour, the old man slept undisturbedly. Then he became restless, throwing off his blanket and tearing open his shirt, although it had grown chilly in the room. Tossing on the bed, he clawed repeatedly at his chest, coughing and groaning.

Bending over him anxiously, Tim noticed a patch of discoloured skin under one of the sick man's ribs. A small red spot was growing rapidly in size. As Tim stared, the spot reddened perceptibly, lapping at the surrounding grey flesh. He made to touch it and then thought better of it.

Dangerfield groaned and cried; Tim caught his wrist helplessly, steadying him against a crisis he did not understand. The growing patch on the chest formed a dark centre like a storm cloud. It oozed, then erupted thick blood, which trailed round the cage of the ribs to soak into the blanket below. In the middle of the bloody crater, something moved.

A flat armoured head appeared. A small brown insect—it resembled a caterpillar larva—heaved itself into sight, to lie exhausted on the discoloured flesh. Overcoming his disgust, Tim pulled a specimen jar from his pack and imprisoned the larva in it.

'I don't doubt that that's what Dangerfield calls a fiffin,' he

158

said. He discovered his hands were shaking. Sickly, he forced himself to disinfect and dress the hermit's wound. He was still bending over the bed when Craig came in to relieve him, carrying a tape recorder. Tim explained what had happened and staggered into the open air.

Outside, in the darkness, the five cayman-heads still fought their intermittent battle. On every plane, Tim thought, endless, meaningless strife continuing; strife and life—synonymous; he wanted to stop trembling.

The dead hour before the dawn: the time, on any planet in the universe, when the pulse of life falters before quickening. Craig, walking a little stiffly, entered the overlander with his tape recorder under one arm. Setting it down, he put coffee on the hot-point, rinsed his face with cold water, and roused the two sleepers.

'We shall be busy today,' he said, patting the recorder. 'We now have plenty of data on Kakakakaxo to work on—very dubious material, I might add. I recorded a long talk with Dangerfield, which I want you to hear.'

'How is he?' Tim asked as he slipped on his tunic.

'Physically, not in bad shape. Mentally, pretty sick. He's a manic-depressive, I should say. Suddenly he is chummy and communicative, then he's silent and hostile. An odd creature. . . . Not that you'd expect other than oddity after twenty years in this stagnation.'

'And the fiffin?'

'Dangerfield thinks it is the larval stage of a dung beetle, and says they bore through anything. He has had them in his legs before, but this one only just missed his lungs. The pain must have been intense, poor fellow. I gave him a light hypalgesic and questioned him before its effect wore off.'

Barney brought the boiling coffee off the stove, pouring it expertly into three beakers.

'All set to hear the play-back,' he said, lighting a mescahale.

Craig switched the recorder on. The reels turned slowly, re-creating his voice and Dangerfield's. Barney and Tim sat down to listen: Craig remained standing.

'Now that you are feeling better,' Craig-on-tape said, 'perhaps you could give me a few details about life on Kakakakaxo. How much of the language of these so-called pygmies have you been able to pick up? And just how efficiently can they communicate with each other?'

A long silence followed before Dangerfield replied.

'They're an old race, the pygmies,' he said at length. 'Their language has gradually worn down, like an old coin. I've

159

picked up all I can in twenty-odd years, but you can take it from me that most of the time, when they sound as if they're talking, they're just making noises. Nowadays, their language only expresses a few basic attitudes. Hostility. Fear. Hunger. Determination. . . .'

'What about love?' Craig prompted.

'I never heard one of them mention the subject. . . . They're very secretive about sex; I've never seen 'em doing it, and you can't tell male from female. They just lay their eggs in the river mud. . . . What was I saying? . . . Oh yes, about their manner of speech. You've got to remember, Hodges, that I'm the only human—the *only* one—ever to master this clicking they do. When my first would-be rescuers asked me what the natives called this place, I said "kakakakaxo", and now Kaka-kakaxo it is; that's the name on the star charts and I put it there. It used only to be called Cassivelaunus I. But I made a mistake, as I found later. "Kakakakaxo" is the pygmy answer to the question, "Where is this place?"; it means "where we die, where our elders died". That's funny, isn't it?'

'Have you been able to explain to them where you came from?'

'That's a bit difficult for them to grasp. They've settled for "Beyond the ice".'

'Meaning the glaciers to the north and south of this equatorial belt?'

'Yes; that's why they think I'm a god, because only gods can live beyond the ice. The pygmies know all about the glaciers. I've been able to construct a bit of their history from similar little items——'

'That was one of the next things I was going to ask you about,' Craig-on-tape said, as Barney-in-the-flesh handed round more coffee to the other listeners.

'The pygmies are an ancient race,' old Dangerfield said. 'They've no written history, of course, but you can tell they're old by their knowing about the glaciers. How would equatorial creatures know about glaciers, unless their race survived the last Ice Age? Then this ornamented cliff in which many of them live . . . You've seen it, I suppose—sort of temple—they could build nothing like that now. They haven't the skill. I had to help them build this hut. Their ancestors must have been really clever; these contemporary generations are just decadent.'

After a brief silence, Craig's voice came sceptically from the loudspeaker: 'We had an idea that the temple might have been built by another, vanished race. Any opinions on that?'

'You've got the wrong end of the stick, Hodges. The pygmies look on this temple as sacred; somewhere in the middle of it is what they refer to as "the Tomb of the Old Kings", and even *I* have never been allowed in there. They wouldn't behave like that if the place hadn't a special significance for them.'

'Do they still have kings now?'

'No. They don't have any sort of rule now, except each man for himself. These five of them fighting outside the hut, for instance; there's nobody to stop them, so they'll go on until they are all dead.'

'Why should they fight over the pelts?'

'It's a custom, that's all. They do it every night; sometimes one of them wins quickly, and then it's all over. They sacrifice their slaves in the day and squabble over their bodies at night.'

'Can you tell me why they attach such importance to these little animals—their slaves, as you call them? The relationship between pygmies and slaves has its puzzling aspects.'

'Oh, they don't attach much importance to the slaves. It's just that they make a habit of catching them in the forest, since they regard the pekes and bears as a menace to them; certainly their numbers have increased noticeably since I've been here.'

'Hm. I don't understand why the pygmies don't kill them. And why do they always keep the two groups separately? Anything significant in that?'

'Why should there be? The pekes and bears are supposed to fight together if they are allowed to intermingle, but whether or not that's true, I can't say. You mustn't expect reasons for everything these pygmies do . . . I mean, they're not rational in the way a man is.'

'As an ecologist, I find there is generally a reason for everything, however obscure that reason may be.'

'You do, do you?' The hermit's tone was pugnacious. 'If you want a reason, you'd better go and find one. All I'm saying is that in nineteen years here, I haven't found one. These pygmies just go by—well, instinct or accident, I suppose. . . . Look, it's no good staring at me with one eyebrow cocked. I don't like your superior ways, whether you're a good doctor or not. I thought you'd come here to make a solid.'

'You were saying the pygmies were not rational.'

'Nor they are. They're not like Earth animals or Earth men. They're living automatically on past glory. You can't do anything with 'em. I've tried. At first I thought I was getting somewhere. At least they acknowledged my authority. . . . It's a terrible thing to grow old. Look at my hands——'

Craig reached forward and switched the recorder off. He lit a mescahale and looked searchingly at Barney and Tim. Outside, beyond their heads, he could see the first light pencilling in the outlines of trees.

'That's about all that's relevant,' he said. 'The rest of Dangerfield's remarks were mainly autobiographical.'

'What do you make of it, Craig?' Barney Brangwyn asked.

They heard the first weaver birds wake and cry in the trees as Craig replied.

'Before Dangerfield crashed on Kakakakaxo, he was a salesman, a refrigerator salesman, I believe, hopping from one frontier planet to another. He was untrained as an observer.'

'That's so,' Barney agreed. 'You obviously feel as I do: that he has misinterpreted just about everything he has seen, which is easy enough to do on a strange planet, even if you are emotionally balanced. Nothing in his statement can be trusted; it's useless, except perhaps as case history.'

'I wouldn't go so far as to say that,' Craig remarked, with his usual caution. 'It's untrustworthy, yes, but not useless. For instance, he gives us several leads——'

'Sorry, but I'm adrift,' Tim Anderson said, getting up and pacing behind his chair. 'Why should Dangerfield be so wrong? Most of what he said sounded logical enough to me. Even if he had no anthropological or ecological training to begin with, he's had plenty of time to learn.'

'True, Tim, true,' Craig agreed. 'Plenty of time to learn correctly or to learn wrongly. I'm not trying to pass judgement on Dangerfield, but as you know there is hardly a fact in the universe which is not open to two or more interpretations. Dangerfield's attitude to the pygmies is highly ambivalent, a classical love–hate relationship. He wants to think of them as mere animals, because that would make them less something to be reckoned with; at the same time, he wants to think of them as intelligent beings with a great past, because that makes their acceptance of him as their god the more impressive.'

'And which are the pygmies in reality, animals or intelligent beings?' Tim asked.

Craig smiled.

'That is where our powers of observation and deduction come in,' he said.

The remark irritated Tim. Both Craig and Barney could be very uninformative. He turned to leave the overlander, to get away from them both and think things out for himself. As he went out, he remembered the jar with the fiffin larva in it; he had forgotten to place it in the overlander's tiny lab. Not wishing to give Craig cause for complaint, Tim slipped it in now.

Two jars were already clipped in the rack above the lab bench. Tim picked them up and examined them with interest. They contained two dead tapeworms; by the labels on the jars, he saw that Craig had extracted them from the entrails of the animals sacrificed the afternoon before. The cestodes, one of which came from the peke, one from the little bear, were identical: white tapes some twenty-four inches long, with suckers and hooks at the head end. Tim stared at them with interest before leaving the overlander.

Outside, the dawn was seeping through the thick trees. He drew the cold air down into his lungs; it was still flavoured with fish. The weaver birds were beginning to call or preen drowsily overhead. A few pygmies were about, moving sluggishly in the direction of the river, presumably in search of breakfast. Tim stood there, shivering slightly with the cold, thinking of the oddity of two diverse species harbouring the same species of tapeworm.

He moved into the clearing. The night-long fight over the dead animals was ended. Of the five pygmies involved, only one remained alive; it lay with the gutted bear in its jaws, unable to move away for its injuries. Three of its legs had been bitten off. Tim's horror and compunction dissolved as he saw the whole situation *sub specie aeternitatis,* with cruelty and kindness as mere facets of blind law, with pain and death an inevitable concomitant of life; perhaps he was acquiring something of Craig's outlook.

With a sudden inspiration, Tim picked up three of the dead pygmies, shouldered them, and, staggering slightly under their combined weight, carried them back to the overlander. At the door, he met Craig about to take some breakfast over to Dangerfield.

'Hello,' Craig exclaimed cordially. 'Bringing home the lunch?'

'I thought I'd do a little dissection,' Tim said guardedly. 'Just to see how these critters work.'

But once in the lab with his burden, he merely donned rubber gloves and slit open the pygmies' stomachs rapidly one by one, paying attention to nothing else. Removing the three intestinal sacs, he found that two of them were badly damaged by worms. Soon he had uncovered half a dozen roundworms, pink in coloration and still alive; they made vigorous attempts with their vestigial legs to climb from the crucible in which he placed them.

He went excitedly in to Barney Brangwyn to report his findings. Barney was sitting at the table, manipulating metal rods.

163

'This contradicts most of the laws of phylogeny,' Tim said, peeling off his gloves. 'According to Dangerfield, the pekes and bears both are recent arrivals on the evolutionary scene here: yet their endoparasites, which Craig has preserved in the lab, are well adapted to their environment inside the creatures, and in all respects resemble the ancient order of tapeworms parasitic in man. The roundworms from the cayman-heads, on the other hand, bear all the marks of being recent arrivals; they are still something more than virtual egg-factories, they retain traces of a previous more independent existence—and they cause unnecessary damage to their host, which is always a sign that a suitable *status quo* has yet to be reached between host and parasite.'

Barney raised his great bushy eyebrows approvingly and smiled at the eagerness on Tim's face.

'Very interesting indeed,' he said. 'What now, Doctor Anderson?'

Tim grinned, struck a pose, and said, in a creditable imitation of Craig's voice, 'Always meditate upon all the evidence, and especially upon those things you do not realize are evidence.'

'Fair enough,' Barney agreed, smiling. 'And while you're meditating, come and give me a hand on the roof with this patent fishing-rod I've made.'

'Another of your crazy ideas, Barney? What are you up to now?'

'We're going hunting. Come on! Your worms will keep.'

Getting up, he produced a long, telescopic rod which Tim recognized as one of their spare, collapsible aerials. The last and smallest section was extended, and to it Barney had just finished tying a sharp knife.

'It looks like a gadget for shaving by remote control,' Tim commented.

'Then appearances are deceptive. I'm still hankering after catching myself one of the local pets, without getting eaten at the same time.'

Climbing up the stepped pole that led into the tiny radio-room, Barney undogged the circular observation dome which gave an all-round view of their surroundings. With Tim following closely, he swung himself up and on to the roof of the overlander. He crawled forward on hands and knees.

'Keep down,' he muttered. 'If possible, I'd like this act of folly to go unobserved.'

Under a gigantic tree which spread its boughs over them, they were well concealed. Cassivelaunus was only just breaking through low cloud, and the clearing below was still fairly

164

silent. Lying flat on his stomach, Barney pulled out the sections of aerial until he had a rod several yards long. Steadying this weapon with Tim's aid, he pushed it forward.

The end of it reached to the nearest pygmy shelter. Outside the shelter, the two captive animals sat up, scratched, and watched with interest as the knife descended. Its blade hovered over the bear, shifted, and began rubbing gently back and forth across the thong which secured the little animal. In a moment, the thong was severed.

The bear was free. It looked owlishly about, hardly daring to move, and undecided as to what should happen next. It scratched its yellow poll in a parody of bewilderment. The neighbouring peke clucked encouragingly at it. A procession of pygmies appeared among the trees some distance away. Hearing them, the bear was spurred into action.

Grasping the aerial in its little black hands, the bear swarmed nimbly up it. It jumped on to the overlander roof and stood facing the men, apparently without fear. Barney retracted the aerial as Tim made coaxing noises. Unfortunately, this manoeuvre had been glimpsed by the returning pygmies. A clacking and growling began and swelled in volume. Other pygmies emerged from their shelters, scuttling towards the overlander and staring up.

The line of cayman-heads emerging from the forest wore the look of tired hunters, returning with the dawn. Over their shoulders, trussed with crude thongs, lay freshly captured bears and pekes, defeated by their opponents' superior turn of speed. These pygmies unceremoniously dropped their burdens and scuttled at a ferocious pace to the P.E.S.T. vehicle.

Alarmed by the sudden commotion, the weavers poured from their treetop homes, screeching.

'Let's get in,' Barney said hastily.

Picking up the little bear, which offered no resistance, he swarmed down inside the overlander, closely followed by Tim.

At first, the creature was overcome by its new surroundings. It stood on the table and rocked piteously from side to side. Recovering, it accepted milk and chattered to the two men vivaciously. Seen close, it bore little resemblance to a bear, except for its fur covering. It stood upright as the pygmies did, attempting to comb its bedraggled fur with its fingers. When Tim proffered his pocket-comb, it used that gratefully, wrenching diligently at the knots in its long coat, which was still wet with dew.

'Well, it's male, it's intelligent, it's quite a little more fetching than its overlords,' commented Tim. 'I hope you won't mind my saying so, Barney, but you have got what you wanted at considerable cost. The wolves are at the door howling for our blood.'

Looking through the window over Tim's shoulder, Barney saw that the pygmies, in ever-growing numbers, were surrounding the overlander, waving their claws, snapping their jaws. Their ire was roused. They looked, in the blue light, at once repulsive, comic, and malign. Barney thought to himself, 'I'm getting to hate those squalid bastards; they've neither mind nor style!'

Aloud he said, 'Too bad we've attracted so much attention. Evidently we have offended against a local law of property, if not propriety. Until they cool down, Craig's return is blocked; he'll have to tolerate Daddy Dangerfield for a while.'

Tim did not reply; before Craig returned, there was something else he wished to do. But first he had to get away from the overlander.

He stood uncertainly behind Barney's back, as the latter lit a mescahale and turned his attention again to his new pet. Seizing the chance, Tim climbed up into the radio nest unobserved, opened the dome, and stood once more on the roof of the overlander. Catching hold of an overhanging bough of the big tree, he pulled himself into it; working his way along, screened from the clacking mob below, he got well away from them before dropping down from a lower branch on to clear ground. Then he walked briskly in the direction of the cliff temple.

Dangerfield switched the projector off. As the colours died, he turned eagerly to Craig Hodges.

'There!' he exclaimed, with pride. 'What do you think of that?'

Craig stared at him. Though his chest was still bandaged, the hermit moved about easily. Modern healing treatments had speeded his recovery; he looked ten years younger than the old man who had yesterday suffered from fiffins. The excitement of the film he had just been showing had brought a flush to his cheeks.

'Well, what do you think of it?' he repeated, impatiently.

'I'm wondering what *you* think of it,' Craig said.

Some of the animation left Dangerfield. He looked round the stuffy confines of his hut, as if seeking a weapon. His jaw set.

'You've no respect,' he said. 'I took you for a civilized man, Hodges. But you've no respect, no reverence; I can tell by your tone of voice; you persist in trying to insult me in underhand ways. Even the Droxy solid makers recognized me for what I am.'

166

'You mean for what you like to think you are,' Craig said, rising. Dangerfield swung a heavy stick. Craig brought up his arm in an instinctive gesture of protection. The blow landed close to his elbow. He seized the stick, wrenching it from Dangerfield's grasp and tossing it out of the door.

The two men stood confronting each other. Dangerfield's gaze wavered, and he turned away.

'You insult me! You think I'm mad!' he muttered.

'Certainly your sanity is not a type that appeals to me,' Craig said.

He left the hut. Dangerfield sank into a chair.

Craig walked briskly across the clearing. The first indication Barney had of his return was when the besieging pygmies set up an increased noise outside. Looking through the windows of the overlander, Barney could see Craig approaching; he drew his blaster, alert for trouble. The cayman-heads were still in an aggressive mood.

Craig never hesitated. As he drew nearer, part of the rabble detached itself from the overlander and moved towards him, jaws creaking open. He ignored them. Without slackening his stride, he pushed between their scaly green bodies. Barney stood rigid with apprehension; he knew that if one of the pygmies moved to the attack, Craig would be finished. The mob would swarm over him before anyone could save him.

But the cayman-heads merely croaked excitedly as Craig passed. Jostling, shuffling their paws in the dirt, they let him get by. He mounted the steps of the overlander and entered unmolested.

The two men faced each other, Craig reading something of the relief and admiration on Barney's face.

'They must have guessed how stringy I'd taste,' he remarked; and that was all that was said.

He turned his attention to Barney's bear-creature, already christened Fido. The animal chattered perkily as Barney explained how he got it.

'I'll swear Fido has some sort of embryo language,' Barney said. 'In exchange for a good rub down with insecticide, he has let me examine his mouth and throat. Appearances suggest he's well enough equipped for speech. His I.Q.'s in good trim, too. Fido's quite a boy.'

'Show him how to use a pencil and paper, and see what he makes of it,' Craig suggested, stroking the little creature's yellow crest.

As Barney did so, he asked Craig what had kept him so long with Dangerfield.

'I was beginning to think the lost race of Kakakakaxo had got you,' he said, grinning.

'Nothing so interesting,' Craig said, 'although it has been an instructive session. Incidentally, I think we have an enemy in Dangerfield; he resents having had to accept our help; it lessens his feeling of superiority. He has been showing me a solid intended to impress me with the greatness of Dangerfield.'

'A documentary?'

'Anything but. A squalid solid made by Melmoth Solids Studios on Droxy, and supposedly based on the old boy's life. They presented him with a copy of it, and a viewer, as a souvenir. It's called "Curse of the Crocodile Men".'

'Ye Gods!' Barney exclaimed. 'I mustn't miss that when it's on circuit again! I'll bet you found it instructive.'

'In many ways, it was instructive,' Craig said. 'The script writers and director spent two days—just two days!—here on Kakakakaxo, talking to Dangerfield and "soaking up atmosphere", so-called, before returning to Droxy to cook up their *own* ideas on the subject. No other research was done.'

Barney laughed briefly. 'It sounds like that sort of thing. Who gets the girl?'

'There is a girl, of course, and Dangerfield gets her. She's a coy blonde stowaway on his spaceship. You know.'

'*I* know. Now tell me why you found it instructive.'

'It was all oddly familiar. After the usual preliminaries—spectacular spaceship crash on mountain-side, etcetera—a Tarzan-like Dangerfield is shown being captured by the bear-race, who stand six feet high and wear tin helmets, so help me. Dangerfield could not escape because the blonde twisted her ankle in the crash. You know how blondes are in solids.

'The pekes, for simplicity's sake, never appear. The bears are torturing our hero and heroine to death when the Crocodile Men raid the place and rescue him. The Crocodile Men are Melmoth's idea of our cayman-headed pals outside.'

'Stop giving me the trailer,' Barney said, feigning suspense. 'Get on with the plot. I want to know how the blonde makes out.'

'The Crocodile Men arrive in time to save her from a fate worse than a sprained ankle. And here's an interesting point—these Crocodile Men, according to the film, are a proud and ancient warrior race, come down in the world through the encroachment of the jungle. When they get Dangerfield back to their village by the river, they don't like him. They, too, are about to put him to death and ravage the blonde when he saves the leader's son from foot-rot or something equally decisive. From then on, the tribe treats him like a god, builds him a palace and all the rest of it.'

'To think I missed it! It sounds a real classic!' Barney cried, overdoing the sham disappointment. 'Perhaps we can get Dangerfield to give a matinée tomorrow. I can see how such a bit of personal aggrandizement would be dear to his heart.'

'It was very sad "B" Feature stuff,' Craig said. 'Nothing rang true. False dialogue, false settings. Even the blonde wasn't very attractive.'

'You don't surprise me,' Barney said. He sat silent for a minute, looking rather puzzledly into space, tweaking his beard. 'But it's odd that, considering this hokum was cooked up on Droxy, it all tallies surprisingly well in outline with what Dangerfield told you last night about the great past of the cayman-heads, their decline, and so on.'

'Exactly!' Craig agreed with satisfaction. 'Don't you see what that means, Barney? Nearly everything Dangerfield knows, or believes he knows, comes from a hack solid shot in a Droxy studio, rather than vice versa.'

They stared at one another with slowly growing amusement. Into both their minds, like the faint sound of a hunter's horn, came the reflection that all human behaviour, ultimately, is inexplicable; even the explicable is a mystery.

'Now you see why he shied away from us so violently at our first meeting,' Craig said. 'He's got almost no first-hand information on conditions here because he is afraid to go out looking for it. Knowing that, he was prepared to face Droxy film people—who would only be after a good story—but not scientists, who would want hard facts. Once I had him cornered, of course, he had to come out with what little he'd got, presumably hoping we would swallow it as the truth and go.'

Barney made clucking noises. 'He's probably no longer fit to remember what is truth, what lies. After nineteen years alone here the old boy must be quietly crazy.'

'Put the average person, with the mental conflicts to which we are all prey, away on an unlovely planet like Kakakakaxo for nineteen years,' Craig said, 'and he will inevitably finish as some sort of fantasist. I don't say he'll be insane, for a human mind is very resilient, but his realities will be those that make his existence tolerable.

'Fear has worked steadily on Dangerfield all this time. He's afraid of people, afraid of the cayman-heads, the Crocodile Men. He takes refuge from his terrors in fantasy. He's become a "B" feature god. And you couldn't budge him off the planet because he realizes subconsciously that reality would then

169

catch up with him. He has no choice but to remain here, in a place he loathes.'

Barney stood up.

'Okay, doctor,' he said. 'Diagnosis accepted. Brilliant field work, my congratulations. But—all we have collected so far are phantoms. Tell me where exactly P.E.S.T. work stands after you've proved the uselessness of our main witness. Presumably, at a standstill?'

'By no means,' Craig said. He pointed to Fido. The little bear was sitting quietly on the table cuddling the pencil.

He had drawn a crude picture on the paper. It depicted a room in which a bear and peke were locked in each other's arms, as if fighting.

A few minutes later, when Craig had gone into the laboratory with an assortment of coleoptera and anoplura culled from Dangerfield's hut, Barney saw the old hermit himself coming across to them, hobbling rapidly among the pygmy shelters with the aid of a stick. Barney called to Craig.

Craig emerged from the lab with a curious look on his face, at once pleased and secretive.

'Those three pygmy carcasses which Tim brought into the lab,' he said. 'I presume Tim cut them up—it certainly doesn't look like your work. Did he say anything to you about them?'

Barney explained the point Tim had made about the roundworms.

'Is there anything wrong?' he inquired.

'No, nothing, nothing,' Craig said in an odd voice, shaking his head. 'And that's all Tim said. . . . Where is he now by the way?'

'I've no idea, Craig; the boy's getting as secretive as you are. He must have gone outside for a breath of fish. Shall I give him a call?'

'Let's tackle Dangerfield first,' Craig said. 'I wonder what he's after now?'

They opened the door. Most of the cayman-heads had dispersed. The rest of them sped away when Dangerfield waved to them. The old man agitatedly refused to come into the overlander, his great nose standing out from his head like a parrot's beak as he shook his head. He wagged a finger angrily at them.

'I always knew no good would come of your prying,' he said. 'It was foolish of me to condescend to have anything to do with you. Now that young fellow of yours is being killed by the pygmies, and serve him right, too. But goodness knows what they'll do when they've tasted human flesh—tear us all

170

apart, I shouldn't wonder. I doubt if I'll be able to stop them, for all my power over them.'

He had not finished speaking before Craig and Barney had leapt from the overlander.

'Where's Tim? What's happened to him?' Craig asked. 'Tell us straightforwardly what you know.'

'Oh, I expect it'll be too late now,' said Dangerfield. 'I saw him slip into the cliff temple, the interfering young fool. Perhaps you will go away and leave me——'

But the two P.E.S.T. men were already running across the clearing, scattering brilliant birds about their heads. They jumped the shelters in their path. As they neared the temple in the cliff, they heard the clacking of the cayman-head pack. When they reached the heavily ornamented doorway, they saw that it and the corridor beyond were packed tight with the creatures, all fighting to get farther into the cliff.

'Tim!' bawled Barney. 'Tim! Are you there?'

The clacks and croaks died. The nearer cayman-heads turned to stare at the men, swinging their green snouts inquisitively round. In the silence, Barney shouted again, but no answer came. The pack continued its struggle to get into the temple.

'We can't massacre this lot,' Craig said, glaring at the cayman-heads before them. 'How're we going to get in there to Tim?'

'We can use the cry gas in the overlander!' Barney said. 'That will shift them.' He doubled back to their vehicle, and in a minute brought it bumping and growling across the clearing towards the temple. The high roof of the overlander snagged several branches, breaking the weavers' carefully constructed roof and sending angry birds flying in all directions. As the vehicle lumbered up, Craig unstrapped an outside container, pulling out a hose; the other end of it was already connected to internal gas tanks. Barney threw down two respirators. He emerged from the cab wearing one himself.

Donning his mask, Craig slung the spare over his arm and charged forward with the hose. The gas poured over the nearest cayman-heads, who fell back like magic, coughing and pawing at their goat-yellow eyes. The two men entered the temple; they moved down the corridor unopposed, impeded only by the bodies fighting to get out of their way. The croaking was deafening; in the dark and mist, Craig and Barney could hardly see ahead.

The corridor changed into a pygmy-sized tunnel, working gently upwards through the mountain. The two ecologists had to struggle past kicking bodies.

The supply of cry gas gave out. Craig and Barney stopped, peering at each other in surprise and some apprehension.

'I thought the gas tanks were full!' Craig said.

'They were. One of the cayman-heads must have bitten through the hose.'

'Or Dangerfield cut it. . . .'

Dropping the now useless hose, they ran forward. Their retreat was cut off: the cayman-heads at the mouth of the temple would have recovered by now, and be waiting for them. So they forged ahead, throwing off their respirators and pulling out blasters.

They turned a corner and stopped. This was the end of the trail. The tunnel broadened into a sort of ante-room, on the far side of which stood a wide wooden door. A group of cayman-heads had been scratching at this door; its panels were deeply marked by their claws. They turned and confronted the men. Tears, crocodile tears, stood in their eyes: a whiff of the gas had reached them, and served only to anger them. Six of them were there. They charged.

'Get 'em!' Barney yelled.

The dim chamber twitched with blinding blue-white light. Blue hieroglyphs writhed on the walls. Acoustics, in the roar of the blasters, went crazy. But the best hand weapon has its limitations, and the cayman-heads had speed on their side. Terrifying speed. They launched themselves like stones from a sling.

Barney scarcely had time to settle one of them than another landed squarely on his stomach. For a small creature, it was unbelievably solid. Every claw dug a point of pain through Barney's thick suit. He jerked his head back, falling backwards, bellowing, as the jaws gaped up to his face. Its grey tongue, its serried teeth, the stink of fish—he tried to writhe away from them as he fired the blaster against a leathery stomach. Even as he hit the ground, the creature fell from him, and in a dying kick knocked the weapon from his hand.

Before Barney could retrieve his blaster, two other assailants had landed on him, sending him sprawling. He was defenceless under their predatory claws.

The blue light leapt and crackled over him. An intolerable heat breathed above his cheek. The two cayman-heads rolled over to lie beside him, their bodies black and charred. Shakily, Barney stood up.

The wooden door had been flung open. Tim stood there, holstering the blaster which had saved Barney's life.

Craig had settled with his two attackers. They lay smouldering on the floor in front of him. He stood now, breathing deeply, with only a torn tunic sleeve to show for his trouble. The three men looked at each other, grimed and dishevelled. Craig was the first to speak.

'I'm getting too old for this sort of lark,' he said.

'I thought we'd had it then; thanks for the *Deus ex machina* act, Tim,' Barney said.

His beard had been singed, its edges turned a dusty brown. He felt his cheek tenderly where a blister was already forming. Sweat poured from him; the heat from the thermo–nuclear blasts had considerably raised the temperature in the ante-room.

'Why did I ever leave Earth?' he growled, stepping over one of the scaly corpses. 'To think I once turned down a safe job in a bank!'

'You got yourself into a nasty spot,' Craig said to Tim. The young man instantly became defensive.

'I'm sorry you came in after me,' he said. 'I was safe enough behind this door. I've been doing a little research on my own, Craig—you'd better come and see this place for yourself, now that you're here. I have discovered the Tomb of the Old Kings that Dangerfield told us about! You'll find it explains quite a lot we did not know.'

'How did you manage to get as far as this without the cayman-heads stopping you?' Craig asked, still stern.

'Most of them were clustered round the overlander calling for Barney's blood when I entered. They only started creeping up on me when I was actually inside. Are you coming to view the Tomb or not?'

They entered, Tim barred the door behind them before picking out the details of the long room with his torch beam. The proportions of the place were agreeable. Despite its low roof, it was architecturally impressive. Its builders had known what they were doing. Decoration had been left at a minimum, except for the elaborate door arch and the restrained fan-vaulting of the ceiling. Attention was focused on a large catafalque, upon which lay a row of several sarcophagi. Everywhere was deep in dust, and the air tasted stale and heavy.

Tim pointed to the line of little coffins, which were embellished with carvings.

'Here are the remains of the Old Kings of Kakakakaxo,' he said. 'And although I may have made myself a nuisance, I think I can claim that with their aid I have solved the mystery of the lost race of this planet.'

'Good!' Craig exclaimed encouragingly. 'I should be very interested to hear any deductions you have made.'

Tim looked at him penetratingly, suspecting sarcasm. Reassured, he continued.

'The mystery is like a jigsaw puzzle of which we already possessed most of the pieces. Dangerfield supplied nearly all of them—but he had fitted them together upside down. You see, to start with, there is not one lost race but two.'

'A nice build-up, Tim. Now let's have some facts,' Craig said.

'You can have facts. I'm showing them to you. This temple—and doubtless others like it all over the planet—was hewn out of the rock by two races who have engraved their own likenesses on these sarcophagi. Take a look at them! Far from being lost, the races have been under our noses all the time: they are the beings we call the pekes and bears. Their portraits are on the sarcophagi and their remains lie inside. Their resemblance to Earth animals has blinded us to what they really are—the ancient top-dogs of Kakakakaxo.'

Tim paused for their approval.

'I'm not surprised,' Barney said, to Tim's regret, turning from an inspection of the stone coffins. 'The bear people are brighter than the cayman-heads. As I see it, the caymans are pretty stodgy reptiles whom nature has endowed with armour but precious little else. I had already decided that that was another thing Great God Dangerfield had garbled: far from being an ancient race, the caymans are neoteric, upstart usurpers who have only recently appeared to oust the peke and bear people.

'Dangerfield said they know about the glaciers. Probably so. Probably they drifted down from the cold regions until the river brought them to these equatorial lands. As for the bear people—and I suspect the same goes for the pekes—their chatter, far from being the beginning of a language, is the decadent tail-end of one. They're the ancient races, already in decline when the parvenu pygmies descended on them and completed their disintegration.'

'The helminthological evidence supports this theory,' Tim said eagerly. He turned to Craig. 'The cayman-heads are too recent to have developed their own peculiar cestodes; they were almost as much harmed by interior parasites, the roundworms, as was Daddy by his fiffin. In a long-established host-parasite relationship, the amount of internal damage is minimal.'

'As was the case with the peke and bear cestodes I uncovered,' Craig agreed.

'Directly I saw these roundworms, I realized that Dangerfield's claim that the pygmies were the ancient species and

174

their "pets" the new might be the very reverse of the truth. I came over here hoping to find proof: and here it is.'

'It was a good idea, Tim,' Barney said heartily, 'but you shouldn't have done it alone—far too risky.'

'The habit of secretiveness is catching,' Tim said.

He looked challengingly at Craig, but the chief ecologist seemed not to have heard the remark. He marched to the door and put an ear to it. Barney and Tim listened too. The noise was faint at first; then it was unmistakable, a chorus of guttural grunts and croaks. The cry gas had dispersed. The pygmies were pressing back into the temple.

The noise took on weight and volume. It rose to a climax as claws struck the outside of the door. Craig stood back. The door shook. The cayman-heads had arrived in strength.

'This is not a very healthy place for us,' Craig said, turning back to the others. 'Is there another way out?'

They moved down the long room. Its walls were blank. Behind them, the door rattled and groaned dangerously. At the far end of the chamber stood a screen. There was a narrow door behind it. Barney pushed the screen away and tried the latch. It would not open. With one thrust of his great shoulders, Barney sent the door shattering back. Rusted hinges and lock left a red bitter powder floating in the air. Climbing over the door, they found themselves in a steep and narrow tunnel. They were forced to go in single file.

'I should hate to be caught in here,' Tim said. 'Do you think the cayman-heads will dare to enter the tomb-room? They seem to regard it as sacred.'

'Their blood's up. A superstition may not bother them,' said Barney.

'What I still don't understand,' Tim said, 'is why the cayman-heads care so much for the temple if it has nothing to do with them.'

'You probably never will,' Craig said. 'The temple must be a symbol of their new dominance for them, and one man's symbol is another man's enigma. I can hear that door splintering; let's get up this tunnel. It looks like a sort of priest's bunk-hole—it must lead somewhere.'

One behind the other, Barney leading, they literally crawled along the shaft. It bore steadily upwards at an angle of forty-five degrees. They seemed to crawl for ever. On all sides, the mountain made its presence felt, dwarfing them, threatening them, as if they were cestodes working their way up a vast alimentary canal.

The shaft at last turned upwards still more steeply. They

had climbed no distance at this difficult angle when Barney stopped.

'The way's blocked!' he exclaimed.

In the confined space, it sounded like a death sentence.

Tim shone his torch. The tunnel was neatly stoppered with a solid substance. 'Rock fall!' he whispered.

'We can't use a blaster on it in this space,' Barney said, 'or we'll cook ourselves.'

Craig passed a knife forward.

'Try the blockage with this,' he said, 'and see what it's made of. Is it rock?'

The stopper flaked reluctantly as Barney scraped. They examined the flakes; Tim recognized them first.

'This is guano—probably from bats!' he exclaimed. 'We must be very near the surface. Thank goodness for that!'

'It's certainly guano,' Craig agreed, 'but it's almost as hard as stone with age. You can see that a limestone shell has formed over the bottom of it: it may be hundreds of years old. Which means there may be many feet of guano between us and the surface.'

'Then we'll have to dig through it,' Barney said.

There was no alternative. It was an unpleasant task. The ill-smelling guano rapidly became softer as they dug upwards, until it reached the consistency of moist cake. They rolled lumps of it back between their knees, sending it bounding back, down into the mountain. It clung stickily to them, and emphasized the parallel between their situation and a cestode in an alimentary canal. They worked at it grimly, wishing they had kept the respirators.

Twenty-five feet of solid guano had to be tunnelled through before they struck air. Barney's head and shoulders emerged into a small cave. A dog-like creature backed growling into the open and ran for safety. It had taken over the cave for a lair long after the bats had deserted it.

Barney climbed out and the other two followed, to stand blinking in the intense blue light. They were plastered with filth. Hardly uttering a word to each other, they left the cave and drew in great breaths of fresh air.

Trees and high bushes surrounded them. The ground sloped steeply down to the left. When they had recovered, they began to descend in that direction. They were high up the mountainside; Cassivelaunus gleamed through the leaves about them.

'Thank goodness there's nothing else to keep us any longer on Kakakakaxo,' Barney said at last. 'We just file our report to P.E.S.T. H.Q., and we're off. Dangerfield will be glad to see the back of us. I wonder how he'll like the colonists? They'll come flocking in once H.Q. gets our clearance. They'll find a quiet little planet—there's nothing here the biggest fool can't handle.'

'Except Dangerfield,' Craig added.

'The man with the permanent wrong end of the stick!' Tim said, laughing. 'He will probably see out his days selling the colonists signed picture postcards of himself.'

They emerged from the trees suddenly. Before them was a cliff, steep and bush-studded. The ecologists went to its edge and looked down.

A fine panorama stretched out before them. In the distance, perhaps fifty miles away, a range of snow-covered mountains seemed to hang suspended in the blue air. Much nearer at hand, winding between mighty stretches of jungle, ran the cold, wide river. On the river banks, the ecologists could see cayman-heads basking in the sun; in the water, others swam and dived, performing miracles of agility.

'Look at them!' Craig exclaimed. 'They are really aquatic creatures. They've hardly had time to adapt properly to land life. The dominating factor of their lives remains—fish!'

'They've already forgotten us,' Barney said.

They could see the crude settlement was deserted. The overlander was partially discernible through the trees, but it took them an hour of scrambling down hazardous paths before they reached it. Never had the sight of it been more welcome.

Craig went round to look at the severed cry gas hose. It had been neatly chopped, as if by a knife. This was Dangerfield's work; he had expected to trap them in the temple. There was no sign of the old man anywhere. Except for the melancholy captives, sitting at the end of their tethers, the clearing was deserted.

'Before we go, I'm setting these creatures free,' Barney said.

He ran among the shelters, slashing at the thongs with a knife, liberating the pekes and the bears. As soon as they found themselves loose, they banded together and trotted off into the jungle without further ado. In a minute they were gone.

'Two more generations,' Barney said regretfully, 'and there probably won't be a bear or a peke on Kakakakaxo alive outside a zoo; the colonists will make shorter work of them than the cayman-heads have. As for the cayman-heads, I don't doubt they'll only survive by taking to the rivers again.'

'There's another contradiction,' Tim remarked thoughtfully, as they climbed into the overlander and Barney backed her through the trees. 'Dangerfield said the peke and bear people fought with each other if they had the chance, yet they went off peacefully enough together—and they ruled together once, as the Tomb proves. Where does the fighting come in?'

'As you say, Dangerfield always managed to grab the wrong end of the stick,' Craig answered. 'If you take the opposite end of what he told us, that's likely to be the truth. He has always been too afraid of his subjects to go out and look for the truth.'

'And I suppose he just doesn't use his eyes properly,' Tim remarked innocently.

'None of us do,' Craig said. 'Even you, Tim!'

Barney laughed.

'Here it comes,' he said. 'I warn you, Tim, the oracle is about to speak! In some ways you're very transparent, Craig; I've known ever since we left the Tomb of the Old Kings that you had something up your sleeve and were waiting for an appropriate moment before you produced it.'

'What is it, Craig?' Tim asked curiously.

Barney let Fido out of the overlander; the little creature hared off across the clearing with one brief backward wave, running to catch up its fellows.

'You were careless when you opened those three pygmies in the lab, Tim,' Craig said gently. 'I know that you were looking for something else, but if you had been less excited, you would have observed that the cayman-heads are parthenogenic. They have only one sex, reproducing by means of unfertilized eggs.'

Tim's face was a study in emotion, then he said in a small voice, 'How interesting! But does this revelation make any practical difference to the situation?'

Barney had no such inhibitions. He smote his forehead in savage surprise.

'Ah, I should have seen it myself! Parthenogenic, of course! Self-fertilizing! It's the obvious explanation of the lack of vanity or sexual inhibition which we noticed. I swear I would have hit on the answer myself, if I hadn't been so occupied with Fido and Co.'

He climbed heavily into the driver's seat, slamming the door. The air-conditioning sucked away the invading smell of fish at once.

'Yes, you have an interesting situation on Kakakakaxo,' Craig continued. 'Try and think how difficult it would be for such a parthenogenic species to visualize a bisexual species like man. The concept would probably be beyond them; it is easier for us to visualize a four-dimensional race. Nevertheless, the cayman-heads managed to do something of the sort—they're not so brainless as you may think, for all their limitations. What is more, they grasped the one fatal weakness of

178

the bisexual system: that if you keep the two sexes apart, the race dies out.

'Without realizing clearly what they were doing, they did just that, separating male and female. That is how they manage to hold this place. Of course, no scheme is perfect, and quite a few of both sexes escaped into the forest to breed there.'

Barney revved the engine, moving the overlander forward, leaving Tim to ask the obvious question.

'Yes,' Craig said, 'As Fido tried to explain to us with his drawing, the "bears" are the males, the "pekes" the females of one species. It just happens to be a dimorphous species, the sexes varying in size and configuration, or we would have guessed the truth at once. The cayman-heads, in their dim way, knew. They tackled the whole business of conquest in a new way that only a parthenogenic race would think of—they segregated the sexes. That is how they managed to supersede the intellectually superior peke–bear race: by applying the old law of "Divide and conquer" in a new way! I'm now trying to make up my mind whether that is crueller or kinder, in the long run, than slaughter. . . .'

Tim whistled.

'So when Dangerfield thought the pekes and bears were fighting,' he said, 'they were really copulating! And of course the similar cestodes you found in their entrails would have put you on the right track; I ought to have twigged it myself!'

'It must be odd to play God to a world about which you really know or care so little,' Barney commented, swinging the big vehicle down the track in the direction of their space ship.

'It must indeed,' Craig agreed, but he was not thinking of Dangerfield.

The old man hid behind a tree, silently watching the overlander leave. He shook his head sadly, braced himself, hobbled back to his hut. His servants would have to hunt in the jungles before he got today's offering of entrails. He shivered as he thought of those two symbolic and steaming bowls. He shivered for a long time. He was cold; he was old; from the sky he had come; to the sky he would one day return. But before that, he was going to tell everyone what he really thought of them.

Going to tell them how he hated them.

How he despised them.

How he needed them.

OLD HUNDREDTH

THE road climbed dustily down between trees as symmetrical as umbrellas. Its length was punctuated at one point by a musicolumn standing on the sandy verge. From a distance, the column was only a faint stain in the air. As sentient creatures neared it, their psyches activated it, it drew on their vitalities, and then it could be heard as well as seen. Their presence made it flower into pleasant noise, instrumental or chant.

All this region was called Ghinomon, for nobody lived here any more, not even the odd hermit Impure. It was given over to grass and the weight of time. Only a few wild goats activated the musicolumn nowadays, or a scampering vole wrung a brief chord from it in passing.

When old Dandi Lashadusa came riding down that dusty road on her baluchitherium, the column began to intone. It was just an indigo trace on the air, hardly visible, for it represented only a bonded pattern of music locked into the fabric of that particular area of space. It was also a transubstantio-spatial shrine, the eternal part of a being that had dematerialized itself into music.

The baluchitherium whinnied, lowered its head, and sneezed on to the gritty road.

'Gently, Lass,' Dandi told her mare, savouring the growth of the chords that increased in volume as she approached. Her long nose twitched with pleasure as if she could feel the melody along her olfactory nerves.

Obediently, the baluchitherium slowed, turning aside to crop fern, although it kept an eye on the indigo stain. It liked things to have being or not to have being; these half-and-half objects disturbed it, though they could not impair its immense appetite.

Dandi climbed down her ladder on to the ground, glad to feel the ancient dust under her feet. She smoothed her hair and stretched as she listened to the music.

She spoke aloud to her mentor, half the world away, but he was not listening. His mind closed to her thoughts, he muttered an obscure exposition that darkened what it sought to clarify.

'. . . useless to deny that it is well-nigh impossible to improve anything, however faulty, that has so much tradition behind it. And the origins of your bit of metricism are indeed embedded in such a fearful antiquity that we must needs——'

'Tush, Mentor, come out of your black box and forget your hatred of my "metricism" a moment,' Dandi Lashadusa said, cutting her thought into his. 'Listen to the bit of "metricism" I've found here, look at where I have come to, let your argument rest.'

She turned her eyes about, scanning the tawny rocks near at hand, the brown line of the road, the distant black and white magnificence of ancient Oldorajo's town, doing this all for him, tiresome old fellow. Her mentor was blind, never left his cell in Peterbroe to go farther than the sandy courtyard, hadn't physically left that green cathedral pile for over a century. Womanlike, she thought he needed change. Soul, how he rambled on! Even now, he was managing to ignore her and refute her.

'. . . for consider, Lashadusa woman, nobody can be found to father it. Nobody wrought or thought it, phrases of it merely *came* together. Even the old nations of men could not own it. None of them knew who composed it. An element here from a Spanish pavan, an influence here of a French psalm tune, a flavour here of early English carol, a savour there of later German chorals. Nor are the faults of your bit of metricism confined to bastardy. . . .'

'Stay in your black box then, if you won't see or listen,' Dandi said. She could not get into his mind; it was the Mentor's privilege to lodge in her mind, and in the minds of those few other wards he had, scattered round Earth. Only the mentors had the power of being in another's mind—which made them rather tiring on occasions like this, when they would not get out of it. For over seventy years, Dandi's mentor had been persuading her to die into a dirge of his choosing (and composing). Let her die, yes, let her transubstantiospatialize herself a thousand times! His quarrel was not with her decision but her taste, which he considered execrable.

Leaving the baluchitherium to crop, Dandi walked away from the musicolumn towards a hillock. Still fed by her steed's psyche, the column continued to play. Its music was of a simplicity, with a dominant-tonic recurrent bass part suggesting pessimism. To Dandi, a savant in musicolumnology, it yielded other data. She could tell to within a few years when its founder had died and also what kind of a creature, generally speaking, he had been.

Climbing the hillock, Dandi looked about. To the south where the road led were low hills, lilac in the poor light. There

181

lay her home. At last she was returning, after wanderings covering half a century and most of the globe.

Apart from the blind beauty of Oldorajo's town lying to the west, there was only one landmark she recognized. That was the Involute. It seemed to hang iridial above the ground a few leagues on; just to look on it made her feel she must at once get nearer.

Before summoning the baluchitherium, Dandi listened once more to the sounds of the musicolumn, making sure she had them fixed in her head. The pity was her old fool wise man would not share it. She could still feel his sulks floating like sediment through his mind.

'Are you listening now, Mentor?'

'Eh? An interesting point is that back in 1556 by the old pre-Involutary calendar your same little tune may be discovered lurking in Knox's Anglo-Genevan Psalter, where it espoused the cause of the third psalm——'

'You dreary old fish! Wake yourself! How can you criticize my intended way of dying when you have such a fustian way of living?'

This time he heard her words. So close did he seem that his peevish pinching at the bridge of his stuffy old nose tickled hers too.

'What are you doing *now*, Dandi?' he inquired.

'If you had been listening, you'd know. Here's where I am, on the last Ghinomon plain before Crotheria and home.' She swept the landscape again and he took it in, drank it almost greedily. Many mentors went blind early in life shut in their monastic underwater dens; their most effective visions were conducted through the eyes of their wards.

His view of what she saw enriched hers. He knew the history, the myth behind this forsaken land. He could stock the tired old landscape with pageantry, delighting her and surprising her. Back and forward he went, flicking her pictures; the Youdicans, the Lombards, the Ex-Europa Emissary, the Grites, the Risorgimento, the Involuters—and catchwords, costumes, customs, courtesans, pelted briefly through Dandi Lashadusa's mind. Ah, she thought admiringly, who could truly live without these priestly, beastly, erudite, erratic mentors?

'Erratic?' he inquired, snatching at her lick of thought. 'A thousand years I live, for all that time to absent myself from the world, to eat mashed fish here with my brothers, learning history, studying *rapport*, sleeping with my bones on stones— a humble being, a being in a million, a mentor in a myriad, and your standards of judgement are so mundane you find no

182

stronger label for me than erratic? Fie, Lashadusa, bother me no more for fifty years!'

The words nattered and squeaked in her head as if she spoke herself. She felt his old chops work phantom-like in hers, and half in anger half in laughter called aloud, 'I'll be dead by then!'

He snicked back hot and holy to reply, 'And another thing about your footloose swan song—in Marot and Beza's Gene-van Psalter of 1551, Old Time, it was musical midwife to the one hundred and thirty-fourth psalm. Like you, it never seemed to settle!' Then he was gone.

'Pooh!' Dandi said. She whistled Lass.

Obediently the great rhino-like creature, eighteen feet high at the shoulder, ambled over. The musicolumn died as the mare left it, faded, sank to a whisper, silenced: only the purple stain remained, noiseless, in the lonely air. Lass reached Dandi. Lowering its great Oligocene head, it nuzzled its mistress's hand. She climbed the ladder on to that ridged plateau of back.

They made contentedly towards the Involute, lulled by the simple and intricate feeling of being alive.

Night was settling in now, steady as snow. Hidden behind banks of mist, the sun prepared to set. But Venus was high, a gallant half-crescent four times as big as the Moon had been before the Moon, spiralling farther and farther from Earth, had shaken off its parent's clutch to go dance round the sun, a second Mercury. Even by that time Venus had been moved by gravito-traction into Earth's orbit, so that the two sister worlds circled each other as they circled the sun.

The stamp of that great event still lay everywhere, its tokens not only in the crescent in the sky. For Venus put a strange spell on the hearts of man, and a more penetrating displacement in his genes. Even when its atmosphere was transformed into a muffled breathability, it remained an alien world; against logic, its opportunities, its possibilities, were its own. It shaped men, just as Earth had shaped them.

On Venus, men bred themselves anew.

And they bred the so-called Impurse. They bred new plants new fruits, new creatures—original ones, and duplications of creatures not seen on Earth for aeons past. From one line of these familiar strangers Dandi's baluchitherium was descended. So, for that matter, was Dandi.

The huge creature came now to Involute, or as near as it cared to get. Again it began to crop at thistles, thrusting its nose through dewy spiders' webs and ground mist.

'Like you, I'm a vegetarian,' Dandi said, climbing down to the ground. A grove of low fruit trees grew nearby; she reached up into the branches, gathered and ate, before turning to inspect the Involute. Already her spine tingled at the nearness of it; awe, loathing and love made a part-pleasant sensation near her heart.

The Involute was not beautiful. True, its colours changed with the changing light, yet the colours were fish-cold, for they belonged to another universe. Though they reacted to dusk and dawn, Earth had no stronger power over them. They pricked the eyes. Perhaps too they were painful because they were the last signs of materialist man. Even Lass moved uneasily before that ill-defined lattice, the upper limits of which were lost in thickening gloom.

'Don't fear,' Dandi said. 'There's an explanation for this, old girl.' She added sadly, 'There's an explanation for everything, if we can find it.'

She could feel all the personalities in the Involute. It was a frozen screen of personality. All over the old planet the structures stood, to shed their awe on those who were left behind. They were the essence of man. They were man—all that remained of him.

When the first flint, the first shell, was shaped into a weapon, that action shaped man. As he moulded and complicated his tools, so they moulded and complicated him. He became the first scientific animal. And at last, via information theory and great computers, he gained knowledge of all his parts. He formed the Laws of Integration, which reveal all beings as part of a pattern and show them their part in the pattern. There is only the pattern, the pattern is all the universe, creator and created. For the first time, it became possible to duplicate that pattern artificially; the transubstantio-spatializers were built.

All mankind left their strange hobbies on Earth and Venus and projected themselves into the pattern. Their entire personalities were merged with the texture of space itself. Through science, they reached immortality.

It was a one-way passage.

They did not return. Each Involute carried thousands or even millions of people. There they were, not dead, not living. How they exulted or wept in their transubstantiation, nobody left could say. Only this could be said: man had gone, and a great emptiness was fallen over the Earth.

'Your thoughts are heavy, Dandi Lashadusa. Get you home.' Her mentor was back in her mind. She caught the feeling of his moving round and round in his coral-formed cell.

'I must think of man,' she said.

'Your thoughts mean nothing, do nothing.'

'Man created us; I want to consider him in peace.'

'He only shaped a stream of life that was always entirely out of his control. Forget him. Get on to your mare and ride home.'

'Mentor——'

'Get home, woman. Moping does not become you. I want to hear no more of your swan song, for I've given you my final word on that. Use a theme of your own, not of man's. I've said it a million times and I say it again.'

'I wasn't going to mention my music. I was only going to tell you that. . . .'

'What then?' His thought was querulous. She felt his powerful tail tremble, disturbing the quiet water of his cell.

'I don't know. . . .'

'Get home then.'

'I'm lonely.'

He shot her a picture from another of his wards before leaving her. Dandi had seen this ward before in similar dreamlike glimpses. It was a huge mole creature, still boring underground as it had been for the last twenty years. Occasionally it crawled through vast caves; once it swam in a subterranean lake; most of the while it just bored through rock. It's motivations were obscure to Dandi, although her mentor referred to it as 'a geologer'. Doubtless if the mole was vouchsafed occasional glimpses of Dandi and her musicolumnology, it would find her as baffling. At least the mentor's point was made: loneliness was psychological, not statistical.

Why, a million personalities glittered almost before her eyes!

She mounted the great baluchitherium mare and headed for home. Time and old monuments made glum company.

Twilight now, with just one streak of antique gold left in the sky, Venus sweetly bright, and stars peppering the purple. A fine night for being alive on, particularly with one's last bedtime close at hand.

And yes, for all her mentor said, she was going to turn into that old little piece derived from one of the tunes in the 1540 *Souter Liedekens*, that splendid source of Netherlands folk music. For a moment, Dandi Lashadusa chuckled almost as eruditely as her mentor. The sixteenth-century Old Time, with the virtual death of plainsong and virtual birth of the violin, was most interesting to her. Ah, the richness of facts, the texture of man's brief history! Pure joy! Then she remembered herself.

After all, she was only a megatherium, a sloth as big as an

elephant, whose kind had been extinct for millions of years until man reconstituted a few of them in the Venusian experiments. Her modifications in the way of fingers and enlarged brain gave her no real qualification to think up to man's level.

Early next morning they arrived at the ramparts of the town Crotheria where Dandi lived. The ubiquitous goats thronged about them, some no bigger than hedgehogs, some almost as big as hippos—what madness in his last days provoked man to so many variations on one undistinguished caprine theme?—as Lass and her mistress moved up the last slope and under the archway.

It was good to be back, to push among the trails fringed with bracken, among the palms, oaks, and treeferns. Almost all the town was deeply green and private from the sun, curtained by swathes of Spanish moss. Here and there were houses—caves, pits, crude piles of boulders, or even genuine man-type buildings, grand in ruin. Dandi climbed down, walking ahead of her mount, her long hair curling in pleasure. The air was cool with the coo of doves or the occasional bleat of a merino.

As she explored familiar ways, though, disappointment overcame her. Her friends were all away, even the dreamy bison whose wallow lay at the corner of the street in which Dandi lived. Only pure animals were here, rooting happily and mindlessly in the lanes, beggars who owned the Earth. The Impures—descendants of the Venusian experimental stock—were all absent from Crotheria.

That was understandable. For obvious reasons, man had increased the abilities of herbivores rather than carnivores. After the Involution, with man gone, these Impures had taken to his towns as they took to his ways, as far as this was possible to their natures. Both Dandi and Lass, and many of the others, consumed massive amounts of vegetable matter every day. Gradually a wider and wider circle of desolation grew about each town (the greenery in the town itself was sacrosanct), forcing a semi-nomadic life on to its vegetarian inhabitants.

This thinning in its turn led to a decline in the birth rate. The travellers grew fewer, the towns greener and emptier; in time they had become little oases of forest studding the grassless plains.

'Rest here, Lass,' Dandi said at last, pausing by a bank of brightly flowering cycads. 'I'm going into my house.'

A giant beech grew before the stone façade of her home, so close that it was hard to determine whether it did not help support the ancient building. A crumbling balcony jutted from the first floor. Reaching up, Dandi seized the balustrade and hauled herself on to the balcony.

This was her normal way of entering her home, for the ground floor was taken over by goats and hogs, just as the second floor had been appropriated by doves and parakeets. Trampling over the greenery self-sown on the balcony, she moved into the front room. Dandi smiled. Here were her old things, the broken furniture on which she liked to sleep, the vision screens on which nothing could be seen, the heavy manuscript books in which, guided by her know-all mentor, she wrote down the outpourings of the musicolumns she had visited all over the world.

She ambled through to the next room.

She paused, her peace of mind suddenly shattered by danger.

A brown bear stood there. One of its heavy hands was clenched over the hilt of a knife.

'I am no vulgar thief,' it said, curling its thick black lips over the syllables: 'I am an archaeologer. If this is your place, you must grant me permission to remove the man things. Obviously you have no idea of the worth of some of the equipment here. We bears require it. We must have it.'

It came towards her, panting doggy fashion with its jaws open. From under bristling eyebrows gleamed the lust to kill.

Dandi was frightened. Peaceful by nature, she feared the bears above all creatures for their fierceness and their ability to organize. The bears were few: they were the only creatures to show signs of wishing to emulate man's old aggressiveness.

She knew what the bears did. They hurled themselves through the Involutes to increase their power; by penetrating those patterns, they nourished their psychic drive, so the Mentor said. It was forbidden. They were transgressors. They were killers.

'Mentor!' she screamed.

The bear hesitated. As far as he was concerned, the hulking creature before him was merely an obstacle in the way of progress, something to be thrust aside without hate. Killing would be pleasant but irrelevant; more important items remained to be done. Much of the equipment housed here could be used in the rebuilding of the world, the world of which bears had such high haphazard dreams. Holding the knife threateningly, he moved forward.

The Mentor was in Dandi's head, answering her cry, seeing through her eyes, though he had no sight of his own. He scanned the bear and took over her mind instantly, knifing himself into place like a guillotine.

No longer was he a blind old dolphin lurking in one cell of a cathedral pile of coral under tropical seas, a theologer, an inculcator of wisdom into feebler minded beings. He was a killer more savage than the bear, keen to kill anything that might covet the vacant throne once held by men. The mere thought of men could send this mentor into shark-like fury at times.

Caught up in his fury, Dandi found herself advancing. For all the bear's strength, she could vanquish it. In the open, where she could have brought her heavy tail into action, it would have been an easy matter. Here, her weighty forearms must come into play. She felt them lift to her mentor's command as he planned for her to clout the bear to death.

The bear stepped back, awed by an opponent twice its size, suddenly unsure.

She advanced.

'No! Stop!' Dandi cried.

Instead of fighting the bear, she fought her Mentor, hating his hate. Her mind twisted, her dim mind full of that steely fishy one, as she blocked his resolution.

'I'm for peace!' she cried.

'Then kill the bear!'

'I'm for peace, not killing!'

She rocked back and forth. When she staggered into a wall, it shook; dust spread in the old room. The Mentor's fury was terrible to feel.

'Get out quickly!' Dandi called to the bear.

Hesitating, it stared at her. Then it turned and made for the window. For a moment it hung with its shaggy shabby hindquarters in the room. Momentarily she saw it for what it was, an old animal in an old world, without direction. It jumped. It was gone. Goats blared confusion on its retreat.

'Bitch!' screamed the Mentor. Insane with frustration, he hurled Dandi against the doorway with all the force of his mind.

Wood cracked and splintered. The lintel came crashing down. Brick and stone shifted, grumbled, fell. Powdered filth billowed up. With a great roar, one wall collapsed. Dandi struggled to get free. Her house was tumbling about her. It had never been intended to carry so much weight, so many centuries.

She reached the balcony and jumped clumsily to safety, just as the building avalanched in on itself, sending a great cloud of plaster and powdered mortar into the overhanging trees.

For a horribly long while the world was full of dust, goat bleats, and panic-stricken parakeets.

Heavily astride her baluchitherium once more, Dandi Lasha-usa headed back to the empty region called Ghinomon. She fought her bitterness, trying to urge herself towards resignation.

All she had was destroyed—not that she set store by possessions: that was man trait. Much more terrible was the knowledge that her Mentor had left her for ever; she had transgressed too badly to be forgiven this time.

Suddenly she was lonely for his pernickety voice in her head, for the wisdom he fed her, for the scraps of dead knowledge he tossed her—yes, even for the love he gave her. She had never seen him, never could: yet no two beings could have been more intimate.

She missed too those other wards of his she would glimpse no more: the mole creature tunneling in Earth's depths, the seal family that barked with laughter on a desolate coast, a senile gorilla that endlessly collected and classified spiders, an aurochs—seen only once, but then unforgettably—that lived with smaller creatures in an Arctic city it had helped build in the ice.

She was excommunicated.

Well, it was time for her to change, to disintegrate, to transsubstantiate into a pattern not of flesh but music. That discipline at least the Mentor had taught and could not take away.

'This will do, Lass,' she said.

Her gigantic mount stopped obediently. Lovingly she patted its neck. It was young; it would be free.

Following the dusty trail, she went ahead, alone. Somewhere far off one bird called. Coming to a mound of boulders, Dandi squatted among gorse, the points of which could not prick through her thick old coat.

Already her selected music poured through her head, already it seemed to loosen the chemical bonds of her being.

Why should she not choose an old hymn tune? She was an antiquarian. Things that were gone solaced her for things that were to come.

In her dim way, she had always stood out against her Mentor's absolute hatred of men. The thing to hate was hatred. Men in their finer moments had risen above hate. Her death psalm was an instance of that—a multiple instance, for it had been fingered and changed over the ages, as the Mentor himself insisted, by men of a variety of races, all with their minds directed to worship rather than hate.

Locking herself into thought disciplines, Dandi began to dissolve. Man had needed machines to help him to do it, to fit into the Involutes. She was a lesser animal: she could unbutton

189

herself into the humbler shape of a musicolumn. It was just a matter of *rearranging*—and without pain she formed into a pattern that was not a shaggy megatherium body . . . but an indigo column, hardly visible. . . .

Lass for a long while cropped thistle and cacti. Then she ambled forward to seek the hairy creature she fondly—and a little condescendingly—regarded as her equal. But of the sloth there was no sign.

Almost the only landmark was a faint violet-blue dye in the air. As the baluchitherium mare approached, a sweet old music grew in volume from the dye. It was a music almost as old as the landscape itself and certainly as much travelled, a tune once known to men as The Old Hundredth. And there were voices singing: 'All creatures that on Earth do dwell. . . .'

NEL BESTSELLERS

Crime

T013 332	CLOUDS OF WITNESS		Dorothy L. Sayers	40p
T016 307	THE UNPLEASANTNESS AT THE BELLONA CLUB		Dorothy L. Sayers	40p
T021 548	GAUDY NIGHT		Dorothy L. Sayers	40p
T026 698	THE NINE TAILORS		Dorothy L. Sayers	50p
T026 671	FIVE RED HERRINGS		Dorothy L. Sayers	50p
T015 556	MURDER MUST ADVERTISE		Dorothy L. Sayers	40p

Fiction

T018 520	HATTER'S CASTLE		A. J. Cronin	75p
T013 944	CRUSADER'S TOMB		A. J. Cronin	60p
T013 936	THE JUDAS TREE		A. J. Cronin	50p
T015 386	THE NORTHERN LIGHT		A. J. Cronin	50p
T026 213	THE CITADEL		A. J. Cronin	80p
T027 112	BEYOND THIS PLACE		A. J. Cronin	60p
T016 609	KEYS OF THE KINGDOM		A. J. Cronin	50p
T027 201	THE STARS LOOK DOWN		A. J. Cronin	90p
T018 539	A SONG OF SIXPENCE		A. J. Cronin	50p
T001 288	THE TROUBLE WITH LAZY ETHEL		Ernest K. Gann	30p
T003 922	IN THE COMPANY OF EAGLES		Ernest K. Gann	30p
T023 001	WILDERNESS BOY		Stephen Harper	35p
T017 524	MAGGIE D		Adam Kennedy	60p
T022 390	A HERO OF OUR TIME		Mikhail Lermontov	45p
T025 691	SIR, YOU BASTARD		G. F. Newman	40p
T022 536	THE HARRAD EXPERIMENT		Robert H. Rimmer	50p
T022 994	THE DREAM MERCHANTS		Harold Robbins	95p
T023 303	THE PIRATE		Harold Robbins	95p
T022 968	THE CARPETBAGGERS		Harold Robbins	£1.00
T016 560	WHERE LOVE HAS GONE		Harold Robbins	75p
T023 958	THE ADVENTURERS		Harold Robbins	£1.00
T025 241	THE INHERITORS		Harold Robbins	90p
T025 276	STILETTO		Harold Robbins	50p
T025 268	NEVER LEAVE ME		Harold Robbins	50p
T025 292	NEVER LOVE A STRANGER		Harold Robbins	90p
T022 226	A STONE FOR DANNY FISHER		Harold Robbins	80p
T025 284	79 PARK AVENUE		Harold Robbins	75p
T025 187	THE BETSY		Harold Robbins	80p
T020 894	RICH MAN, POOR MAN		Irwin Shaw	90p

Historical

T022 196	KNIGHT WITH ARMOUR		Alfred Duggan	50p
T022 250	THE LADY FOR RANSOM		Alfred Duggan	50p
T015 297	COUNT BOHEMOND		Alfred Duggan	50p
T017 958	FOUNDING FATHERS		Alfred Duggan	50p
T017 753	WINTER QUARTERS		Alfred Duggan	50p
T021 297	FAMILY FAVOURITES		Alfred Duggan	50p
T022 625	LEOPARDS AND LILIES		Alfred Duggan	60p
T019 624	THE LITTLE EMPERORS		Alfred Duggan	50p
T020 126	THREE'S COMPANY		Adam Hardy	50p
T021 300	FOX 10: BOARDERS AWAY			35p

Science Fiction

T016 900	STRANGER IN A STRANGE LAND		Robert Heinlein	75p
T020 797	STAR BEAST		Robert Heinlein	35p
T017 451	I WILL FEAR NO EVIL		Robert Heinlein	80p
T026 817	THE HEAVEN MAKERS		Frank Herbert	35p
T027 279	DUNE		Frank Herbert	90p
T022 854	DUNE MESSIAH		Frank Herbert	60p
T023 974	THE GREEN BRAIN		Frank Herbert	35p
T012 859	QUEST FOR THE FUTURE		A. E. Van Vogt	35p

T015	270	THE WEAPON MAKERS	A. E. Van Vogt	30p
T023	265	EMPIRE OF THE ATOM	A. E. Van Vogt	40p
T017	354	THE FAR-OUT WORLDS OF A. E. VAN VOGT	A. E. Van Vogt	40p

War

T027	066	COLDITZ: THE GERMAN STORY	Reinhold Eggers	50p
T009	890	THE K BOATS	Don Everett	30p
T020	854	THE GOOD SHEPHERD	C. S. Forester	35p
T012	999	P.Q. 17 – CONVOY TO HELL	Lund & Ludlam	30p
T026	299	TRAWLERS GO TO WAR	Lund & Ludlam	50p
T010	872	BLACK SATURDAY	Alexander McKee	30p
T020	495	ILLUSTRIOUS	Kenneth Poolman	40p
T018	032	ARK ROYAL	Kenneth Poolman	40p
T027	198	THE GREEN BERET	Hilary St George Saunders	50p
T027	171	THE RED BERET	Hilary St George Saunders	50p

Western

T016	994	EDGE No 1: THE LONER	George Gilman	30p
T024	040	EDGE No 2: TEN THOUSAND DOLLARS AMERICAN	George Gilman	35p
T024	075	EDGE No 3: APACHE DEATH	George Gilman	35p
T024	032	EDGE No 4: KILLER'S BREED	George Gilman	35p
T023	990	EDGE No 5: BLOOD ON SILVER	George Gilman	35p
T020	002	EDGE No 14: THE BIG GOLD	George Gilman	30p

General

T017	400	CHOPPER	Peter Cave	30p
T022	838	MAMA	Peter Cave	35p
T021	009	SEX MANNERS FOR MEN	Robert Chartham	35p
T019	403	SEX MANNERS FOR ADVANCED LOVERS	Robert Chartham	30p
T023	206	THE BOOK OF LOVE	Dr David Delvin	90p
P002	368	AN ABZ OF LOVE	Inge & Stan Hegeler	75p
P011	402	A HAPPIER SEX LIFE	Dr Sha Kokken	70p
W24	79	AN ODOUR OF SANCTITY	Frank Yerby	50p
W28	24	THE FOXES OF HARROW	Frank Yerby	50p

Mad

S006	086	MADVERTISING	40p
S006	292	MORE SNAPPY ANSWERS TO STUPID QUESTIONS	40p
S006	425	VOODOO MAD	40p
S006	293	MAD POWER	40p
S006	291	HOPPING MAD	40p

NEL P.O. BOX 11, FALMOUTH, CORNWALL.

For U.K. & Eire: customers should include to cover postage, 15p for the first book plus 5p per copy for each additional book ordered, up to a maximum charge of 50p.

For Overseas customers & B.F.P.O.: customers should include to cover postage, 20p for the first book and 10p per copy for each additional book.

Name ....

Address...

....

Title ....
(MAY)